PROXIMA DYING

Hard Science Fiction

BRANDON Q. MORRIS

BRANDON Q.
MORRIS
HARD SCIENCE FICTION

Contents

Proxima Dying

February 19, 19

They actually did it! Marchenko 2 shakes his head, but immediately rejects this human gesture. That ungrateful pack —they threw him out of his own base! And he had been so full of hope when he finally saw Adam and Eve again. *My children!* He had recognized them immediately, even though he had not seen them for 14 years. They had grown into beautiful children. *What am I thinking? They aren't children anymore, they're grown-ups.*

Marchenko 2 thought about it for a long time. Should he try to avenge this betrayal? Should he lie in wait for them when they leave the station? On the second day he stopped outside the range of all sensors, sat on the ocean floor, and pondered his options and strategies.

His hardware, J the robot, gives him freedom to endure. He can exist underwater for as long as he wants, because he has all the resources he needs. He is able to generate energy by using the temperature differences between various water levels. Using this energy, his fabricators can produce anything he needs to get along in this underwater world.

I have decided—I am going to accept their judgment... He is already on the way to the dark hemisphere of this planet, a planet that always faces its same sunburnt and hot side toward Proxima Centauri, its sun. The decision has not been easy for him. It might be interpreted as acceptance of the injustice done to him. That was the only reason he hesitated so long, because he obviously did not accept the verdict of his children. His children... When he thinks of them he feels the infinite love he had to suppress for so many years. He is not responsible for what happened, not he, because he is the victim.

It wasn't easy sweeping away this argument, but finally a probabilistic analysis opened his eyes. He calculates which courses of action were open to Adam and Eve. He knows a lot about Proxima b, things that they have yet to find out. They are stupid—they should have disassembled his body in order to extract his knowledge. This would have saved them a lot of disappointment in the near future. But the knowledge he acquired over the years also tells him that Adam and Eve will inevitably venture into the dark hemisphere during their search for the former inhabitants of this planet. It is only a question of time, but he will see them again. If he gets going now, he will have a chance to thoroughly prepare for their arrival.

The ground ahead of him is sloping down slightly. The pressure sensors report a cool current moving towards the north-northwest. He scans the ocean floor with his search-light. That is an old, deeply human habit. He does not need light to discover obstacles, but now and then he feels the need to see, just like he used to in his former life. He decided a long time ago to put away such behavioral patterns. They do not belong to him anymore. They are part of what he once was, a human being with all his shortcomings.

Today he is much more than that. He can be whatever he wants to be. For humans, that is a utopian idea and will always remain so. For him, it is a reality. During the first four years of his space voyage, he still believed he owed something to humans. But after the flare killed Adam and Eve, and the ship denied him a new start-up for the Adam and Eve project, he realized he owed humans no debt. He is alone, but that doesn't matter: He can learn indefinitely, and his power is without limits. Still, he can clearly feel something is missing. The Creator has denied him the ability to create life, and it logically follows that his omnipotence is wasted if he has nobody to protect and to support with it. He needs Adam and Eve, and he knows they will come to him.

February 21, 19

"SHIT! IT'S COLD!" ADAM YELLS. THE WATER LEVEL IN *VALKYRIE* sinks as fast as the bilge pumps can manage.

"Don't make such a fuss," Eve replies, already starting to take off her thin pressure suit.

I can easily understand Adam. Taking a short trip in *Valkyrie* is much too cumbersome. The battle with the other Marchenko—Marchenko 2—for the station set us back seriously in terms of technology. My robot body, J, still has not been completely repaired. We also haven't yet had the time to upgrade *Valkyrie* with a real airlock, or at least with a coupling port to attach itself directly to the station, meaning Adam and Eve have to swim through cold water. While the suit-heating mechanism is working at its maximum, trying to keep them warm, water has a high thermal conductivity and the cold ocean quickly reduces their body heat.

The problem down here at the bottom of the sea is energy supply. The nano-fabricators can produce almost anything from practically any material, but they need the energy to do so. On the surface of the planet, the local sun— Proxima Centauri—provides more than enough energy, but the underwater station laboriously generates it from currents and the temperature differences between various water layers. That limits our options.

It is Eve's fault we are starting our first excursion today, only a week after the dramatic conflict. She complained until I finally gave in. The two of them were not convinced by my counterargument that Marchenko 2 might have chosen to lurk nearby and, if so, I could not help them without J.

Our destination is the alien transmitter, the only still-working—possibly—trace left of the former inhabitants, as far as we know. It must have some function!

"Well, shall we go?" Eve is really in a hurry. Is this caused by curiosity, or by boredom with life at the bottom of the sea? She and Adam spent many years on board *Messenger*, which is very similar to the station down here. It is clear Marchenko 2 deliberately placed his ship here and then expanded it.

"Another 37 seconds," I answer via the loudspeaker. "The pumps are almost finished."

"And then?" Adam asks.

"We will have to see," I say. "Eve is in charge today."

Adam sits down in the seat near the stern end of the cabin and buckles himself in. Eve sits down as well and turns the monitor towards herself. She checks where the transmitter is shown on the map, but she doesn't yet choose a course. Adam gives her a puzzled look, but she does not notice it. Then she reaches for the control levers to the right and left of the monitor. *Valkyrie* starts moving. For a few seconds a metallic scraping can be heard, until the vessel rises far enough above the sea floor.

Eve does not seem to be taking the direct way. The small arrow on our screen indicates our direction of travel, and it points into areas we haven't yet explored. At this depth there is eternal darkness anyways, which makes it hard for me to talk of a dark hemisphere.

"What would happen if we just keep going straight?" Adam wants to know.

"We know too little about that," I reply. Yet the very question feels good. Columbus and his crewmates must likewise have agonized about that.

"Couldn't it just go on forever? The hair plants on the bottom seem to have adapted to the environment."

"We don't know, though, whether the ocean covers the entire dark hemisphere. Perhaps there are gigantic mountain ranges there. Think of the Antarctic on Earth."

Adam glares at me. "I don't give a shit about Earth!"

"I just wanted to say that, on a certain planet in the solar system, the South Pole is not accessible by submarine, but the North Pole is."

"I did understand," Adam says, abruptly turning away. He doesn't realize that this gesture is futile, because there is always a camera I can use to look at his face. But I better not rub his nose in it.

"Stop arguing," Eve says. She calmly focuses on the screen that shows the radar scan of the environment. "There are no discernible changes in the surface structure as far as the instruments reach… but that doesn't mean anything."

"Shouldn't we start thinking about what to do next?" asks Adam with his head lowered. He has gotten out of his seat and is slowly pacing.

"Yes, Adam, I am setting course for the transmitter. Perhaps that will give us a clue." Eve uses the right lever to control the thrust of the jets. I notice a force seeming to act on us from the outside, but it is really just our own inertia. Adam places a hand on the steel wall of the inner hull. The vessel changes its course.

WHILE WE APPROACH OUR DESTINATION, EVE HAS THE SENSORS checking in all wavelengths. The first measurement spike we detect is in the infrared range. The water temperature at the bottom is almost universally at four degrees. But on the monitor displaying infrared intensity, it looks as if, far away from us, somebody lit a candle in the dark. As I know more than the infrared sensor, namely the exact position of the object, I can calculate its emissions. This is definitely not a candle but rather a small heating plant. I try to match this with the image of the transmitter I remember, but that doesn't work.

What will Adam and Eve say about it? I am very curious. While I have described the transmitter to them, my words seemed insufficient to me.

Within half an hour the candle flame grows into a bright glow such as might come from a burning torch. The monitor displays an elongated oval, perhaps two meters high, that seems to hover above the ground.

"Is it floating?" Eve asks.

Adam points at the gap between the ground and the oval. "Zoom in on this area so it fills the entire screen."

Without the blinding brightness of the oval it becomes clear that there is a connection to the ground, but it radiates much less heat. I readjust the image to show the entire object. Something is bothering me. "There is something wrong here. You notice anything?" I am not sure myself what I am looking for. The whole scene does not feel dangerous, just strange.

Eve zooms in again and focuses on the transition between the brightness of the oval and the darkness of the water it swims in.

"Do you mean this?" she says.

Of course. The water is too dark. It should absorb much more heat from direct contact with the heat source. What we are seeing here would be normal in a vacuum, but on the ocean floor?

"The source seems to be very well shielded against its environment," Adam says. "But what's so unusual about that?"

"The fact that we can see it so brightly," Eve says, anticipating my own explanation. "The shielding seems to work only for thermal conduction but not for infrared radiation, which we see as brightness here."

"And what's strange about that?"

"Thermal conduction works via direct contact," Eve says, really getting into it. "The particles transfer heat by colliding with each other. While radiation can be blocked quite well by using absorbent or reflective materials, that is more complicated with thermal conduction."

"You would have to prevent contact between the source and the outside."

"Yes, Adam. But regardless of which material you use for it, that material itself is made up of particles that collide and can conduct heat."

"Unless there is a layer containing nothing," Adam says.

"A vacuum. Exactly. Without particles there is no thermal conduction. Marchenko, can you calculate for us how thick this layer would have to be?"

"No," I reply. "I am missing too much data to do that. We have to get more precise measurements for the transmitter."

A TENSE SILENCE REIGNS OVER THE NEXT FEW KILOMETERS. ON the radar display, the transmitter—or what we assume to be one—only appears during the last minute. It is hard to say whether it was deliberately designed this way, since the delicate construction might be responsible for the small radar signature.

Valkyrie's searchlights shine on the dish-shaped object. Adam and Eve marvel at it on the monitor. The instruments indicate that the dish is 15.7 meters wide. It sits horizontally on the bottom and no mountings can be seen. In the shine of the searchlights the material appears thin and bright, like porcelain. A mast rises from the center of the dish. It has a thickness of about half a centimeter. We cannot measure this more precisely from inside the vessel, particularly as the mast doesn't seem to be evenly shaped. There are small bulges at regular intervals, the function of which is not identifiable.

Most impressively, spheres circle the mast within the radius of the dish. They are concentrated on the side from which we approached the transmitter. At first glance they seem to be made of the same material as the dish. These are precisely-shaped spheres, each with a diameter of 98 centimeters, floating in the water at different heights and distances from the pylon.

Adam points at one of the spheres. "I wonder what their function is."

"I have no idea," I reply. "Maybe they are ornaments? On..." I start, and then swallow the next word before starting over. "Elsewhere, some structures are just built for esthetic reasons."

"The dish alone shows that the inhabitants value beauty," Eve postulates.

"Or valued it," Adam adds, and Eve nods.

"Sometimes the beauty of an object derives from its purpose," I say, "but you will have to get out to answer the question."

I have to admit I envy the two of them right now. *If I only had a body!* I wish to myself. While I can see the transmitter on all wavelengths, only Adam and Eve will be able to touch it.

"Done!" Adam is already wearing his pressure suit.

Eve shuts down her terminal just to be on the safe side. While the hardware is supposed to be waterproof, caution can't hurt. We have to flood *Valkyrie* again to allow the two of them to exit. Hopefully for the second-to-last time.

Eve signals by giving a thumbs-up after she has donned her suit. I let the water flow in, and *Valkyrie* sinks to the bottom. Then Adam opens the hatch. I imagine the blackness he sees above, and in the camera image I watch him push off and swim outside. Eve follows him, and I accompany both of them with the searchlights. They are real naturals at this. I never managed to give them practical swimming lessons, but they move elegantly toward their destination. Near the dish they let themselves sink to the bottom.

"Wow," Eve says. "From close up it is even more impressive than on the screen."

Adam carefully touches the edge of the dish, which is about at chest height. I wonder whether I should stop him, but he probably would not listen to me anyways. Nothing can happen, I think, as the dish will hardly give him an electric shock! In slow motion Adam first closes the fingers of his right hand around the edge, then those of his left. Nothing happens. All of a sudden he jerks violently.

"Hey!" Again I yell, "Hey!" not knowing what else to do in my panic. From here I cannot help him. Eve pulls on Adam's shoulder, but I already hear his laughter via helmet radio.

"You! You..." I shout. "That wasn't funny at all! Don't you dare do that again!" I am beside myself and feel my heart beating wildly, even though I don't have one... anymore.

"And if I do? Don't be so touchy," Adam replies.

Eve also reaches for the edge of the dish and pulls herself up. I realize what she is planning to do. A bit further inward, and perhaps a meter and a half above her, floats one of these strange spheres. She goes directly for it, arms outstretched. One hand touches the sphere first, then the other. Due to her momentum, the sphere is pushed slightly to the side. I record the exact position. What happens next is something I already suspected. The sphere slowly moves back to its original position, pulling Eve along. Considering that it looks perfectly round, and seems to have no propulsion system, that is a phenomenal achievement. In addition, the sphere must account for Eve's weight while moving back.

"Did you see that?" I ask. I'm not sure whether the movement could be seen well from below.

"Yes, very distinctly. The sphere moved back after I pushed it out of position," Eve replies.

"One moment," Adam says. He turns aside, obviously aiming for another sphere. He pushes off much more strongly than Eve did, also kicking his feet. He hits the sphere perfectly and drags it along. One meter, two meters, but he is already slowing. The sphere decelerates, brings both of them to a stop, and then they float back to the sphere's original position.

"Not bad," Adam says. "I wonder what else this sphere can do. Should we try to kidnap it using *Valkyrie*?"

"I don't know," Eve replies. "This is alien technology we don't really understand. We'd better not stress it to its limits."

Strictly speaking, we shouldn't have touched anything, I think, *but how else are we supposed to find out anything?*

"The positions of the spheres must be very important to the aliens," Adam says. "This means they are probably more than just decorations. You were here before, Marchenko. Has anything changed?"

"I did not record the exact positions, but I remember one particular feature concerning the placement of the spheres. If you measure their distances, you get a geometric progression." I check the numbers again. *No, that is not correct.* "Sorry, it's not a single progression. There are several. One might assume that the spheres are arranged in circles around the pylon. There are three circles. The distances between the spheres of a particular circle form one progression. For the innermost circle, for example, this is 1, 1.5, 1.75, 1.875..."

"And what does this mean?"

"I don't know, Adam. It must have meant something to the builders of the transmitter."

Now Eve moves from sphere to sphere. She measures each of the distances again using the laser rangefinder from her tool belt. "Marchenko," she says, "did you notice all these progressions converge on a natural number?"

I calculate the limits of the three progressions. And indeed they all are fixed values, rather than infinity. That is a strange coincidence. *Why didn't I notice this earlier?* "Correct," I confirm. "But does this mean something?"

On the camera image I see Eve shrug her shoulders.

"It is probably due to the fact that mathematics is universal," I say. "One plus one is always two, on any planet and in any language."

"Too bad," Eve says. "I was hoping we had discovered some kind of code."

"Or at least identified its purpose," Adam adds.

"Concerning its purpose, we might have a chance to find that out. Please describe the material of the sphere, as well as that of the central mast."

"One second. I have an analyzer," Adam says as he reaches into his tool bag and pulls out a device that looks like a stubby pistol. The device bombards an object in as many wavelengths as possible and uses the reflected radiation to find out what it is made of. Adam starts with the sphere he is still holding on to. He pushes a few buttons, mumbles something incomprehensible, and then swims down to the transmitter dish. After repeating the procedure he compares the data.

"Ceramic," he says, "so our first impression concerning porcelain wasn't far off."

"What are its components?" I ask.

"Just a sec, I am going to send you the data."

The analysis appears in my memory unit. "Magnesium, calcium, titanium, cobalt," I read out loud. "What does that remind you of?"

"Could be some high-temperature superconductor," Adam says.

"Perhaps," I reply, "but unfortunately we only get integrated values instead of an exact structural analysis. There might be several layers of different materials, or a thick layer in which all of these components occur. Those would lead to two completely different scenarios."

"Couldn't we find out more inside the station?" Eve asks. "*Messenger* had a scanning tunneling microscope."

"There is probably something like that in the station, Eve, but for that purpose we would need to extract some material and take it with us."

"Should I break something off?" Adam asks, acting as if he were about to hammer the analyzer against the edge of the dish.

"Don't you dare!" I warn him, though I know he couldn't be that irrational.

"The sensor is much too pretty to do that," Eve says. "And what kind of impression would we make if we come here from far away and start smashing their china?"

"Never mind," Adam says. He pushes himself off again and swims toward the central mast.

Oh yes, I think, *we haven't examined it closely yet.*

Adam stretches out his arms in front of him. I am watching him through the camera. He is just about to grab the mast when his hand is suddenly stopped. Adam tries it a second time, but once more he can't get closer than arm's length.

"What is going on?" he yells, and turns toward the *Valkyrie* as if I could give him an explanation. Eve now also moves toward the mast. Does she think Adam is playing another trick on us? But she is also unable to touch the mast.

"Remember the infrared images?" I ask.

"I've been thinking of that," Eve says. "The thermal conduction insulation is probably located inside this layer. But what exactly does it contain, and why is it invisible?"

"Adam, why don't you try..." I don't even have to finish the sentence. Adam takes the analyzer and aims it at the mast underneath the boundary layer. Silence reigns for several seconds. Time seems to stretch on. The device takes much longer than usual for its task. Adam stares intently at its display, though I know there won't be anything to see there except for the message, 'Please wait.'

"The numbers are puzzling," Adam says after precisely one minute and 37 seconds.

"How puzzling?"

"I am sending them to you." He pushes a button.

Now I see the data. Adam has not exaggerated. "The numbers really are baffling," I say in agreement.

"In what way? Don't leave me hanging here," Eve says.

"The analyzer found nothing," I say.

"Nothing? But there certainly is something there. You can see it, and it affects the thermal conduction, doesn't it?" asks Eve.

"The device functions by examining reflected radiation at different wavelengths. But it didn't find any. Either the radiation is completely absorbed by the material around the mast, or it is passed through just as completely," I surmise.

"The first case is highly improbable," Eve says. "Otherwise we wouldn't have been able to detect the heat signature of the transmitter so clearly from far away. So the material must let anything coming from the inside pass through."

"Correct," I say in agreement. "It is much more likely that any radiation can pass through. We can test this with an experiment. Adam, set the analyzer to the maximum level and repeat the analysis."

"What good will that do?" he asks.

"If all radiation truly goes through the material, it would hit normal materials behind it and be partially reflected by them. This should appear as a background signal in the analysis. We need maximum performance for this. Otherwise the signal would stay below the detection threshold.

Normally, the analyzer is not supposed to measure the environment as well."

"Okay." Adam holds the analyzer gun as close to the mast as possible. We wait. This time, the procedure finishes faster. The device might have interpreted the background reflections as a measurement signal. Adam looks at what is happening on the display.

"Your theory is correct, Marchenko," he says. "Water, silicon dioxide, various salts, exactly what one would expect of an ocean." He presses the send button again. "So we know the stuff in there does not shield from radiation. Not one bit. Therefore it could only be a vacuum, or something close to it, right?"

Eve pushes off and swims upward along the mast, her arms outstretched so she can feel the invisible boundary. She reaches the top.

"The cover reaches all the way up here and is closed at the tip," she reports via radio.

"I don't understand," Adam says. "That doesn't make any sense! A transmitter that does not send, but uses energy? That's totally inefficient! Why should somebody construct something like that, and even build it to last an eternity?"

It can't be denied that the transmitter consumes energy, because it must somehow receive the heat it then radiates. Where does it come from? That is another question for which we do not yet have an answer.

"Perhaps it is not a transmitter, but rather a receiver that needs energy while waiting for a signal?"

Eve's idea cannot be easily dismissed. A switched-on radio uses electricity, even during times when no programming can be heard. "And the spheres?" I ask.

"Perhaps they serve to adjust the frequency. Like tensioning or pressing guitar strings."

Maybe Eve is on to something here. I am not quite convinced, but I feel we are getting closer to an answer.

"You mean the spheres are like knobs on a radio receiver, adjusting it to a particular frequency?" Adam asks with a laugh. "That sounds so crazy it might actually turn out to be true. But who is supposed to turn them?"

"Maybe they are not meant to be changed. Then the receiver would be tuned to a fixed frequency, set to stay that way. That would explain why the spheres obediently return to their original positions," Eve says as she slowly sinks down from the top of the mast.

"I think we are wrong concerning the type of receiver. We are thinking too much in terms of Earth."

"What do you mean, Marchenko? I definitely don't think in terms of Earth," Adam says.

"I wanted to say we are thinking in categories like radio communication. What if this has nothing to do with radio waves? Perhaps not even electromagnetic waves, but something altogether different?"

"You are considering something like sound waves? Not a bad idea," Eve says. "Sound waves are pressure waves within a medium. If I change the medium—meaning the water—by means of the spheres, that would be a kind of frequency modulation."

"But sound waves don't make sense, because the range is much too short. The antenna is obviously aimed upward. Sound waves would stop at the vacuum and not get past the atmosphere."

"The direction of the antenna, Marchenko, that is an important clue. It doesn't look like it can be changed, so during the orbit of Proxima b around its sun it can reach only certain targets," Eve says.

Or be reached by certain targets, I think. I simulate the course of the planet around its central star. I know the position of the antenna, as it sits vertically to the round exterior of the planet. Which planets or stars could it possibly send a signal to or receive one from, at least once a year? My program routines take a while to go through the entire star catalog. Finally, I get a result.

"Alpha Centauri," I say.

"The neighboring star?" Adam asks.

"Yes, what else?" Eve says. "It is obvious it had to be something nearby. Perhaps that is the star they escaped to?"

"I don't know... It could just be a coincidence," I say.

"It certainly is," Adam says. "Just take a look at the dimensions of the antenna. It has a diameter of just under 16 meters, and is even under water. That would never be sufficient to reach Alpha Centauri with a clear signal that could be distinguished from background noise."

"You are thinking of a transmitter again," Eve retorts. "A receiver could be much smaller, if the transmission power on the other side is large enough."

"I still don't believe we are dealing with a rather undersized radio receiver here," I say.

"Could we check your theory?" Eve asks.

I think about this question. Whatever material the mast is made of, its outer skin exists in our world and therefore must obey our laws of physics. Seismographs explore the interior structure of the world by sending vibrations—in their case, soundwaves—downward and receiving the reflected signals. This should also work with the mast. We only have to strike it like a bell on top. Then the vibrations would propagate along its length and spread out. A large part would be absorbed, but some should return. Those signals will tell me everything about the mast.

"Okay, then let's play 'The Hunchback of Proxima b,'" I say.

Adam and Eve stare toward the *Valkyrie*, obviously confused. I don't feel like explaining this to them. If it works, I can add the explanation later. After all, the two of them don't explain all their ideas to me.

Valkyrie is not equipped with sonar, as a submarine would

be. But a loudspeaker or microphone could fulfill the same function. The helmets of Adam and Eve contain sensitive microphones that can also receive sound from the outside. I would simply have to precisely log the vibrations caused by the measurement signal. I can get these data live thanks to the suit telemetry.

"Could you two swim up to the tip of the mast and hit it with some object?" I ask.

Adam follows my request, but asks in a puzzled voice: "Can I use anything, no matter what?"

"Yes, it's your choice."

Eve conspicuously shakes her head so that I can see it even through the helmet visor, but she doesn't say anything. She swims upward with deliberate slowness and pulls a tool from her front suit pouch.

"You can start whenever you are ready," I say.

The monitoring system of the suits will automatically record the two of them hitting the mast, along with the resulting sound waves. In the meantime I am preparing some algorithms to automatically extract the data relevant for me. The measurement method might be primitive, but I am not aiming for high precision. I just want to know one thing: Does the mast end shortly below the ocean floor, or does it reach far down?

I take a look through the cameras. Both of them are having fun. Hammering something in a seemingly-meaningless fashion seems really enjoyable. In a way it looks odd, as they are not really hitting the mast, but instead are striking the invisible barrier around it. Also, the water slows their arm swing so they are unable to hit with their full strength.

"But watch out. You'd better stop if you get the feeling something is about to break."

"Certainly, boss," Adam replies.

After five minutes I have enough measurement data to get a meaningful result. "You can stop now," I say.

"So what was this supposed to do?" asks Eve, who is slowly swimming toward *Valkyrie*.

"Just a moment, I am running some calculations."

"Don't keep us in suspense," she says.

"Let's get back inside already," Adam says with a bored voice. "I don't believe we can find out anything else here."

I hope to show them soon that the opposite is true. I nod my head until I remember that nobody can see this, because I currently have no head. "Yes, why don't you come back inside? As soon as I have the results, we are traveling back to the station."

The answer appears in my consciousness. It is an impressive feeling having the results of extensive calculations suddenly materialize inside my mind. When I was still a human being I occasionally caught a glimpse of this when a sudden inspiration made me slap my forehead with my hand. *How could I have overlooked this obvious fact until now?* I would think. I have a similar reaction to the result of the soundwave measurement. The insight appears out of the blue, right in the part of my consciousness that is actively dealing with this strange transmitter or receiver. Something—and I know that it is the algorithms running in my subconscious—drops it down. And then knowledge opens, as though previously hidden in a box, and it feels as though it should have always been here.

"People, the mast reaches down several kilometers," I say.

Adam and Eve have already closed the hatch and are waiting for the water to drain. That's perhaps why they don't appreciate my insight the way I had hoped they would. Or perhaps I have to give them some background information.

"This makes it clear what kind of receiver we've got here."

"Oh, really?" Eve says, sounding as if she is not truly interested in an explanation.

"It is a gravitational wave receiver. It is meant for..."

"... receiving gravitational waves, sure," Adam interrupts me. "I already thought something like that."

"Is that so?" I reply.

"Yes, really. It was somehow logical, so far under the sea. The device won't be disturbed here."

"But you didn't say a word."

"Well, I didn't want to spoil your fun."

No matter. I shouldn't get upset now. If this is a gravitational wave receiver, this means there must be a transmitter somewhere. And that technology would not just be able to generate gravitational waves, but also to modulate them. This is far beyond mankind's current abilities. Learning how to do this would provide an enormous advance for us.

"If this is a receiver, then where is the transmitter?" Eve asks as if reading my thoughts.

"Alpha Centauri?" Adam suggests.

"No, Adam, the position of the antenna then makes no real sense for gravitational waves," I say. "Those can be detected more efficiently if they arrive parallel to one of the arms."

"To one of the arms, precisely. Perhaps what we see here," Adam says, pointing at the screen he just switched on, "is the arm of the sensor providing the control signal. The gravitational wave changes the lengths of the two arms, which are perpendicular to each other, differently. This allows the actual signal to be detected."

"You don't have to explain the principle of a gravity wave detector to me," I say. My voice sounds angrier than I intended.

"You would have done it, too, in his place," Eve says.

I have to laugh. Eve is not completely wrong. "Well, you two smart alecks," I say, "then what about the spheres? What is their function? Do they serve just as decoration?"

"Each mass influences the spread of gravitational waves. Thus they could function as a kind of tuner," Adam says.

"They are much too light for that. Gravitational waves are created through the interaction between black holes or neutron stars, not by a few spheres with a diameter of one meter."

Of course I know this is not exactly true, but only limited by our measurement precision. The gravitational waves generated by a collision of the spheres would be minimal and impossible to measure, even for a technologically-advanced civilization.

"How do you know their weight?" Adam asks.

"That's not hard to estimate. The volume of the sphere multiplied by the density of the heaviest known material..."

"And what if the contents of the spheres are an unknown material?"

"That is pure speculation, Adam."

"Everything we do here is a wild guess, so why shouldn't we engage in some reasoned speculation? What if the spheres contain dark matter? The lambda-cold dark matter model assumes that its particles would have to be very dense and heavy."

"But we haven't measured anything."

"Exactly," Adam says. "Dark matter would not interact with electromagnetic radiation. That's why we can't see it."

"I know all that," I say, "but so far, all that is only a theory. Nobody knows what dark matter is made of. We are only pretty sure that it must exist."

"My thoughts exactly!" Adam replies.

"So how would the builders of this device have collected dark matter?"

"A cubic centimeter of space contains on average dark matter equivalent to the mass of a proton. They just would need a very fine-meshed sieve."

"And how would they lock the dark matter inside the spheres? As it does not interact with normal matter, no wall would keep it in."

"The spherical form is perfect for that purpose. Once you collect enough particles of dark matter, they would form a ball under the influence of their own gravity," Adam says.

"A fascinating idea, Adam, I have to admit," I say in a congratulatory tone. "But is it even remotely connected to reality? Wouldn't there be a danger of the super-heavy dark particles turning into a kind of dark black hole?"

"So what? Black holes are among the most stable objects in the universe. They will not evaporate until long after the last star has ceased to exist."

"Nevertheless, nobody would like to have one of those in close vicinity, let alone 15 of them."

"The black hole was your speculation, not mine. There might just be a lump of dark matter inside the spheres."

"'Could, would, might,' doesn't help us."

"Pull yourselves together, guys!" Eve says in a loud voice. "This is ridiculous. Would you rather split hairs than solve our problems? Then let's just weigh the spheres!"

"That would hardly be possible," I reply. "Remember how you pushed the sphere aside with your body? You could scarcely have done that if the sphere had an enormous mass. You simply would not have overcome its inertia so easily."

"Or the sphere has a kind of motor that provides the required energy. Otherwise it couldn't float."

"Correct, Adam. Perhaps the sphere does not contain any dark matter at all. That would be the simplest solution."

"Yes, I know, Occam's razor. The simplest solution is preferable."

"I just can't believe these sophisticated spheres are only a pretty decoration," Eve says. "Who would do something like that?"

"Humans might," I reply. "But they could not send messages via gravitational waves. The very fact that we understand the functioning of this receiver is already a great success. And we have a lead: Alpha Centauri."

"We can hardly reach that star, and I would not bet on our having truly understood this receiver," Adam says. "I don't know what else we can achieve here. Let's go back."

We prepare *Valkyrie* for the return trip. This time I take the helm. While Adam and Eve are dozing in their seats, I use all my sensors to observe the strange and simultaneously beautiful device left behind by the previous inhabitants of this planet. *Will we ever be able to find them?*

February 23, 19

My soul floats above my body. Is this like one of the out-of-body experiences some humans reported having had in extreme situations? I feel a shiver running over my skin, even though I currently do not even have an external casing. A phantom pain stabs my left arm. There is nothing mystical about this. While my consciousness is in the onboard computer of the station and watches the world through alert senses, my physical sense lies below me, under the ceiling camera through which I examine it, to be exact. Marchenko 2, who reached Proxima b before us, executed this body with an electrical shock. My body, paralyzed and burnt out, will now be resurrected. I've had to do without it for nine days. It became harder and harder for me as the days went by, but now this period is almost over.

Currently J the robot is still connected to thick power and data cables that provide his system with all it needs. The body is in an upright position. It is wedged into a steel frame specially built by Marchenko 2 to support the weight of the heavy metal robot. The outer skin is damaged in many spots. The access points through which invisible streams of nano-fabricators move could be mistaken for open wounds. They are roundish, very dark, and they bleed the oil that facilitates the movement of the fabricators and is in turn spread by them.

Adam and Eve help repair my body. It would be possible to just use the fabricators, which are smaller than bacteria, but just like with diseases of the human body, macrophysical operations sometimes offer a shortcut to healing. Eve, for example, drilled most of the access holes into my body, while Adam optimized the shapes for some of the limbs by using a grinding machine. The goal was to keep the mass low while maintaining full functionality. Mechanical instruments can often achieve this more quickly than a host of tiny fabricators —just like cutting down a tree would be faster using a good old ax than employing termites that digest the wood fiber by fiber.

Soon I should be able to get up again. My robot body will be more powerful than before. It will be able to run faster, jump higher, and lift heavier loads. Adam and Eve suggested interesting ideas. It has been fun working with them, and I think that Adam's mood has improved in the meantime. I am sure he is carrying around a problem he does not want to discuss. I mentioned this to him, but he won't say anything. This bothers me, as I cannot solve the issue with my nano-fabricators. Only Adam can do that.

Lunch break. On the way from the landing site to this place, Adam and Eve had to live on what my fabricators could produce from biomass we found on the way. The nutrients fit human needs, but not much could be said for looks, consistency, and taste. Compared to that, the station is a paradise. Marchenko 2 must have done everything to ensure two humans might have a pleasant stay here—even though those two no longer existed, having died long before. Was he aware of this fact? I don't know, but I am aware that a consciousness separated from a body, like he and I both are, is able to suppress unpleasant facts.

Eve has ordered a steak from the 'kitchen'—a box that produces food on request—while Adam just asked for 'something.' Therefore he lifts the flap on the box to retrieve a dish of greenish sauce with nondescript lumps in it. He doesn't ask what it is supposed to be, but sits down at the table next to Eve and starts shoveling down the food listlessly. Eve cuts off small pieces of artificial meat and writes down her observations. She is always trying to improve the recipes that were probably developed by Marchenko 2. She seems to be 'nesting,' preparing for a long stay here.

I tell them to enjoy their meal. I would love to participate in this ritual, to feel food in my mouth, its consistency and smell, to experience the taste variations on different sides of the tongue. I always believed I would forget that feeling someday, but it hasn't happened. Quite the opposite—my imagination becomes livelier and more precise. In the past, when I was a human being, I never focused on food so consciously, but today I can't help doing it even though I am unable to eat.

Did Marchenko 2 experience similar feelings? Or did he develop totally different obsessions? His presence here shocked me less than I would have thought possible. Does this mean I expected it? Or, am I simply not bothered by it? Objectively speaking it was almost logical that the Creator—Shostakovich—would copy me, even though this was illegal. While he had stated the opposite, it would have been foolish to bet everything on a single horse and send out only one *Messenger* probe with a copy of my consciousness. But how thorough was the Russian billionaire? Is Marchenko 2 my only sibling, or are there currently thousands of us on the way? I don't know, and I have no idea how I could find it out. One thing is clear: Adam and Eve must not be told. They certainly wouldn't like the idea that there might be hundreds of copies of them, and possibly even more.

"So, what do we do now?" Adam asks the question with his mouth full, interrupting my musings.

"Yes, that's what I wanted to ask," says Eve, who has finished half of her steak in the meantime.

"To be honest, I am not sure."

"We could just stay here," Eve says. "I wouldn't mind doing that for a while."

"Certainly, for a while," I reply. "But then the question will return, so we might as well answer it now."

"Can we really do that?" Adam says, touching a sore spot.

"We don't have enough information. We have the spaceport on the coast," I say, starting my list. "The buried wall that mentions the guardians in the east. There is the gravitational wave receiver, even though we don't really understand its functionality."

"And a crazed robot we banished to the dark side of the planet," Adam adds.

"He probably doesn't have much to do with our journey," I reply.

Eve nods. "We did decide we would move further east at some point. After all, we've already been in the west."

"This is useless if we don't have a specific destination. The hemisphere facing away from the sun is huge. And a voyage there won't be a walk in the park. Therefore we should be certain it's worth our while. Otherwise we'd better stay here," I say.

"As I already mentioned, I've got nothing against that, nothing at all," Eve says somewhat sheepishly.

"Don't you really want to know why we are here?" Adam asks.

"Because the Creator sent us? Is it so important?"

"Yes, Eve, for me it is," Adam replies.

The young woman shakes her head and focuses again on her steak. "*This* is why I am here," she says, cutting off a piece and holding it up.

"We can't just march off on a whim," I say. "Therefore we need ideas to help us find a potential destination."

"Perhaps we'll find something on the shore that will tell us the way. Like another wall with texts on it, a traffic sign, whatever," Adam suggests.

"You mean we try digging in random places across the planet?" I ask.

"No, you can scan the ground to see whether it is worthwhile to start digging."

"That is a possibility. It will cost us a few days per square kilometer. But we have plenty of time. As soon as a flare threatens us we return to this base."

"You'd better leave me here, then," Eve says.

"We'll gladly manage without you," Adam grumbles.

"In any case, it is going to be a very lengthy search without a guarantee of success," I say.

"Maybe we could shorten the scanning process for the upper ground layers? If we had a balloon, for example, we could measure from up there."

"Great idea, Adam," I say. I run some calculations about this method. Unfortunately I find a problem. "It won't work with my technology. Sorry. In order to find anything, the scanner cannot be higher than 50 meters above the surface."

Adam crosses his arms in front of his chest. "Then *Messenger* won't help us either, will it?"

That is the ship that brought us here. We only separated the landing module. *Messenger* itself is still waiting for us in orbit. Could it possibly aid us, and if so, how?

"The orbit of *Messenger* is too high for it to employ its ground radar. The planet has a dense atmosphere," I say.

"What about the camera?"

"If an artificial structure could be seen from space, we would have noticed it during our approach, Adam."

"Perhaps we didn't check carefully."

"That is unlikely. You can't ignore the cloud cover, the

vegetation, the areas in the shadow, and the long time that must have passed. We had to dig out the spaceport and the wall."

"Could we see something in a different wavelength range? Gamma rays? X-rays?"

"They would only scan the surface."

Adam's question makes me think. One of the last Mars probes tried to find hidden structures on the red planet using a gradiometer, which measures variations in the gravitational field. The structure of the planetary crust is not identical everywhere. According to its thickness and composition, it changes the gravitational field above it. If you know the flight altitude of a satellite, you can determine the vertical component of gravity.

"The force of gravity," I say, "that could give us clues."

"Sure," Adam replies. "Any artificial structure changes the gravitational field all the way out into space."

"But we can only measure it if there is a large change."

"Then we'd better hope the inhabitants of this planet built high-rises rather than huts."

"There is only a slight problem: *Messenger* does not have a gradiometer on board. There simply was no plan to scan the planet that way. After receiving the radio message asking for help, we assumed there would be direct clues."

Adam gets up from his place at the table. "Why don't you say something, Eve?"

His sister looks up at him and crosses her arms. "So we have to improvise something, as usual?"

"Unfortunately, due to lack of ongoing maintenance, there are no more working fabricators left on board the spaceship. So constructing something new is out of the question."

"How exactly does a gradiometer work when it measures a gravitational field?" Eve asks.

"Basically, those are simple but very precise acceleration sensors," I explain. "Something like the step counters you have in your suits. A change in the gravitational field generates a force that the sensor records as acceleration."

"The greater the acceleration, the higher the force," Adam says.

"And the higher the change in the gravitational field. The instrument always measures the spot directly below it, or the line through the center of the satellite orbit, to be more exact," I add.

"So if Messenger had a gradiometer, it would have to first fly across the entire planet?" Eve asks.

"That's what it looks like. Depending on the size of the structure we are looking for that shouldn't take too long, though," I reply.

"Okay, then we just need such a gradiometer. Couldn't we just use an existing acceleration sensor?"

"We would need at least two, which are at some distance from each other, but three would be better. The attitude control system definitely has one," I say.

"Just one? Isn't every functional unit duplicated for the sake of safety?"

"You are right, Eve. That would make it two."

"I left my tablet on Messenger," Adam says. "It also has an acceleration sensor."

"That is not as precise as the one in the attitude control module, but it might be used as a check value."

"So... do we have our gravitation measurement device?" Adam asks, giving me a hopeful look.

I don't want to disappoint him now. Normally, these sensors are placed on the outside of a satellite, preferably at the end of a boom, so that they are not affected by the mass of the spacecraft. I have no idea how precise our gradiometer is going to be. If we are unlucky, it will only confirm that Proxima b has an approximately spherical shape. Everything will depend on which dimensions the inhabitants used for their buildings.

"*MESSENGER*, PLEASE COME IN." TWO HOURS LATER OUR mothership is in range again, and I describe to the ship's control system how to calibrate and connect the three sensors. The signal evaluation has to happen on board the spaceship, because our daily radio communication window only lasts a few hours, and it shifts from day to day.

Messenger will have to adjust its orbit in order to cover as much of the planet as possible. I calculated that after two weeks it will have checked about 50 percent of the surface, including almost 80 percent of the dark side. While I hope we won't have to start an expedition to the dark hemisphere, I somehow have the feeling if we find any remaining inhabitants it will be there.

Eve will be able to rest for a while longer. I just hope the delay won't drive Adam crazy during the coming days.

March 4, 19

Sometimes he thinks he is the only sane person in the station, while at other times he feels he is slowly going insane. Perhaps he has some genetically-based nervous disease nobody has noticed so far? Adam turns over in his bed without opening his eyes. He understands neither Marchenko nor Eve. His sister has settled in here, all nice and cozy, using all the comforts of the station without thinking of the future.

And Marchenko doesn't seem to be all there. He is constantly working out plans. Adam particularly dislikes that Marchenko is everywhere and nowhere. It is about time J—the robot in which Marchenko had lived since their landing—becomes functional again. Adam suspects that Marchenko secretly does not want to move back into J, preferring to have complete control over the onboard systems.

It's no use. Adam simply cannot go back to sleep. He opens his eyes. Eve lies in the other bed. Her deep breathing shows she is fast asleep. The room is not completely dark. It never gets totally dark, because there are always a few indicator lights monitoring some vital signs. Adam has no idea which light signifies what. Marchenko 2 did not leave them an instruction manual for the station. Adam throws off his blanket. Once he gets up he realizes he really has to use the bathroom. The dim light has the advantage that he can find his way to the exit located in the floor without bumping against anything. He glances at Eve's bed. She is still asleep. Then he slowly descends the ladder.

The light in the command module switches on immediately. Adam hurriedly closes the hatch above him. He hopes the bright light did not wake Eve.

While he is in the bathroom he wonders, *What now?* He leaves the room deciding he might play some games on the terminal. Adam sits down on the chair in front of it. The station offers a surprisingly large selection of games. This is particularly amazing because their Marchenko only gave them access to a very few games on *Messenger*. Both of these ships should have been launched with the same basic software assortment. Their Marchenko probably wanted to keep them from gaming because he thought it was bad for their development. That's so much like him. At the bottom of his heart he is still an old, conservative Russian who was young almost a hundred years ago.

Adam quickly notices he is not in the mood for gaming. He walks aimlessly through the command module, but he can't come up with an idea. Should he go back to bed and spend the rest of a sleepless night there?

He stands below the hatch and looks down at his feet. The service module is located beneath him. It wasn't that long ago that he frantically searched for a switch there to turn off Marchenko 2. Adam steps aside, leans down, and takes the round rug off the hatch. He opens it and climbs down the ladder. The light down here is also switched on automatically. Adam well remembers the smell of grease and oil, like in a workshop, which this place actually is. He looks around. The room looks comfy in an odd way. It is dirty, that's true. But putting that aside, it does not have the sterile feel of the command module. Adam imagines Marchenko 2 spending most of his time here, brooding in solitude. He probably would have gone crazy during such a prolonged period of loneliness.

In the corner Adam sees the control console that he had used to deactivate Marchenko 2. That was almost two months ago. Had it been a mistake? No, certainly not. Marchenko 2 would have considered Adam to be his property. That AI acted for years as if his Adam and his Eve were still alive, so you never knew what he might do.

But are the actions of their own Marchenko really much different? Adam realizes that finding the right balance is difficult. He sits down in front of the console. It is a simple electrical cabinet that has no inputs or outputs. But he should be able to establish wireless communication. Adam takes his universal device out of his pocket and taps it a few times to launch a connection.

"User identification required."

How did Marchenko 2 log on? Adam tries 'Marchenko' and 'Adam' as passwords, but the device rejects them. However, he is offered the option to create a new account. Adam does so. The password, he is told, has to be at least seven characters long. There seem to be no rules concerning the user name. Adam interrupts the connection and restarts it.

"User: Marchenko."

"Password: AdamEve."

"Welcome, Mitya," the device displays. That had been too simple. However, Marchenko 2 did not have to worry about illegal access to his files, living all alone down here. Accordingly, he has minimal access-controls standards. Mitya is a term of endearment for Dimitri. Why is the computer system addressing the second Marchenko this way?

"Who am I talking to?" he types.

"My name is Francesca."

Adam laughs at this answer. No programmer would ever call a semi-AI 'Francesca.' This electrical cabinet is not powerful enough for a true AI. SAIs lack the ability of autonomous learning. Yet they can be programmed so that they are able to solve some types of problems.

"What can you do for me, Francesca?"

"Calendar, notebook, maintenance, settings."

"Explain maintenance."

"The maintenance menu offers access to all basic systems in the station. Warning: Immediate execution of all commands is the default setting."

So the software will not warn him if he is about to deactivate the life-support system. That's too dangerous and he should not touch this menu.

"Explain 'notebook,' please." He can imagine what a notebook would be, but it is better to ask.

"You saved your entries in the notebook, Mitya. I do not have the ability to understand their content, but I can read them out loud to you."

"Can you also display them?" Adam asks.

"Yes."

"Is there a particular order?"

"The entries are in chronological sequence."

"How many entries are there?" Adam wants to know.

"Three thousand, seven hundred and forty-four."

It's going to be a long night, Adam thinks. He does not feel bad about reading the second Marchenko's diary. The AI endangered all of them and obviously did not consider these notes important enough to take them along.

"Entry One."

Marchenko 2 describes waking up and his first days on board *Messenger*. It sounds as if he was very optimistic back then, eager for adventure. Did their own Marchenko think that, too?

"Entry Two."

The story continues. This is a period long before Adam's own birth, so he is not really interested in it. He continues reading up to Entry 5, but then decides to jump closer to the present.

"Entry five hundred and twenty-two."

Adam spontaneously thought of this number. The tone of the text has changed radically. This Marchenko is extremely saddened. It seems his two children were killed two weeks ago. It is not clear how they died, but at this moment the reason for their death is obvious to Marchenko 2. He keeps asking how he is to blame for it. In spite of this, there appears to be an undertone of hope. It is not all over yet.

"Entry seven hundred and nine."

By choosing this number Adam has jumped ahead about a year and a half. The Marchenko in this text is almost unrecognizable. He is cynical, evil, and completely disillusioned. Adam has never experienced their own Marchenko this way. Does this mean he might exhibit the same behavior? Adam simply does not know enough. Yet he does not feel like reading these complete memoirs. He is not interested in Marchenko, this one or the other. This is about himself, Adam from space.

Can he ask the notebook questions? Perhaps he might find out something about himself that way.

"Is there a search function, Francesca?"

"Of course. Use the command 'Search' in order to search for something."

The programming of this software is really primitive. Maybe the designers erroneously believed that simple software would be especially reliable? What should he ask? What is the core of his story? He has an idea, and suddenly his face feels all hot.

"Search for Creator."

"Thirteen references."

"Display all."

Tightly-spaced text appears on the screen of Adam's universal device. The first two passages just briefly mention the term 'Creator.' In the third text, however, the word appears in almost every other sentence.

"Today I made a shocking discovery related to the Creator. If it weren't so terrible I would have to be glad Adam and Eve are no longer alive."

The entry appears to be from a time long after the death of both of them.

"I have always wondered about the sectors in my memory I could not access. My kind interpretation was that the Creator used these to store a message to my children that would be revealed to them in due time. Perhaps when they came of age? I was wrong, because the Creator had something very different in mind. In a few words, he explained the true dimensions of his project. The mental block was probably removed because Adam and Eve should be adults now. It is very hard for me to write down the whole truth. It is so monstrous that my mind refuses to grasp it completely. Or perhaps I am simply not willing to accept this betrayal by the Creator. I have always attempted to convey to Adam and Eve how unique they are. I told them the Creator, and thus all mankind, chose them for an important mission, and that they alone could fulfill this task. But the truth looks very different. The Creator sent thousands of Adams and Eves, in the form of their DNA, on space voyages. They flew to different destinations that had one thing in common—they possessed potentially habitable planets."

Here the text ends. Adam feels cold, his limbs tremble and his back is sopping wet. This is impossible. Marchenko 2 must have imagined this in his madness. Or is this perhaps a trap, designed in such a way that he or his sister would find it at some point, the mean-spirited revenge of a defeated AI? Of course not—that is nonsense. They discovered the station more or less by accident. Marchenko had no opportunity to prepare for their visit this way.

So everything is true. His presence here, his entire life, is meaningless. Who knows how many beings of his kind are currently exploring Proxima b? Or are they especially lucky to arrive here as the first or perhaps only team? Well, Marchenko 2 landed before them, even if he lost his passengers on the way.

Adam wonders what to do. Should he tell Eve about it? Adam checks his surroundings. Did their own Marchenko realize what he just found out? He tests the console. No, it is not possible to access it from outside. Of course their Marchenko might guess the password, just like he did. But even then he would not find out who logged into the electrical cabinet beside him.

"Francesca, delete access and search logs."

"Logs deleted."

Adam's palms feel moist. He wipes his hands dry on his pants. "Francesca, maintenance."

"Which systems do you want to access, Mitya?"

"Radio."

"Not accessible. Should I display a list of accessible systems?"

"I need to establish a channel to my mobile unit."

"I understand. Opening communication system. Searching mobile unit. Please wait. Please wait. Mobile unit found. Current position 140 kilometers east/southeast. Channel capacity not sufficient for spoken communication."

"Can I send a message electronically?"

"Of course, Mitya."

Adam puts his hands in his pockets and takes them out again a moment later. He wants to establish contact with the second Marchenko. He needs the full truth, as quickly as possible. But why should Marchenko 2 be interested in talking to him and answering his questions? Adam himself immobilized him and initiated his banishment. Adam crouches in front of the console, places an elbow on his knee and massages his aching temple with one hand. If he stays down here too long, Eve will show up at some point. What should he write?

"I want to dictate a message to the mobile unit, Francesca," he says.

"You can start, Mitya."

"Marchenko: I have been skimming through your notebook." Should he apologize for it? He shakes his head. "I need more information about the Creator and our mission. Let me know whether you are willing to discuss this and what I can do for you in return. Please use this channel. Signed, Adam. End of dictation."

"End of dictation," Francesca confirms.

"Display text."

His message appears on the screen. The voice recognition has worked perfectly. The text does not sound groveling, but neutral. It's just about some information, nothing more, nothing less.

"Send message," Adam says.

"Message sent."

March 7, 19

For a few days, Adam has been even more withdrawn than usual. I don't think I hear him say more than ten words a day. Is that normal? Eve also seems to be concerned. I saw her trying to confront him about this. In the end she even yelled at him. That's not like her at all, but he still only gave one-syllable answers.

I guess I have to accept the fact that I can't get through to him anymore. Perhaps it is only a phase. Could he be entering a delayed adolescence, even though he will soon be 17 years old? Or might he be ill? In my former life I was a doctor, but not a psychologist, let alone a psychiatrist. Is Adam suffering from depression? I have consulted various textbooks, but I am not sure.

Perhaps he just needs something to divert him. Should we start another excursion to the gravitational wave receiver? I don't think we would gain any new insights, but it is possible. This time I could participate better in the research, because J, the robot that serves as my mobile platform, has finally been fully repaired.

I just asked Adam and Eve to help me activate the robot. The complete transfer of my consciousness into the machine is a tricky process, and I am a bit afraid of it. It is as if my own heart were going to be deactivated for a few minutes before a new one is implanted. Who likes such an uncertain intermediate phase? What if the body exhibits a severe fault and destroys itself?

J is still hanging inside his steel scaffolding. The bleeding wounds have disappeared. His skin is shiny, as Eve just covered it with machine oil. She is really putting in a lot of effort. She seems to be glad about the fact that I am regaining my physical form.

Starting the robot is a complicated procedure. While the robot is only a machine, he's a very sophisticated one. It is not possible to turn on all modules simultaneously. We have to activate the individual components in the proper order. If we mess up, the best outcome might be having to start the process over again, while the worst-case scenario would be damage to some of his parts.

Right now, the robot still seems completely dead. When I am not on board, it is controlled by a semi-AI. We will use this SAI to start up the robot now. Eve has asked to be in charge of the procedure. I have agreed. She can see the process and the block diagram on her monitor. Eve carefully touches an on-screen button. Adam jerks back when J opens both eyes. But nothing else happens. J's limbs are still slack. Eve gradually increases the energy supply. While she is doing this, Adam removes the power cables. J looks like a patient whose IV lines are being taken off after a complicated surgery.

"Watch out, I am going to activate the motors in his upper body."

A moment ago, J seemed soft, despite his metallic body, but now he exhibits a dynamic tension. His arms are no longer controlled strictly by gravity, but swing slightly of their own accord. One can see the robot testing one muscle after the other. Now and then something moves somewhere.

"You can remove the scaffolding now," Eve says.

They had already unscrewed most of the fastening bolts beforehand. Adam only has to work on four spots, and then J's upper body no longer has support. The motors move jerkily and the robot begins to straighten himself.

"Please move back a few steps," Eve warns. Now comes the decisive moment. J is supposed to rise again. Eve quickly presses two buttons. The robot gets up almost noiselessly. I am watching him through the camera. J has changed. Due to the cramped circumstances down here, he is smaller than before, and he also moves on two legs. J takes a step forward so that he can turn around. Now I can see his third arm located on his back. It will help him carry loads or pull a sled.

"Marchenko, it is about time," Eve says. The robot is functioning perfectly, so I can transfer my mind inside his metal body.

But now a message arrives and distracts us. Eve looks annoyed. She pushes a few buttons. Then her eyes widen in amazement.

"It's *Messenger*," she says. "It must have found something. I can't recognize what it is, though."

"One moment, I'll take a look," I say. Our spaceship just sent us a mountain of raw data. There must be something interesting hidden in the data, as otherwise the ship would not have sent it. But the detailed evaluation is left up to me.

First I detect coordinates. I match them with my internal world map. "There is something pretty close to the center of the dark hemisphere," I tell them.

"What is it?" Adam steps up to the robot and stares into the eyes, as if I were already inside.

"Please be patient for a while."

"That's easy for you to say, after we've been waiting more than two weeks," Adam replies.

I scan the measurement data. *Messenger* found something enormous indeed. There is a high concentration of mass.

However, the data don't indicate what specific object is located there. It could be remnants of an iron meteorite core, or a giant volcano, or a city... It is also unclear how large the object is. It is only certain that its mass is very large.

"Well, the thing has a diameter of between 500 meters and 25 kilometers," I say, explaining the margin of error, "and it weighs as much as two or three skyscrapers."

"It could be all kinds of things," Eve replies. I have to agree with her.

"Can't we see anything at that location? *Messenger* must have photographed everything."

"No, Adam," I say, and display the location in question on Eve's monitor. "All we can see is a solid ice layer at least 50 meters thick. We will have to find out what hides beneath it."

Suddenly Adam can't wait to be going. "When are we starting?"

"I don't know. First we have to consider the best way to reach this location—through the ocean or on top of the ice?"

March 8, 19

"WAKE ME UP IN HALF AN HOUR!" EVE CALLS FROM ABOVE.

That's so typical, Adam thinks. *She could have set an alarm, but she doesn't like its noise.* Yet Adam does not complain about Eve taking a nap, because this suits his purposes well. Marchenko is currently testing his new body at the bottom of the ocean and probably won't be back for an hour or more. This gives Adam enough time to check whether Marchenko 2 has replied to his message.

"I am closing the hatch so you won't be disturbed," he calls out to Eve. Then he shuts the hatch leading to the upper room. He bends down, opens the matching hatch to the service module, and climbs down. It looks much tidier now. Marchenko must have cleaned it up yesterday. He obviously wants to live down here.

Adam looks around. The data console in the corner appears untouched. Marchenko probably doesn't need it, as he can access the computers in the station in much simpler ways. Adam crouches down in front of the metal console and establishes a connection.

"User identification required."

I hope Marchenko hasn't changed anything! Adam enters the same user name and password he had used four days ago.

"Welcome, Mitya!"

Either the service program is running separately from the rest of the station technology, or Marchenko saw no reason for selecting a new password. Adam hesitates. He wonders whether Marchenko also found the entries left by his alter ego.

"Open communication system," he says.

"Channel is being opened."

"Francesca, is there something like an inbox?"

"There is a saved message."

Adam rubbed his hands. "Who is the sender?"

"Mobile unit one."

That designation is new, but also logical. Four days ago there was only one mobile unit—Marchenko 2. Now there are two, as the 'real' Marchenko has regained his body. Adam has to be careful not to send his messages to the wrong address.

"Display saved message."

The text appears on the screen of his universal device. Adam squints because the font is so small.

"Adam, my dear," he reads. The salutation gives him the creeps. Marchenko 2 seems to live in his own private world. "I am so glad you want to contact me. You have no idea how much I missed you and your sister. Excuse me for using that term, but emotionally I still consider you siblings, even though genetically—as you probably know—you are no more closely related than any random man on Earth is to any random woman."

Eve, whom he has known for so long, the only human being he knows, and the one whose reactions he can predict almost as well as his own, is not really his sister? That's impossible. Marchenko 2 must be up to something, must be trying to stir up trouble between them. Adam massages one hand with the other, making his joints crack.

"I will gladly tell you what I found out about the Creator, our shared mission, but also about Eve and you. However, I have to insist that we meet for that purpose."

This is it. He wants to get one of us in his power. What is Marchenko planning? Does he need leverage?

"You can't imagine how much I long to see your familiar face again. Therefore please forgive an old man this harmless request."

A harmless request—who would be naive enough to believe that?

"For obvious reasons we cannot meet near the station. Your Marchenko would prevent it. I am not entitled to criticize his motives. Yet you might ask yourself sometime why you asked me to tell you the truth, and not him. I don't want to interfere with your decisions, though. It is your life, and you are an adult. The fact is, we need to meet on neutral ground for practical reasons."

Adam hesitates. He can't simply sneak out of the station. Plus, they are about to leave on their journey to the dark side of the planet. How can they arrange a meeting, then? They can't. Somehow, he must persuade Marchenko 2—the *fake* Marchenko—to communicate what he knows.

Adam's thoughts suddenly stop. He just called the banned AI 'fake.' Is this just force of habit, or is there more behind it? What is the real relationship between the banished Marchenko and their own Marchenko, who is currently testing his new body in the ocean?

He goes on reading.

"I am already more than 100 kilometers from the station, and I cover 5 to 10 additional kilometers every day. If you want me to, I will slow down so you can catch up with me. Once you are ready you should contact me, preferably via this channel. I am sending you an attachment listing other frequencies you can use to reach me if you are unable to stay on this one. These frequencies are outside the commonly used spectrum. Therefore your Marchenko won't be monitoring them. However, you will have to manipulate the communication system in order to transmit on these frequencies. You need to come up with an idea. I know you can do it, and I am sure we will meet again. Best wishes, Marchenko."

Adam collapses. Crouching becomes too exhausting, so he sits on the floor. A meeting in the middle of nowhere, how would that even work? He can't escape their Marchenko's supervision that easily. However, it might be possible once they are on the way. Marchenko won't always be able to focus on him and Eve simultaneously.

But what would be the use of meeting with Marchenko 2? Adam can never be sure Marchenko 2 is telling the truth. When they arrived at the station, he definitely lied to them. He only had one goal. Who knows whether it would be any different next time? Adam knows he should not have sent that message four days ago. It would have been better to ignore the digital journal. *What right do I even have to read a stranger's diary? Yet don't I also have the right to know the truth?* Adam sighs out loud. His thoughts are muddled like never before. As soon as he thinks he has developed a logical series of arguments, he comes up with a refutation, which makes it all appear meaningless.

He has to formulate a reply. By now he's been sitting down here for three-quarters of an hour. He should have gotten Eve up a while ago. Time is running short, and their Marchenko will probably return soon.

"Marchenko," he starts to write. That sounds neutral. He isn't actually writing to his own Marchenko, even though the two Marchenkos are probably based on the same elements of consciousness.

"We are going to leave the station in a few days. Our destination is an object in the center of the dark hemisphere. I hope we can meet along the way. I will try to contact you during our voyage using one of the frequencies you mention. Have a nice journey. Adam."

He reads the text one more time. While doing so, he feels a faint rumbling in the floor of the station. Their Marchenko has probably just closed the airlock door from the inside. He has to go up again. How will Marchenko 2 interpret his text? Adam hopes it won't trigger any unfounded expectations. He knows, though, that he can't completely avoid the possibility. He has no control over what his recipient is going to read between the lines.

There is another noise. Marchenko is back inside the actual station.

"Send message," Adam says. Francesca confirms his command. "Delete logs." Then he ends the connection.

Adam gets up and climbs the ladder to the command module. Adam looks around, but he is still alone. Therefore he won't need an excuse. He carefully closes the hatch leading down. Then he knocks loudly on the entrance of the cabin above him.

"Wake up, sleepyhead," he says. "Marchenko is back."

Ten seconds later the door is opened. The robot body carrying Marchenko's consciousness enters the room. One can see Marchenko is in a hurry, as there are still some water-streaked areas on his torso.

"What is going on?" Adam asks.

Marchenko stops abruptly. The robot's mouth region opens and forms a kind of smile. "Oh, nothing," he says. "I just suddenly started to worry. I had the feeling something happened to the two of you."

The cabin's hatch opens and Eve climbs down the ladder. Eve, the woman he always considered his sister, but who supposedly is not even related to him. *What does this mean for the future, if it turns out to be true?* He studies Eve carefully. With every step she takes down the ladder, the thin fabric of her pants stretches over her backside. It is nice to watch. So far, Adam has never dared to look at her this way. No, that's not right, he simply had not thought of doing so. It never bothered or worried him when she sat topless next to him on the bed. He hopes that won't change! Is it the fault of Marchenko 2? Has he ruined their relationship? Perhaps he should talk to their Marchenko, who has always behaved like a father to him. Yet Adam does not dare to do so. What he is now doing feels like a betrayal.

"Why are you looking at me as if I were a ghost?" Eve asks.

Adam is glad she cannot interpret his gaze correctly. He turns toward Marchenko. "So, is everything working?"

"Yes, the body works excellently. Good work from all of us."

Eve steps closer to him and wipes a few drops of water from the metal. "I don't want you to get any spots," she says.

Marchenko laughs. "As you are already here, we might talk about our expedition, okay?"

"Good idea," Adam says. He finds a place to sit down. Eve sits on the table, dangling her feet.

"I took a look at it. We can reach our destination by crossing the ice or by going underwater," Marchenko says.

"Really?" asks Adam.

Marchenko looks at him. "I mean, in principle. Unfortunately it is impossible to predict whether the path across the ocean floor is free all the way to the center of the dark hemisphere. We simply lack the data. However, we know that the entire rear side of the planet is covered by ice. And the model of global circulation I calculated assumes that there is a continuous ocean below the ice, with a depth of at least one kilometer. There might be a mountain range blocking the way, though, that reaches all the way up to the ice layer."

"If we go below, wouldn't we have to drill through the ice to reach our destination?" Eve asks.

"Maybe. We don't really know what kind of object this is.

Perhaps it is a gigantic tower that has a door at its base on the ocean floor? In that case we would have to drill through the ice from above while being able to enter it easily from below."

"A tower? You think that, Marchenko? A black tower?"

"It could be black, Eve."

"I am for going through the ocean," Adam says. *That would offer me the only chance for meeting Marchenko 2,* he thinks. *Marchenko 2 would stay in the ocean.*

"Can you give a reason for that, dear brother?"

He feels a stab of pain in his chest. *Damn.* If only he had left that electronic notebook alone. No, he will never again be able to listen to Eve's words innocently.

"It concerns the resources," he says. "We have everything we need on the ocean floor. Or Marchenko can create it from the available compounds and elements."

"But what about the energy we require? Without it, the fabricators can't work. I would think our chances would be better on top of the ice. And oxygen is freely available up there, while we have to generate it down here," Eve argues.

"The oxygen is an important argument," Marchenko agrees. "As far as energy generation is concerned, we would get about the same amount above or below. On top of the ice we have wind energy, down here the ocean currents. But if we travel across the surface of the ice, we have more than enough air and fresh water, without having to expend energy. We don't need to worry so much about energy during the voyage if we pack plenty of food supplies. We would travel faster and return sooner. We always have to monitor our air supply in the ocean. If an obstacle shows up... well, I experienced this once and would like to avoid it."

"And if we have to get below the ice layer nevertheless?" *Looks like I won't be able to meet Marchenko 2,* Adam thinks. He feels disappointed, but somehow relieved at the same time.

"Then we will have to come up with something. But perhaps we won't have to get through the layer of ice."

"What do you think we will find at our destination, Marchenko?"

The robot turns toward Eve. "A building, I hope. Something the inhabitants of Proxima b created, something that fulfilled some function for them."

"And why didn't they build it at some location that is easier to reach?"

"Maybe they didn't want everybody who just happened to come by to find it."

March 14, 19

Eve is tossing and turning on her bunk. Marchenko and Adam had insisted on leaving the station two days ago, much to her regret. If she'd had her say, they would have taken a break there, for a year or two. Why are the other two so eager to continue this expedition? Whatever awaits them in those icy wastes will wait for a few more months or years. And nobody will be there. The famous emergency signal that lured them here to Proxima b was certainly misunderstood. Perhaps it was meant for someone else, or it wasn't a request that they should come here, but rather a warning telling them to stay away. Who could know?

She closes her eyes, but there is a recurring sound that keeps her from falling asleep. It is a cracking sound, very faint, which repeats about every 30 seconds. The hissing of the jets driving *Valkyrie* forward is much louder, but she simply can't ignore the cracking.

Crack. There it is again. Eve presses her eyes shut. If she could only fall asleep quickly enough! Now she has 30 seconds of quiet. *Sleep, Eve sleep! Crack. Too late.* She opens her eyes. Would it help if she turned onto her other side? Eve tries it, though she knows it won't make a difference. *I hope we get there soon!*

Something touches her legs, just for a moment, but noticeably. What was that? Eve opens her eyes. She must have actually fallen asleep. The second bunk, closer to the stern, is empty. Adam should be sleeping there. *Where did he disappear to?* She sits up cautiously. His bed is definitely empty. *Is he also having a hard time sleeping?* Eve closes her pajama top.

Recently, Adam has been staring at her in a strange way. Actually not at her, but at her breasts. Since then she has stopped sleeping topless. She will have to talk to him about it. Maybe it's all a misunderstanding. Nudity was never an issue between them, so why should this change now? Eve is reminded of that famous story from Earth in which an animal —a snake?—causes a young woman named Eve to feel ashamed about being naked. *What animal is behind this?*

She stands up. The floor feels cold beneath her bare feet. In the bow, numerous small lights shine on the robot. Marchenko has deactivated the robot body. In the evening he announced he would try to calculate and plot the entire route based on data from orbit. Eve slowly walks around Adam's bunk. She does not want to scare him. Or perhaps he has fled from the cracking sound and is now sleeping in some recess.

After two steps toward the stern, Eve realizes that her brother is obviously not sleeping. The cover of the engine room shaft is open. A faint light shines from below. Eve knows how crowded it is down there. That is not a place where you would lie down to sleep, even if the cracking sound bothers you elsewhere. *Adam must be up to something.*

She approaches until she can look down into the shaft. She recognizes Adam's legs. Slowly, she crouches. Should she touch him? What is he doing down there? Eve listens. She hears the sound of typing. *Adam is writing something! But why down in this hole?* She ponders this question. If she confronts him now, he will feel like she is spying on him. She does not want that. Perhaps she can talk to him about it tomorrow without Marchenko noticing.

Adam's right leg is moving. Eve is startled. Has he noticed her? He definitely shows signs of trying to crawl out of the hole. She gets up as quietly as possible and tiptoes back to her bunk. She turns around before sitting down. Adam is already standing over the hole, looking in her direction. *Damn.* She sits down on her bunk, cross-legged.

Her brother slowly comes closer. He seems to be taking a lot of time. He looks like he feels guilty about something. What was he doing down there? He reaches Eve and sits down next to her. She turns sideways and looks him in the face. His brow is furrowed. His gaze is aimed directly at her cleavage. She raises her left hand and gives him a slight slap on the cheek. He looks at her. It is obvious he doesn't know what to say. She can feel his thoughts wrestling inside his head. There is something he wants to tell her, and at the same time, something else keeps him from doing so. She knows this well and gives him an encouraging smile.

Unfortunately, she gets no answer. "I had to check something," Adam says. "The system reported a potential malfunction down there."

Eve knows this is only a made-up excuse, and he must be aware that she knows this. Yet he still attempts to lie. *What does this mean?* She shakes her head. *If he wants to keep the truth to himself, oh well. But he can spare himself the excuses.* He wants to say something, but she places her index finger on his mouth. While she is moving forward, he retreats.

He smells good. She briefly inhales through her nose, and yes, he really smells good. It must be the scent of the engine room. Eve has to laugh at herself. Is she going crazy now? With her right hand she gives him a slight push against his shoulder. It is supposed to mean he should go to his bed, and he understands her gesture. Adam gets up, walks five steps to his bunk, and settles in. Eve also lies down. She pulls the blanket over her body and rolls up in a fetal position. Soon she is asleep.

March 16, 19

VALKYRIE IS BOBBING UP AND DOWN IN A BLACK HOLE THAT seems to have suddenly appeared in the ice. It is a painful memory. Everything looks like it did back then, on Enceladus. Even the environment is similar. It is icy cold, and the sky is black. At first we tried to moor on the edge of the ice layer, where you can still see the expanse of the ocean, but the ice was too thin there. Therefore I had *Valkyrie* dive and continue underwater a few more kilometers before melting a hole through the ice. Here the ice is three meters thick and can therefore support my heavy body and the even heavier sled.

Now it is time to load the sled with everything still stored inside *Valkyrie*. In order to unload the vessel more easily, I set up two strong searchlights, lighting a scene that looks rather eerie in black and white. But there are a few differences between this place and Enceladus. On the ice moon, for instance, Saturn always hung above the horizon, so it never became completely dark. I am afraid we will encounter darkness in its most severe form on Proxima b. The planet does not even have a moon. If the clouds hide the stars, we will feel like we are deep inside a dark cave.

On the other hand, the air up here on top of the ice is breathable. While it is icy cold—in the center of the hemisphere it might drop to minus 80 degrees—Adam and Eve can just wear warm clothing instead of their spacesuits. Marchenko 2 put lots of supplies in the station, and they will now be used to good purpose. The distance we have to cover is unbelievably long. On Proxima b the eternal ice starts about 3,000 kilometers past the borderline between day and night. Therefore we have to cover almost 8,000 kilometers. If we manage to travel 50 kilometers a day, our voyage will require 160 days. And that is only the way to our destination. We will spend almost a whole terrestrial year in continuous darkness, a strain I can hardly imagine.

Our most important means of transportation will be the sled I built. I can't force Adam and Eve to walk the whole way. On the platform of the sled I constructed a small, well-heated tent where Adam and Eve will spend most of their time. It does not offer a lot of room, but enough to stretch their legs and sleep. I hope this will allow us to move without taking long breaks.

According to the surface conditions I might not just cover 50 kilometers a day, but 100 or even 200 kilometers. My robot body, as I have tested, can reach a speed of approximately 12 kilometers per hour if the sled carries its maximum weight, including the two passengers—at least on level ground. One-sixth less might not be an unrealistic value. This way we might reach our destination in as little as 40 days.

Adam emerges from the hatch. He turns around and bends down. One hand—it has to be Eve's, of course—passes him a sack. He pulls it up, holding it in front of him. I am standing at the edge of the ice, using my third arm like the boom of a crane in order to take the sack from him. I have to be careful not to lose my balance, so I simultaneously lean in the other direction. My spine is more flexible than that of a human, so I can bend it in any direction and at almost any angle. I trained for days to master every function my body offers. I toss the sack onto the sled.

"Man, it is really cold," Adam says. Clouds of vapor issue from his mouth and nose when he talks.

"It's only minus 15," I hear Eve say from inside *Valkyrie*. "Don't make such a fuss, sissy!"

He laughs. I would never have been allowed to talk to Adam like this, but he doesn't complain. "What's the weather report for the coming days?" he asks me.

"Mostly fair weather until tomorrow, with temperatures falling."

The planet is tidally locked in its motion around its sun, always facing it the same way, but this does not mean there is no weather. *Messenger*, high above us in orbit, keeps us up to date. It is predicting gale-force winds for the day after tomorrow. We are no longer in the storm zone, where the energy exchange between the light and the dark sides occurs, but particularly strong cyclonic winds also affect the adjacent areas.

"After that it will get stormy, unfortunately," I say.

"How stormy?" asks Adam.

"Very, if I can trust the *Messenger* data. I think we had better find shelter before then."

It doesn't look too good for covering 200 kilometers per day, at least for the day after tomorrow.

"Couldn't this planet leave us alone with its storms?"

"You'd be surprised, Adam. If the energy exchange between the two hemispheres didn't exist, our destination would be as cold as outer space. You should be glad about any storm bringing some warmth we wouldn't have otherwise."

"Can we go on now? My feet are falling asleep from standing around," Eve calls from inside *Valkyrie*. Adam takes the next sack from her, passes it to me, and I place it on the sled. I inspect the cargo area and estimate that we can leave in half an hour.

March 18, 19

If something can go wrong, it will go wrong, Adam thinks. *Can't we catch a break?* He fell into the hole of the alien spider, he got caught by Eve while communicating with the enemy, and now the storm is on time and as bad as *Messenger's* forecast. Adam clings to the sled. Gusts of wind repeatedly hit the tarp of their tent, and the fact that Marchenko has increased his speed does not make the voyage any more comfortable. Marchenko has supposedly detected a cave in a low slope. However, as he avoided mountainous areas during route planning, the cave is significantly off our path, and it is doubtful whether we will reach it in time.

"Can't we just melt our own cave into the ice?" Adam asks via radio, the way they now must communicate between the tent and the robot.

"We don't have enough time for that. And look around, it's all flat. Do you want to melt the cave into the ground?" replies Marchenko.

"Why not?"

"I thought we needed a cave, not a swimming pool."

Eve laughs at Adam.

Of course—the ice would turn into water.

"But thanks for your suggestion," Marchenko adds, while the sled still flies across the ice.

Adam imagines the mountain toward which they are heading. On the warm side of the planet the mountain might rise on an island, or actually form an island, if there was water there. Couldn't these creatures have constructed their important building in the warm hemisphere? Here the ocean has a depth of several thousand meters. Measuring from the ocean floor, this mountain must be enormous. Perhaps a volcano?

"Marchenko... are we approaching a volcano?" Adam asks. He does not receive an immediate answer. The AI is probably checking all the data first.

Finally Adam hears, "I quickly downloaded the altitude profile from Messenger. You are apparently right. The slope seems to be part of a gigantic caldera surrounding the crater."

"Isn't that somehow dangerous?" Adam asks.

"It doesn't look like the volcano has been active in recent times."

"*Messenger's* measurement of the gravitational field did not detect it, did it?"

"No," Marchenko says and pauses. "You are right—that's interesting. But it probably is not significant."

"Good," Eve says.

"I don't want to worry you," Marchenko says, "but it might be a close-run thing."

"How close?"

"Very close, Adam. The storm is approaching at 180 km/h. I can see its edges already on the radar. It's 20 kilometers away, I would say."

"That's barely seven minutes. And how long will it take to reach the cave?" Adam asks.

"At least ten minutes."

"Marchenko, stop right away," Adam exclaims. Eve looks at him. He realizes at once that she understands him.

"Perhaps I can move somewhat faster."

"Marchenko, we really have to stop," Eve now calls.

The robot abruptly stops the sled.

"No time for long discussions," Adam says to Marchenko. "We turn the sled over and you lie on top of it. How much do you weigh?"

"About one and a half tons. I would crush you."

"Nonsense. Take a look at the side walls of the sled. They can withstand a lot of pressure. It is a classic U-shaped profile."

"How do you know that?"

"Just something I recall. Turn the sled over. Now."

"What about the supplies?"

"No matter. We can cram some of them under the sled, whatever fits. It is going to get rather tight. How long do we have to wait for the storm to move past us?"

"The worst should be over in four or five hours, according to *Messenger*."

Adam puts a blanket on the ice. It is coated with metal foil. "Eve and I will lie down on that. You place the sled over us and plug all the holes with the sacks, so we won't get any areas of low pressure in there."

"Are we going to have enough air to breathe?" Eve asks.

"The volume should last for several hours. In case of emergency Marchenko would have to blow in fresh air from above," Adam says.

"Okay." Eve is already lying down. Adam lies down next to her. He is briefly annoyed because he does not know how to place himself. He decides for the position in which his back faces Eve. Marchenko sweeps the supplies off the cargo area, turns the sled over, and carefully places it over Adam and Eve. He tries to put as many sacks as possible inside the shelter of the inverted sled, with help from Adam and Eve. They have the impression their surroundings are already getting darker, even though they can no longer see outside.

"There isn't enough space for everything. I hope I picked the most important things," Marchenko finally says. By now, the roar of the storm can be clearly heard.

"Then place yourself on top and we will see what happens," Adam asks him.

The roof of their little shelter lowers by one or two centimeters once Marchenko situates his robot body on top.

"Best of luck down there," he says.

"We're doing fine," Eve replies.

Adam's heart is beating faster. He hopes this construction will withstand the storm. A gale can develop enormous force. He read a lot about natural disasters as a child and was fascinated by these primal forces that humans are powerless against. They would have to stay as low as possible and not give the wind a chance to create a low-pressure area.

This seems to be working well. He can hardly feel any draft. It is almost as if they had voluntarily walled themselves up inside a crypt. What if Marchenko's robot body fails for some reason and he won't be able to get up after the storm? They would never manage to push away 1,500 kilos from down here. They would suffocate.

Suddenly Adam jerks. Something soft is touching his back.

"I feel cold," Eve whispers as she moves closer to him, and then she places her left arm on his belly. He realizes he can feel her breasts against his back, in spite of the warm clothing they are wearing, and he is terrified. She does not know what he knows. He has to be careful so that she does not misunderstand him. And she will, if her hand accidentally moves any lower. Oh man, oh man, they are in great danger—a gale is raging that could kill them and very well might—and he has to worry about sporting an erection. What kind of strange and embarrassing reaction is this? For safety's sake he moves her hand a bit higher. He starts feeling hot.

Eve doesn't seem to realize his problem, because ten

minutes later he hears her snoring behind him. That's unusual for her. Perhaps it's caused by the lack of oxygen? While that is unlikely, he still wants to check the air with his universal device. He takes the device from his bag and activates the oxygen display. Everything is okay. They still have at least seven hours of safe breathing left. Humans don't suffocate that quickly, as they can exhale and inhale the same air three or four times without any problem. And if the air supply gets tight, Marchenko can help them. Adam slowly calms down. Maybe he should try to sleep, too. But then he would miss the most precious moments of his life—and he won't be able to spend another night in this pleasant, yet completely innocent, position for some time.

THE STORM IS HOWLING ABOVE THEM. WHILE ADAM DOES NOT feel the slightest breeze down here in their crypt, forces rage not far away that not even Marchenko can stop. He hopes Marchenko calculated everything correctly. In the middle of these plains there is nothing to temper the fury of the storm. The sled protects them, but if the wind manages to reach underneath it with its strong arms... Adam does not want to think about it, but he can't help imagining the scene. *It is utterly impossible for me to sleep under these circumstances. How does Eve manage it?*

There are some rumbling sounds a few times, twice especially loud ones.

"Everything is fine," Marchenko just says. But Adam cannot hear any movement above him. Marchenko obviously is not even checking whether everything really is fine. Should he go and see for himself?

After the second loud noise he cannot help but ask, "Is the luggage still there?"

"Probably not," Marchenko answers.

"Don't you want to check?"

"Much too dangerous."

"And the crates with the supplies?"

"What's gone is gone."

Adam sighs. It would be best to fall asleep. He tries to do so, but just when he gets used to the howling of the storm, Eve starts to snore again.

March 19, 19

"INVENTORY," A DEEP VOICE CALLS FROM OUTSIDE.

Adam opens his eyes and blinks as Eve shines her flashlight at him. "Get out of bed, sleepyhead," she says.

"I didn't sleep at all," Adam mumbles. But his eyes feel crusted over, so he realizes this isn't true.

"Watch out!" Marchenko calls. Eve pushes Adam's head down. Marchenko lifts the sled and turns it back upright. "Wait, I am going to put up the tent in a moment."

Adam feels terribly cold. A moment ago the temperature was 10 degrees, now it is minus 80 degrees. His suit heater cannot adapt so quickly. Therefore Adam is very grateful when Marchenko finally finishes setting up the tent. "And what about our supplies?" he asks.

"Well, to put it positively, we still have about half," Marchenko says.

"And that doesn't bother you?"

"No, Adam, I packed more than enough. And I still can produce most things."

"Maybe we should still look for those supplies?" Adam suggests.

"You can forget about it. Whatever the wind swept off the

sled has been carried many kilometers away. We will never find it in the darkness."

"Then we can be glad that Eve and I were not blown away."

"Indeed," Marchenko says. "You would not have stood a chance all alone out there. I would never have found you. I'm glad you made me turn the sled into a shelter."

March 31, 19

LUNCH BREAK. MARCHENKO HAS STOPPED THE SLED. THE entrance to the tent is half open. Eve sees how the moist air from their shelter freezes immediately when it gets outside. Now and then the lamp at the tent entrance shines on metal. That is Marchenko, who is currently running a routine check of his robot body.

"Well? Is everything okay?" Eve asks.

"So far no failures."

Adam is 'cooking.' They still use this term, even though now it is more accurate to say 'warming up', and it is really related to chemistry. One mixes a few freeze-dried components with water according to Marchenko's instructions and then adds energy. The results are underwhelming. Eve has to force herself to eat, but she knows she would kill herself if she does not act in a disciplined fashion. Her body needs carbohydrates, protein, fat, and so on. If they follow Marchenko's instructions, they get nutritious meals. Taste is a secondary issue.

Eve's main problem is hygiene. During the first few days she forced herself to go outside and rub her body with snow.

By now it is too cold for that. It's not worth losing a small toe in order to get rid of body odor. *I really would love to take a shower again!* Eve remembers the spray of water that had covered her—like she imagined warm rain would feel—when she showered in the station. They will have to do without showers for at least three more months, and that is if everything goes smoothly.

The problem gets worse, because the growing darkness makes all of their senses more acute, day by day. Sometimes Eve escapes the stuffy atmosphere of the tents for a few minutes. Then she sits at the front of the sled. A thick layer of clothing protects her body. She has completely wrapped up her head and face, and her eyes are protected by large goggles. Only a thin scarf covers her mouth, which lets a little of the icy air move through.

By now she has learned to taste the air. Its flavor changes according to the weather and their surroundings. She concentrates on this for a while and then asks Marchenko for current data, which she predicts more accurately day by day. When there are clouds in the invisible sky, the air tastes saltier than usual. It also has a different consistency, like a very thin version of the cotton candy Marchenko once had fabricators make for them. When the stars shine, though, the air seems intoxicating. Eve looks up to the dark sky, in which an immense number of lights glitter.

Eve sucks in the cold air like it's a sparkling cocktail with a lot of ice. The smell seems to be more related to the environment. When they cross broad plains, she smells dry summer grass illuminated by a hot sun. When their ride gets bumpier, due to crevices and chunks of ice blocking the way, there is an aroma of moss and fungi in the air, mixed with the sharp smell of ozone after a thunderstorm. What came first, her imagination or the changes in her perception? Eve cannot tell, but whenever she compares her sensations with Marchenko's data, she finds a surprisingly strong correspondence.

Yesterday she tried to tell Adam about this, but he seemed totally uninterested. He doesn't mind the smell inside the tent very much, and it is always Eve who insists on opening the tent flap. Then Adam just whines about being cold. She admits it gets very cold inside the tent quickly, but as long as they are wearing their LCVGs, the heated underwear, they can't ever feel really ice-cold. Unless they run out of energy.

When Eve is sitting out there all bundled up, the scarf can only keep the cold away for a few minutes. However, Marchenko adapted the helmets of their pressure suits so they can be directly connected to their LCVGs. When she puts on her helmet, Eve turns from a fascinated traveler into an omniscient researcher. She regrets this slightly, because the role of the traveler allows for a closer contact with the environment and herself. Adam would laugh about such ideas, but it is true—the helmet turns uncertainty into certainty. The inside of the faceplate shows her a radar scan of the surrounding area, based on Marchenko's sensors. The eternal darkness disappears and is replaced by a constructed reality in which hard objects shine brightly, and soft ones more dimly, while potential dangers appear in red. While it is still the world they are moving through, it is also like a game world—a virtual reality—but with real dangers.

"How dangerous are the things marked in red?" she asked Marchenko.

"Once the system recognizes them as hazards they really aren't dangerous anymore, as I move around them," Marchenko answered.

Afterward she realized why the red markers seemed so unreal. She does not really have to be afraid of things appearing in red, but of anything without special markings. The next step or the one after that might reveal a hitherto unknown danger, such as a crevasse hidden from the radar below a thin layer of ice.

Eve is glad the human mind is so adaptable. One cannot

simply be afraid of every step one takes. The brain gets used to the warnings from the unconscious and quickly learns to ignore them. This is the only way Eve can so thoroughly enjoy the ride on the sled.

April 6, 19

THE ICY PLAIN IN FRONT OF THEM SEEMS TO STRETCH INTO infinity. They have been crossing this formation for three days, a giant, trough-shaped valley with an unusually smooth ice sheet. Perhaps a meteorite crashed here a long time ago. Its impact liquefied the ice, which then froze again. Of course this is only a somewhat dubious theory, because no crater could be detected from orbit—and the object might have completely destroyed itself during impact.

The ridge surrounding the valley, approximately a thousand meters high, keeps clouds from getting here. For this reason there is hardly any snow in the area. In addition, it is significantly colder than outside the valley, as all warmth is lost into space. The smooth surface does have one advantage, though. It allows them to advance more quickly.

Marchenko remembers the conversation with Eve about possible dangers. He did not tell her that the true threat did not come from the environment. They lost half of their supplies during the gale near the beginning of the expedition. Marchenko constantly worries about this. They certainly will not suffer from lack of air and water. The atmosphere will stay breathable, and they would never find cleaner fresh water than in the several-kilometers-thick ice sheet below them.

Yet almost all other elements are missing. His nano-fabricators could produce almost anything from single atoms. But they don't have the skills of an alchemist. They cannot change one element into another one, as that would require a nuclear reactor. Air and ice offer them hydrogen, oxygen, carbon, nitrogen, and a few noble gases. But elements such as potassium, calcium, or magnesium, which the human body needs, are rare. He could extract some of it from his own robot body, iron for instance, but the longer the expedition goes on, the more Adam and Eve will develop signs of malnutrition. This will weaken them, their bodies will fail, and he won't be able to help them.

Marchenko's imagination constantly tortures him with this worst-case scenario. He has to hurry to prevent it from becoming a reality. If they manage it in 50 days, Adam and Eve will be safe. He has already started recycling their excretions, the way it had been necessary during the long space voyage to Proxima Centauri. Psychologically, Adam and Eve still seem to be in good shape. It might be the force of habit, because they have spent all of their years cooped up together. Eve is definitely the more stable of the two. Adam is often moody and then he takes it out on Eve or Marchenko, who has recently started deliberately offering himself as the target of Adam's anger by provoking him now and then. Is this a clever idea? Time will tell.

Now *Messenger* reports in. Two weeks ago, Marchenko sent the spaceship into a lower orbit. He hoped to receive more accurate data that would tell him more about their destination. The ship has been sending him updates on a regular basis. By now, evaluating the data has become routine. Until today the results had not been exciting.

"We have news about our destination," he tells Adam and Eve via radio.

"Yes?" says Eve's sleepy voice.

"We can now determine the size much better, in all dimensions. The change in the gravitational field caused by the object indicates a kind of cylinder."

"So it really is a tower?" Adam speculates.

"Yes, or a gigantic spaceship. Or an exhaust pipe. What we know for certain is that its shape is cylindrical," Marchenko explains.

"And how big is it?" Eve asks.

"It is long and thin, one could say. A diameter under 200 meters and a length of several kilometers. The object seems to be completely stuck inside the ice."

"Doesn't it reach into the ocean?"

"No, Adam, in its center the ice sheet is at least eight kilometers thick."

"And we definitely could not reach the object from below?"

Adam is asking strange questions. It is obvious what the answer would be. Marchenko remembers Adam voting for going through the water. Maybe Adam is thinking of that.

"No, we could not reach the object from the bottom of the ocean. Or only with great difficulty."

April 7, 19

HIS BACK IS ITCHING. ADAM IS SCRATCHING IT, BUT THERE IS ONE spot he cannot reach. Should he ask Eve? He listens to the eternal night. She is breathing evenly. Eve is probably asleep. He shouldn't wake her up. It's actually day now, at least according to the schedule Marchenko brought with him from Earth. *Why are we still keeping terrestrial time?* he wonders. His body does not seem to be convinced. Each day Adam finds it more difficult to fall asleep at the agreed-upon time and then wake up refreshed in the so-called morning.

He stands up. It is only now he notices he cannot hear the sound of the runners moving over the ice. The sled has stopped. Adam puts on his jacket and pants, slips on his boots, sets his helmet over his head, and crawls to the tent door. There he looks around. Eve is still sleeping soundly. He envies her slightly. He crawls further toward the outside. It is dark. Adam is surprised and at the same time marvels at his own surprise. *Human beings are strange and unpredictable creatures, aren't we? Or perhaps it is I who am strange, and everyone else is normal?*

He does not want to wake Eve. "Marchenko," he whispers. No answer.

He activates the lamp on his helmet and aims the light forward. The glow is soon lost in the darkness. Marchenko is not there. Adam sits on the edge of the sled for a moment and then slips down to the ice. He moves very cautiously. A primal fear has taken hold of him. He is afraid of stepping further onto the ice because it might break. At the same time, he knows that the ice sheet has a thickness of several hundred meters. It is crazy! He is applying experiences from Earth, which he never could have made, to this alien world. This information must be lodged in his genes.

Gradually, Adam feels safer. Sometimes the ice creaks below his feet. He shudders the first few times this happens, but then he realizes these sounds are meaningless. The ocean is so far below him, utterly inaccessible. He is reminded of Marchenko 2, who right now is on his way to the center of the dark hemisphere. *That Marchenko won't have a chance of reaching the alien object—unless I help him. I have to warn him!*

Adam checks his universal device. The frequencies for reaching Marchenko 2 have not yet been stored into its memory. Yet he has to send a message. Adam shines his helmet lamp in all directions. Marchenko is nowhere to be seen. Adam walks around the sled. When he reaches its back, the blue-white light of his lamp reveals a rough block of ice perhaps 15 meters away. There he could formulate his message without anyone hearing him.

Adam turns around and scans the area again. *No Marchenko. Good.* He walks toward the block of ice. He must have misjudged the distance. It is more like 50 meters. The block is huge. *How could it have developed here?* It looks like someone froze water inside a cube. Adam shines the light of his lamp on the ice. He sees delicate structures that branch as they move further inward and shine in the light. *Really pretty,* he thinks. *I should show this to Eve.* But he has to send the message first.

He walks behind the block so he can no longer see the

sled. Then he takes the universal device from his pocket and sets it to the first of the frequencies, or at least he tries to. But this model seems not to be prepared for it. The frequency band he is supposed to use has been deactivated on this device. *What now?* If he is lucky, he can run a software update.

Adam turns the device over. There is a service-panel cover on the back. It is obvious it was designed for technicians rather than for normal users. Adam opens the cover and shines his light inside. He sees a primitive circuit board. Something like this might have been mass-produced about a hundred years ago. Such designs are still popular in spaceships because they are quite resistant to radiation and can easily be repaired. That's his chance.

Adam launches the service menu of the software and checks the source code. *Lucky me!* In one spot a module on the circuit board generates a value. The software then uses it to calculate the transmission and reception frequencies. If he removes the module, the value should be cut in half. Then he simply has to double the frequency to get the channel he needs. He works quickly. Soon he is able to close the cover again. The device still works, but now it transmits in the range he needs. *What should I tell Marchenko 2?*

"Hello Marchenko," he dictates out loud. His voice sounds hollow. He hasn't heard it in a while without the background noise of the sled runners rubbing against the ice. "We have new data from our spaceship. It does not look like the alien object will be accessible from the ocean. Either you turn around, or you can tell me everything I don't know through this channel. From now on I will check this frequency regularly. I hope to hear from you." He pushes the send button. This should be enough.

Just so he won't forget, he sets his universal device to reception standby mode for the selected frequency. Of course there is the risk that their Marchenko might notice something, but Adam doesn't think this will happen. He turns around and walks past the edge of the ice block. From here he has to follow a course at a 90-degree angle. He looks ahead. He can't see anything in the light of the lamp. The sled must be too far away. And it is not illuminated.

Adam starts walking, looking for the sled to appear in his field of view, but the plain before him remains empty. He has probably gone in the wrong direction. He turns around 180 degrees. There is the block of ice, his reference point. He doesn't want to make a mistake, so he returns to the cube and then goes away from it at a slightly different angle. He walks 20 meters, 30 meters... and once again finds nothing. The plain has no landmarks and is completely uniform. Adam still refuses to admit it, but he knows that he has made a huge, idiotic mistake. His sister Eve and Marchenko have no idea he is out here. He is breathing heavily. He stomps back to the ice block and tries a different direction. The sled must be somewhere!

That was a silly thing to do, you dumb shit! he thinks. Marchenko must have come back, taken up the sled, and started sprinting onward. Marchenko is in a hurry. He wants to reach the destination before his passengers die. While Marchenko has never mentioned this, Adam can do the math. He knows they lost about half of their supplies in the storm. He can imagine what they are lacking. He and Eve would not die of hunger or thirst, nor would they suffocate or freeze to death. Rather, they would succumb to malnutrition after some organ in their body ceased functioning.

Oh, well. For Adam, this became irrelevant a few minutes ago. Now he will either starve or freeze to death. He has no food with him, and he lacks the technology to make edible organic material from the carbon dioxide in the air and the water in the ice. And the energy required by his heated underwear will eventually fade away. What talents does he really have? He is great at getting himself into dangerous situations, where he has to be rescued by others—not exactly something to be proud of. Adam smashes his fist against the block of ice, spraining his middle finger. "Shit!" he yells, but of course nobody can hear him. He laughs out loud.

Adam, get a hold of yourself, he tells himself. *What are your chances? Marchenko is moving away from you at 20 kilometers per hour. At some point Eve will notice you are no longer lying next to her. If you are lucky, she will search for you outside. Otherwise the sled will move further away. And then?* Adam hits his visor with his hand. The helmet radio has a limited range, at most a hundred meters, he would estimate. But he still has the universal device. He should easily reach Marchenko with it.

He takes it from his pocket, but then remembers he modified it a short while ago. Now it only transmits in frequencies Marchenko does not automatically monitor. That was the purpose of his modification. *Where is the module I removed? Perhaps it can be inserted in again?* He remembers dropping it. It must be somewhere behind the block of ice.

Adam kneels down and starts searching. The part he needs is about four millimeters long and one millimeter wide. He can't find it. He moves around in wider circles. His knees are starting to feel cold. He brushes his gloves across the ice. He can already feel the desperation in a corner of his mind, waiting for his next mistake. He does not yet know what that mistake will be.

How many other foolish things has he done? What can he expect? *This stupid module must be lying here somewhere!* Did he accidentally step on it and then move it elsewhere with his boots? Adam sits down and then looks at his boot soles in the light of the helmet lamp. Nothing on the left side. On his right sole he finds a piece of bluish metal in a tiny crack. It must have stuck to the special rubber of the boot when he crushed the module.

April 7, 19

Eve opens her eyes. She feels disoriented. A moment ago she was a little girl playing a board game with J the robot. It was a strange dream, because she simultaneously was an adult looking over J's shoulder. She saw how little Eve snuck one of her opponent's game pieces and how the robot graciously ignored it. The little girl was happy she had finally won a game.

Now Eve moves her hand upward. The tarp of the tent is above her. It is cold and slightly damp. That is the moisture she and Adam are sweating off all the time. Eve reaches for the spot next to her. She feels the thin blanket that usually covers Adam, but her sibling is not there. *He is probably getting some fresh air outside.* Eve is glad, because recently Adam has been spending too much time holed up in the tent. The runners of the sled make a steady crunching sound. Marchenko seems to be making good headway.

Then she feels the pressure of her bladder. She needs to pee. That always takes some time, as she has to get completely dressed. Marchenko suggested several times they could pee into bags. Eve suspects why he is so intent on capturing all their excretions, particularly the salts concentrated in urine. But she would be too embarrassed relieving herself in front of her brother, or being present when he does it. She would rather get dressed and go outside, even if Marchenko has to stop the sled for a few minutes.

Eve is going to hurry. Her pants have a flap at the bottom that she can open. Then she will squat behind the sled, and they can go on two minutes later. She certainly does not want to expose any bare skin to the cold much longer than that. If Marchenko's predictions are right, it will soon be so cold that she won't be able to relieve herself outside. But until then it is worth the three or four minutes they have to spend on it. Even if, as Adam calculated, the sled would stand still almost three hours during 40 days with two bathroom breaks each, it is still worth it to her.

After putting on her clothes she crawls on her knees to the exit. The tent flap is not fastened. She pushes the thick tarp aside and feels around for Adam. But there is nothing there. He must have picked a different spot. She turns on her helmet lamp and shines it in all directions. She only sees the tent and the supplies in the sled. Ahead of her she detects Marchenko, who is leaning against the ropes, pulling their vehicle towards its destination with quick steps.

"Adam," she calls. No answer. She calls again, and still no answer.

After her third call, Marchenko turns around and slows down. "Pssst," he says via helmet radio. "Adam is asleep in the tent."

"He is not in the tent. How did you get that idea? I am searching for him out here."

"Say that again."

"He is not in the tent. Didn't you hear me?" At that moment Eve realizes what this means. "Shit! Adam is gone! Stop right..."

Marchenko abruptly stops the sled. Eve slides forward, but he grabs her before she can fall from the sled. One supply container gets past him. He bends down and puts it back in the sled. *Why doesn't he say anything?* Eve is surprised. *Adam is missing! Adam! Missing! Why is Marchenko so calm?*

"Adam is missing! Adam is missing!" she screams.

"I can hear you perfectly," Marchenko says to her. He seems too calm and collected. Where is his agitation, his despair?

Doesn't he feel anything? That is not right. It must be the shock. "We have to turn around right away," she exclaims.

"Just stay calm. We must not rush things," Marchenko answers in a deliberately calm tone.

What the heck? He is treating me like a little girl! I can decide for myself when to stay calm, and right now is not the time for calmness. Adam is gone!

"I stopped a while ago to check a joint in my right leg. I moved away from the sled so the inevitable noise would not disturb the two of you. You were sleeping so soundly. Adam seems to have left the sled during that time."

"I didn't even notice we stopped."

"You were asleep."

"How long ago did this happen?"

"An hour and 38 minutes."

"That doesn't sound like much," Eve says, hoping for a reassuring reply.

"*Not much* is a relative term. I am just checking our route. During that time we covered 30.5 kilometers."

"So Adam is standing some 30 kilometers from us on the ice, in utter darkness and all alone?"

"We have to assume so, Eve."

"Perhaps he walked in the direction we were moving? During this length of time he could have walked almost eight kilometers toward us."

"Unless he walked away from us. Imagine everyone is gone and you are alone on the ice. Now, which direction was the sled going a moment ago?"

She looks at Marchenko's massive robot body and feels tears welling up. *I don't want to cry now,* she thinks. *No crying. Concentrate.*

"I hope he is smart enough not to move from the spot," Marchenko says. "Then we really have a chance."

"How high?"

"What?"

"The chance. How high is the chance that we are going to find him? Please tell me the truth."

"We are not following a perfectly straight line, Eve. Now and then I have to move around obstacles. Over a distance of 30 kilometers, this would create a relatively wide corridor."

"But you know where you stopped."

"I remember an unusual block of ice there. I tried to develop a theory about how it might have come into being. But I don't know the precise location itself. Here there is no positioning system supported by satellites orbiting the planet. I have to rely on the compass and the rangefinder."

"What about two-way radio?"

"I have been sending messages to him the whole time, but he does not react. Either his universal device is broken, or Adam is unable to answer."

"And the helmet radio?"

"That will only work once we get close to his location. Its range is very limited."

Eve thinks about this. *Is there anything we have overlooked?* "Could *Messenger* help us? Could it search for Adam?"

"From orbit? Not a chance. Its cameras are not precise enough for that."

Eve's visor fogs up. She has to return to the tent. She can't help out here anyway. She sighs out loud.

"We have to find him," she says. "We simply have to!"

"We will," Marchenko replies while turning the sled around. Thirty seconds later they are racing across the ice, in the direction from which they had come.

April 7, 19

I FEEL LIKE SLAPPING MYSELF. IT IS MY FAULT THAT ADAM IS gone. I should have made sure, should have looked into the tent to see whether he was still as soundly asleep as before! I neglected my duty. I should be turned off, because I am a worthless piece of metal with a dimwitted mind, and I should suffer death by being melted down! *How could this happen?* I think.

I run through the dark night, dragging the sled behind me. I even considered leaving the sled behind. Then I could cover 35 or perhaps 40 kilometers per hour. But I would risk losing Eve, too. I didn't even dare to ask her what she thinks of this idea. She certainly wants to be there when we find Adam.

The only problem with that is, she would also have to witness it if we cannot save Adam. I am not sure which pain will be worse: having lost Adam, or having to watch Eve grieve for the loss of her sibling. *But that's a wrong assumption,* I tell myself, without really believing it. *We are not going to lose Adam. He will be waiting for us at the ice block.*

Adam is clever. A few hours in the darkness won't be a problem. He could stand this for days. While he does not have any food with him, the ice is made of fresh water, and a human being takes three or four weeks to starve to death. His suit will keep him warm for about one week. He has air to breathe, unlike Francesca and Martin back when they had to walk through the vacuum on the surface of Enceladus to reach the lander. And I managed to save them even under those circumstances. Now my task is much easier. I have to return to the block of ice, pick up Adam, and go on toward our destination.

Whether it is really that easy depends on one issue—will Adam still be waiting for us at the ice block? That is the decisive factor. I know roughly where the ice block is located. From a distance of two or three kilometers I will be able to detect it via radar. Once I am only a few hundred meters away, I can contact Adam by helmet radio. But if he set out on his own, I won't have much of a chance of finding him. He is too small for the radar to detect, and I would only discover him once he is also within helmet-radio range.

I hope Adam is level-headed enough not to leave the area of the ice block! He might never find the block again if he moves just 50 meters away in this eternal darkness. Walking in a straight line in absolute darkness is impossible for a human being. Adam might believe he is walking straight toward the north. Instead, he could be walking in a curve. At some point he might turn around to walk back but just walk in a curve again. But it wouldn't be the same curve. *Please, Adam, sit down and wait for us!*

It is time to warn Eve. While the environment looks just as bleak as before, the ice block should soon appear in the radar image.

"Shouldn't you be able to see the ice block?" Eve asks. She must have been thinking along similar lines.

"Just a moment... yes, there it is!" A dot is blinking on the radar horizon, and it is slowly getting larger.

"Marchenko," Eve says.

"Yes?"

"We will find him."

"Yes," I reassure her.

It is definitely the ice block. Now it can't be long before we are in helmet radio range.

"Eve, you can start trying to reach him via helmet radio. We are getting close enough."

Her messages sound calm, almost stoic. "Adam, please come in," she says. Marchenko can imagine how much self-control this requires.

Adam does not answer. I aim a brief laser pulse at the ice block. The distance is approximately 500 meters. Now the helmet radio definitely should be able to reach Adam. Yet Eve's calls trigger no reply. I slow down. If Adam does not answer, I have to start scanning the surroundings more carefully. Perhaps Adam's helmet radio has failed, or he is unable to answer for some reason. He might be standing or sitting somewhere around here, waving at them. Or he could be asleep and not even notice they are here.

The ice surface shows no sign of Adam. They reach the block and circle it. Still no sign of Adam. Eve keeps calling him via helmet radio. She is probably clutching at straws, fulfilling her part of the job to the bitter end. It is unreal. I circle the ice block several times, hoping that Adam might suddenly appear. I increase the radius of the search circles. *At least his body should be somewhere, shouldn't it?* In this area there are no deep fissures he could have fallen into. I remember the mishap in the forest, when Adam fell into the pit. That was only a few weeks ago, yet it seems to have happened in another lifetime.

This planet means bad luck for Adam and Eve. The Creator's plan must have had gaps from the very beginning.

Nothing fits the story they were given at the beginning of the journey. Had they ever really stood a chance?

No, none of us did, I tell myself, *but you are just avoiding the issue.* It's true. I am trying to lessen my own guilt. It is my fault Adam is out there somewhere. I am responsible if he dies on the eternal ice. I failed to protect and save him. And I am probably going to kill Eve the same way.

Eve. I have to get a grip on myself. I am not alone. Nobody can absolve me of the responsibility for Adam's death. Yet I have to take care of Eve.

"It doesn't look good," I say via helmet radio.

"We can't give up," she replies. I am surprised, because I did not expect such a clear-cut voice.

"He is not here anymore."

"As long as we have not found his corpse, he could still be alive."

That is true, as I know from experience. In my former life, I rose from the dead myself. I never told Eve about it. Ultimately, Proxima b is not Enceladus. *Having been lucky once does not give you the right to be lucky again.*

"Just a moment, I am stopping the sled," I warn Eve. I take the ropes off my shoulder. "Don't move away from the sled. I just want to take a closer look at the area around the ice block."

I leave the sled standing about ten meters from the block. Then I activate all my sensor systems and scan a three-meter-wide strip around the block. I notice something near one corner. In the infrared image, an unremarkable spot appears in front of it. It is not quite as dark blue as its surroundings. I increase the contrast. The spot is approximately one-tenth of a degree warmer than the ice. *Did someone sit there for a while?* I cannot detect any natural cause for it.

I start a simulation. *What kind of traces would a medium-sized man in a thermal suit with a specific heating capacity and a body temperature of 37 degrees leave behind?* The program concludes that a human being might have been sitting there. But it cannot calculate when exactly he got up and left. It is only clear that it can't have been more than an hour ago. If we had arrived faster, Adam would have been still here. But why didn't he wait, rather than march off, obviously in the wrong direction?

I am scanning the ground using high resolution. Half a meter from the block I notice a bright spot. That is not ice, and it looks as if it did not originate on this planet. I carefully dig the object from the upper ice layer, melt the surrounding ice, and analyze it. The artifact consists of ceramic, metal, and plastic. It appears to be an electronic module. It is damaged. Did Adam try to repair his universal device? That would explain why we cannot contact him.

"He was here," I say, "just an hour ago."

"Yes, I can still feel him," Eve says.

That is impossible, I think, but I don't say that out loud. I am willing to grasp for any straw. "Eve?"

"Yes?"

"Can you feel where he went?"

"Unfortunately, no. And you, Marchenko, can you somehow measure it?"

I admire Eve. She seems so cool and calm, so composed. "No, I am not able to do that. He might have gone in any direction. An hour on foot means three-quarters of a circle with a five-kilometer radius. That is almost 60 square kilometers. It would be easier for us to find a grain of sand on a beach."

"What can we do, Marchenko?"

I think about this question. I really would like to answer with a whole list of options. But there is nothing there. Should we randomly search an area which increases with each minute he keeps walking? *Messenger* is currently on the other side of the planet, but even if the ship were directly overhead it could not detect Adam from orbit. What if we simply wait to see whether he will return to the block of ice?

"I have no idea except to wait for him here," I say.

"That makes no sense. Adam left because he had a reason to. He is not going to come back."

I know. Even if he wanted to turn around, he would hardly find the ice block. Adam is all alone in icy darkness, without the technologies built into my robot body. He wanders around aimlessly out there, and it is my fault. But I cannot give in to the pain.

"Marchenko?"

"Yes, Eve?"

"We should get on the way. Adam would have wanted us to. He is not stupid. He did not wait for us here, so he had a good reason, a way of getting to safety some other way. Right now we cannot help him."

"That is true." I look at the ice block where Adam was sitting. I use the arm on my back to scratch a message into the hard ice: 'We are waiting for you at our destination, Adam.' Then I return to the sled and take up the ropes again.

"Can we get going?" I ask.

"Yes," says Eve. Suddenly her voice sounds quiet and brittle. I pull on the ropes and start running. It feels good to be moving. I run as fast as I can. But it is in vain. Even if I put all my energy into locomotion, I can still easily think about things. I am launching a complex climate simulation for Proxima b, which uses up a large part of my computing capacity. Now and then I listen to the helmet radio channel. I can hear Eve sobbing quietly. My robot body cannot shed tears.

April 10, 19

He is not going to die, not here and not now. Adam trudges across the icy plain in utter darkness. He cannot waste any more time—unlike what he'd done three days ago when it took him half an hour to get the idea of asking Marchenko 2 for help. It had been the worst half hour of his life, a time during which he had felt like a living corpse sentenced to death by freezing and, most of all, having to wait passively for the end.

Then his eyes fell on the universal device that he had already written off as useless. It wasn't defective at all, because he had recently used it to transmit a message. While he still considers Marchenko 2 weird and mad, it would be better to be rescued by a madman than to die a miserable and senseless death on the ice.

It turns out his hope was well-founded. Marchenko 2 is more than ready and willing to race to his rescue as quickly as possible. They were not able to talk long, as Adam had to conserve power in his device, but it was obvious Marchenko 2 was very pleased with the opportunity to see his lost son soon. He would bend over backward to save Adam from certain death.

Of course, Adam realized his own Marchenko would be on the way back to pick him up. But when would they have noticed his absence? What if Eve slept through the rest of the day? And how are they supposed to find each other in this seemingly-endless darkness, without any radio contact? The idea of waiting for his possible rescue—without any message, blind and deaf—seemed many times worse than the possibility of definitely meeting his rescuer in a week.

However, that option meant walking ahead into the thick blackness surrounding him. When he had left there were clouds in the sky, so he could not use the stars to orient himself. However, the radio connection with Marchenko 2 helped. He only had to take a bearing of his transmissions now and again in order to correct his route. They exchanged a few words every two hours. This did not just show Adam the right way, but also freed him for a brief moment from his utter isolation.

Adam could have never imagined having endless space around himself, yet feeling locked up in a tiny cell at the same time. But the darkness seems like an enclosing wall to him. He takes one step after the other, always carrying his prison with him. He can't even hit his hand against the wall to make sure it is still there. Adam had once read that, back on Earth, confinement in a darkened cell was used as a form of punishment, a kind of torture. Now he understands how cruel this method can be.

Whenever he cannot stand it any longer, he briefly switches on his helmet lamp. For that moment he feels released from his dungeon. He looks at his surroundings and sees the ice shimmering in bluish colors. His destination is the open sea, where they started out with their sled. His rescuer is moving toward him from there. In the light of the lamp, Adam searches for the tracks the sled left behind when they came this way before. He hopes this might relieve his loneliness, but he doesn't find a trace.

The icy plains look like nobody ever walked here before, and there probably won't ever be anyone after him. In different circumstances he might feel great now. He is setting foot on places where no human being had ever traveled before. He could give names to each ice formation because he is the discoverer of this area, the secrets of which are shrouded in great darkness.

It is a real pity he cannot enjoy his hike. But that is only natural, because he is far from being safe. For one thing, there are crevasses in the ice that might appear at any moment. Luckily, these don't occur too often, because the surface in this basin is very homogenous and relatively young compared to the age of the planet. Didn't Marchenko mention that a meteorite must have crashed here several hundred thousand years ago?

Adam is not afraid of crevasses. It's not because he is particularly courageous. No, it is simply not possible to be afraid of them, just like you don't worry about being struck by lightning when the weather is fine. If he should really encounter a crevasse, it would happen all of a sudden. He would only notice it at the instant his foot stepped into empty space. He would have no chance to undo the step. He would simply fall into the crevasse, never to be seen again. He hopes —should that happen—to die instantly. Otherwise something else would happen that he is even more afraid of: His suit heater will eventually fail, causing him to freeze to death.

According to the onboard suit system, the heater can function for eight days. Three of them have already passed...

Together with Marchenko 2, he has analyzed how far he can deactivate certain subsystems. But there are few options. He only switches on the helmet lamp when he really cannot stand the darkness any longer. He limits the communication with Marchenko 2 to what is absolutely necessary. As long as he keeps walking, the suit heater runs at minimum power. But now and then he has to rest, has to sleep. Then his body does not generate enough heat. While the overcast sky hides the stars from him, the clouds at least keep the temperatures from dropping even further. It gets slightly warmer with every kilometer he advances toward the day-hemisphere.

Yet it is going to be a tight race. He has been lucky that Marchenko 2 took his time traveling across the ocean floor. By now, he is moving toward Adam on the ice. If everything works out, they will meet on the 16th. However, the energy supply of his suit will run out a day sooner. Adam runs the calculations again and again. No matter how he figures it, he will have to survive 24 hours in the cold. The system forecast might not be completely accurate, as it could be only 22 hours, or perhaps 26 hours, but it will be somewhere within that timeframe.

Perhaps he can keep walking for those 1,440 minutes. That is the only solution he can come up with right now. As long as he keeps moving, his body will function as a heater. Once the support of the LCVG fails, he will gradually cool down, but it might be enough to keep him going. He is still not nearly close enough to the edge of the ice sheet. As soon as he lies down and falls asleep, the cold will overpower him, mercilessly. Then he will never get up again.

Marchenko 2 promised him this would never happen. Yet Adam knows the difference between wish and reality. Even a robot equipped with a human consciousness cannot defeat the laws of nature. Adam keeps adding one more step, one more step... He will try to keep to his part of the agreed-upon meeting plan. He almost hopes to be surprised by a crevasse. By now, the idea of a quick, painless death no longer seems so terrifying. Perhaps such an ending would be better for anyone who ended up on this planet under circumstances like his. Adam feels like he has been bad luck for everybody. That's probably not what his Creator intended for him.

April 11, 19

It always happens when she is still half asleep: Eve's arm feels around for Adam, but his spot is empty. Then she is startled, and abruptly wide awake. Her subconscious, which takes over control while she sleeps, must not have accepted the fact she has lost her sibling.

She doesn't discuss it with Marchenko. Overall, they talk much less than they used to. Eve tells herself there is simply less for them to talk about. Previously, she quite often spoke for both herself and her sibling. Adam is gone now, and their voyage also goes on without incident.

"Are we making good progress?" Eve asks. She wipes the salty moisture from her face. *Since when have I been sweating so much at night?*

"Yes, very much so," Marchenko answers. "At this pace we are going to get there before the end of the month."

Months, weeks, days, these terms have lost much of their meaning for her. When she wakes up, it is dark. While she sits outside and listens to the creaking of the sled's runners, darkness envelopes her. And when she rolls herself up in her blanket again, it is dark. She does not even notice whether her eyes are open or closed. *I hope it is only the terms which have lost their meaning*, she thinks.

Since Adam is no longer on board, they only stop sporadically. Eve relieves herself in the tent, as Marchenko suggested a while ago. She tries to not pay attention to the stench of her urine, nor the smell of sweat that permeates her clothing. Under these conditions it is impossible to follow even minimal standards of hygiene. Her hair is matted. She does not even dare dream of taking a shower, like back in the station, as that would trigger painful memories of Adam. Eve just wants to arrive at their destination.

She also doesn't sit outside as often anymore. To her, the surroundings seem to have changed, becoming harsher and more inhospitable. Marchenko tells her that they are still traveling through the long valley. Tomorrow they will cross the ridge at its end. However, Marchenko does not expect this to cause any problems. He thinks that the incline should be easy to manage.

Eve, who is currently sitting on the front part of the sled, raises her nose. She has partially separated the connection between her helmet and her LCVG. If she tilts her head back slightly, some fresh outside air will flow in under the visor. The air is considerably drier than it was at the beginning of their journey. It is not only her nose that tells her that, as Marchenko confirms the fact. Even though they are still zooming over an ocean, the climate is a continental one. The air is so chilly that it can absorb little moisture. This has the advantage that Eve can almost always see the night sky. Clouds only appear rarely now, and then only at a high altitude.

The sky with its myriad stars is her only escape. That is the place where she belongs. She was born there. She would rather fly aimlessly through space than move through this harsh environment towards a destination they won't be able to comprehend in the end. The planet imprisons her, while space seems to offer unlimited freedom.

Of course this is only a naive wish that most likely will never come true. She has been created to fulfill a task, and it is only afterward that she will be free to think about the realization of her own wishes. That is, if she is still alive then. This is the reason she wants to find and examine—as quickly as possible—the object they noticed through gravitational measurements. She wants it over with.

"Marchenko?"

"Yes?"

"How do you think Adam is doing now?" Eve holds her breath.

"If only I knew..."

"Can you generate a forecast?"

Silence. He is probably calculating all possible options right now. Finally, Marchenko says, "There is a likelihood of 80 percent he is doing fine. Meaning he is alive. The risk of him falling into a crevasse is low."

"Why is the value then only 80 percent?"

"The fact that he cannot be contacted by radio lowers the probability of him still being alive."

"Oh. And how long will he be able to hold out?"

"I would assume four or five more days."

"And then?"

"Lack of energy," Marchenko says. The searchlight on his head turns in her direction. She can see that his hands are trembling. Trembling robotic hands? That seems scary to her. "You know what this means," he adds.

Yes, she knows. Eve tries not to think about it, but Marchenko's words got her thoughts moving, and she cannot stop them. She imagines Adam's skin gradually turning white, cracking and bursting. A tear runs down her cheek. *No, Eve, it is not yet the time for a farewell.* She will do that five days from now.

And what if he somehow gets help? Perhaps he is walking straight back toward *Valkyrie* and will soon radio them from there. No, that is absurd. Marchenko's analysis is correct. She knows what will happen to Adam once his energy runs out, and there is no chance to save him. She reaches a fingertip under the edge of the helmet and wipes the tear from her cheek.

April 15, 19

The systems of Marchenko 2 are running at full tilt. He is proud of his technology. He can move across the eternal ice significantly faster than that *other* Marchenko. Continually optimizing his robot body during all those years in his station under the sea is really paying off. He needs less energy relative to the distance covered, runs faster, and is equipped with better sensors.

But unfortunately none of this changes the fact he will be one day late. Adam—his Adam, his lost son—is almost within his reach, yet too far away. Marchenko 2 had been glad when Adam contacted him. He always knew his children would return to him, but he had not expected it to happen so soon. If only he did not have to deal with the next 24 hours! It will be the *other* Marchenko's fault if he loses Adam for the second time. If the terrible event occurs, which right now seemed so likely, he will destroy his alter ego. That consciousness, no matter how similar it was to him, did not deserve his children, did not deserve to live. The Creator must have made a terrible mistake in creating or transferring that *other* Marchenko, and he himself will have to set it right.

Marchenko 2 feels anger rise inside himself. He nourishes this rage by imagining Adam freezing to death, and it rises even higher. It drives him forward, leaving him with the impression it enables him to cover two or three additional kilometers per hour.

Nevertheless he will arrive too late, unless Adam performs the impossible feat of walking nonstop for a day and a night. And even then it is not knowable whether that would be enough. Adam has a test ahead of him nobody ever passed.

It is time for their last conversation. Afterward, Marchenko 2 will only send short navigational impulses. Adam will turn his universal device to receiving mode once every hour, so he won't lose his way.

"This is Marchenko. Adam?"

"I can hear you. This is Adam." There is a lot of static. Adam obviously has switched the device to low-power mode, as recommended.

"How are you progressing?"

"Fine," Adam says, concise as usual. "And you?"

"Better than expected."

"But not much better?"

"There are still about 24 hours during which you will be on your own."

"I understand," Adam says after a brief pause.

Was that a swallowing sound? Marchenko wonders. "See you later. Otherwise, everything as agreed upon."

"See you tomorrow."

"Adam?"

"What is it?"

"You are going to make it. Marchenko, out." He ends the connection.

It is odd. He feels his throat tighten, even though he does not have one. *Stupid phantom pains.* He searches for the anger inside himself. *If this goes wrong, Marchenko, then God have mercy on you. I will rip you apart and hang your brain above Adam's corpse. But, you will keep your optical sensors and I will build you an energy supply lasting for eons. Then you can watch as Adam's body merges with the planet, atom by atom.*

April 16, 19

AT 1800 HOURS I STOP THE SLED. I REALIZE HOW RANDOM THIS time measurement is. I simply counted the seconds since the moment of waking up. When necessary I use leap seconds and leap days, as if we were still on Earth. But we are on Proxima b, four light years away. Right now the planet is reminding us of this fact in a very harsh way.

I can see it when I look at Eve: She knows why I have stopped.

"It is time now, isn't it?" she asks.

"Yes. With a likelihood of more than 95 percent, Adam will have frozen to death by now. We should say farewell to him."

"At 95 percent?"

"That is the point where an event is usually assumed to have happened for sure."

"Shouldn't we wait until it reaches 100 percent?"

"The probability will approach 100 percent, but it will never reach it."

"Does this mean Adam's chance of survival never reaches zero?"

"Not until we find his corpse." Probabilities. I should

know better. My friends at one time estimated my own chance of survival to be zero. Yet I now feel 100 percent alive. But it would be wrong to cling to this hope. Just like my friends were acting correctly back then when they wrote me off. I don't blame them for it.

"Agreed," Eve says.

She surprises me, again and again.

"We have to let go of Adam."

Before stopping I did not plan anything, no ceremony, no speech, not even a few simple words. I had hoped these would come by themselves. Yet my mind is blank. While I can elucidate the climate on Proxima b, I fail at finding a few words to say about Adam. Therefore, I would rather stay silent.

"I also don't know what to say," Eve starts after a moment. Then silence reigns again.

"Adam, it brought me great joy to be able to spend so many years with you," she finally says. "You didn't have a choice and had to tolerate me. And I also did not choose you. But if I had the opportunity today to select a brother, I would pick you again. One is not supposed to say bad things about those who have to go, but in your case that is no restriction, because I only have good memories. So, wherever you are, I wish you a good journey."

Eve's last words sounded slightly nasal. She sniffs. I wish I could cry. And I wish I could find words for my feelings, but I fail to do so.

"Marchenko?"

"I am here."

"That's good," Eve says, and I understand what she means. She puts her head back and looks at the sky. "Did you see that? A shooting star," she says after a while.

I did not see a shooting star. I wonder whether I should look at the recording of the last few moments, but then I understand. "Yes, a shooting star," I say.

We continue gazing at the sky in silence. It looks almost like what you would see from Earth's southern hemisphere. Except that the binary star Alpha Centauri shines much more brightly... And there is a main sequence star that is missing from Earth's night sky. Cosmically speaking, we are only a stone's throw away, but our home planet is so remote we cannot reach it.

I hear a rattling sound from the sled. Eve has gotten up and is retreating into the tent. "Is that enough?" I ask her.

"No, that is not enough, not even close."

I sigh and pick up the sled ropes again and push on. The ice creaks under the runners.

April 28, 19

FOR THE LAST THREE HOURS I HAVE REDUCED OUR SPEED TO 15 kilometers per hour. According to the data sent by *Messenger,* we should be in the vicinity of the alien object. Yet the data for the position may have an error margin of two or three kilometers.

Eve notices the change and leaves the tent. "Are we almost there?" she asks.

"It must be somewhere around here."

"What are we supposed to be looking for?"

"Unfortunately, the gravitational field scan cannot tell us that. It must be something that doesn't belong here."

"And what if it is covered by the ice?"

"I hope not! And that is not very likely. When the inhabitants built this thing, it must have been accessible."

"But that could have changed."

"Due to the dry conditions here, the ice layer only grows a few millimeters per year."

"Yet in a thousand years that would be several meters."

I cannot contradict Eve. "Let's just hope the builders accounted for it."

While I slowly drag the sled, I use radar to scan the

surrounding area in all directions. Here the ice is as smooth and unwrinkled as a baby's bottom. Any artificial structure should show up on radar. Yet there is nothing to see.

"Are you excited?" asks Eve.

An interesting question. How should I answer? *Am I excited?* I check my neural activity. It is two-thirds higher than usual. "My neural activity has increased by two-thirds," I tell her.

Eve laughs. "Mine by 100 percent."

There! There is a dot on the radar. It is a bit sideways from the exact center, perhaps 500 meters to the right, from our perspective.

"I think I found something," I say. And yes, I am excited. I can feel the anticipation. I would like to run there right away. But there is also the fear of being disappointed. Have we only found the core of a meteorite?

I transmit the radar image to Eve's universal device so she can form her own opinion. The closer we get, the larger the object becomes.

"Looks thrilling," Eve says.

"I think this is what we are looking for," I reply.

The shape of the object gradually becomes clearer. The dot becomes a cuboid shape, which seems to be slightly tilted. According to the gamma analysis, its outer surfaces are made of metal. Therefore it cannot be some random ice formation. The thing seems to be hardly larger than a house. Hadn't the first Messenger scans indicated an object with a diameter of 500 meters, and then refined it to 200 meters?

"It looks rather small," Eve says. "I expected something much bigger."

She seems to be reading my thoughts. Yet it is too early to be disappointed. What we can see is probably only a small part of the entire object. What would Adam have been thinking right now? Which questions would he have asked?

'Faster! Faster!' I thought. This much I'm sure of. Adam

definitely would have been urging me to go faster. I involuntarily move several steps forward.

"What function did it have?" Eve asks, interrupting my musings.

I stop again. My thoughts of Adam will have to wait. "I hope it is an entrance," I reply. If I were constructing a building out here on the ice, I would place an entrance at the very top, where it can be reached.

"Let's move closer," Eve says impatiently.

"We should not rush things. Perhaps it is dangerous. Maybe these beings don't like visitors."

I bombard the object with scans in all kinds of different wavelengths. It is dark in infrared, so it doesn't radiate heat. I send the infrared image to Eve. "Take a look."

"No activity," she says. "That's good, because then there certainly won't be any danger."

Her idea cannot be readily dismissed. I pull the sled and move us to within a kilometer of the object.

"If there was any daylight, I could already see it with my own eyes," Eve says.

"Just a moment." I am sorry I must tell her to wait longer, but I want to check first to see if this thing has noticed our approach. The object remains as inactive as before. I am not sure whether this is good news or bad news.

"Okay, we can go closer, but we are going to leave the sled here."

"I could never find it again on my own," Eve says.

Damn it! She is right. This is too dangerous. But it might be risky to approach the object with everything we have. I think about this question. Eve is about to get off the sled.

"You are right," I say. "Stay seated. I will park the sled close enough to this object that you can see it with your helmet light."

Eve does not answer. However, she aims her helmet light

forward. When we are still about 100 meters away, she says, "Wow!" for the first time.

I stop and aim my own searchlight at the object.

"Wow," Eve says again.

The building is not particularly impressive—a simple cuboid shape—but it looks strangely alien, even from afar.

"Do you feel it, too?" Eve asks.

I know immediately what she is referring to, though I am unsure if this is caused by psyche or reality. The object radiates something that feels like attraction and repulsion at the same time. It is as if an exotic spider were sitting in front of me. I feel incredibly curious and would like to examine it. At the same time, I shiver and want to immediately run away.

"It is both fascinating and frightening," Eve says, as if she is the voice of my thoughts. "I wonder whether this is related to the fact that it was built by a completely different species?"

"I don't know. We simply have to be careful, and not expect too much," I say. "This might look like a building, but it could have simply grown. Not like a plant, but like a crystal."

"But we can only find out if we actually go there," Eve says. She gets up, climbs down from the sled, and starts marching. If Adam were here he'd probably be running ahead of her.

"First I want to..." I start saying. Then I change my mind and follow her. I quickly catch up. It is only a few steps compared to our long journey here, but the excitement we feel seems to extend the distance.

"One moment," I say. Eve is standing directly in front of the cuboid shape. Her helmet lamp casts a yellowish glow on the material. She is raising her hand, trying to touch the material. *Should I allow her to do this? What might happen?*

Eve seems to have second thoughts. She lowers her arm again. Then she uses her other hand to pull off her glove. I see her small, naked hand. I am afraid for her, but I also feel paralyzed while Eve places her bare hand on the object. Suddenly I remember: Skin on ice-cold metal—that cannot end well. I want to tear her away, but Eve already raises her hand again. Nothing has happened.

"Cold," she says, putting her glove back on. "Completely inactive. What a pity. Of course I put lotion on my hand." She turns towards me. I see her smile behind the visor of her helmet.

From close up we see that this cuboid shape is not as uniform as it appeared from afar. Here and there pieces stick out, and there are bulges and holes. I cannot see what function the irregularities serve.

We move around the object several times. There are no doors, nothing that would indicate an entrance. We found this thing, but so far none of our questions have been answered. I imagine Adam climbing all over the structure and realize how much I miss him.

"What do you think?" Eve says, interrupting my thoughts.

"I still don't understand it at all."

"It's not a work of art, is it?"

"What do you mean?"

"If it were a work of art, its very existence would be its function. Then we wouldn't have to try to understand it any further."

"That is true. But who would create a work of art in a place where nobody can see it?"

"Then we agree," Eve says. "It must serve a function. Therefore it also must possess an entrance."

"What about a letter opener? That doesn't have an entrance," I say.

"Oh, so now it's a giant's letter opener?" Eve says with a laugh.

"Okay, let's assume it has an entrance," I say. "But where is it?"

"The object does not reach down into the ocean, so the

entrance must be up here. Or once was up here. Either the entrance is here, and we did not recognize it, or it is buried by a layer of ice several meters thick."

"Correct."

"Then I hope it is located below the ice. Because we will never find the entrance if we cannot recognize it."

"You realize a layer of ice presents a real obstacle, don't you?" I warn her.

"Nothing we could not get rid of. Meaning you could do it... Couldn't you?"

I really hope you are right, Eve. Unfortunately, I am not very optimistic right now.

April 29, 19

EVE IS STARTLED, CAUSING HER TO WAKE UP INSTANTLY. Something is different now. What's happened? Then she notices it. The noise is gone. For four weeks she has been sleeping to the sound of steel runners gliding across the ice of the Proxima b ocean. She is no longer used to silence. She realizes this is the third time she has awakened due to the quiet.

She looks at the time indicated on her universal device. It is shortly after three o'clock. She is awake enough, so she will get up now. Marchenko should be glad about it. She asked him to wait with his examination of the object until she could be with him. He promised to do this, even though it meant having to stand around all night long, doing nothing.

She runs her hands through her hair. It feels disgusting and really should be washed. If she just didn't have to wear a helmet all the time. Her scalp is starting to itch the moment she even sees the helmet. The sweat of several weeks is sticking to its inside.

She rummages through her pocket. There should be a rubber band in there. She finds it and ties her hair into a braid. *Brushing teeth, oh well.* She reaches for the water bottle in the rear corner of the tent. She uses the water to moisten her toothbrush. Adam swears by ultrasound brushes, but she never liked those.

Adam. It is terrible he can't be here with her at this moment. A part of her is missing, and it hurts. Shouldn't she have noticed sooner when Adam had disappeared from the sled? They really could use his ideas right now. And his enthusiasm, though lately there had been little sign of it. Something must have happened, right before they left the station. Why is she just now making this connection? And is whatever happened somehow related to Adam's disappearance? She should have asked him then, though she probably would not have received an answer. Still, it might have made a difference. Sometimes just asking can be enough to make someone think twice about life's happenings.

She packs her toothbrush. Then she pulls the practical urination bag from its box. She relieves herself and closes the bag. That will have to do for her morning hygiene. It was sufficient for the last four weeks. She puts on her external suit and her helmet, though she feels like holding her nose while doing so. Then she crawls from the tent.

"Good morning, Marchenko," she says. J the robot turns around and seems surprised. He obviously did not expect her so early. *Has he been watching the alien object all night long?*

"Good morning, Eve. You got up early today," Marchenko replies.

"I have something for you." She hands him the urine bag. Marchenko will recycle it and its contents. The carbon in the plastic might end up in her food, and the salt from the urine will for sure. The fact that Adam is gone makes the lack of supplies less dramatic than expected. *Even the darkest cloud has a silver lining,* Eve tries to convince herself. "I couldn't sleep any longer," she says.

Marchenko nods. "I was afraid of that. It is a change, as

we are no longer traveling. But your body will soon adapt to everything."

How would you know? she wants to ask him. Yet she suppresses the impulse. Marchenko does not deserve that. Since Adam has been gone, she sometimes feels the urge to hurt Marchenko. Luckily, she has more self-control than her brother. "What about it, do you have a plan?"

"Most certainly. I thought about nothing else all night long."

"Your plan probably involves a lot of measurements, and my participation is urgently needed."

"No—I mean, yes, I really wanted to measure some things, but as far as a specific task for you—"

"I know that, Marchenko," she interrupts him. "I would like to take a close look at this object."

"What do you mean?"

She points toward her eyes with her left index finger. "Look. With these here."

"I understand," Marchenko says reluctantly, and Eve knows quite well he does not understand her. But that's not so bad. Humans, and she counts Marchenko among them, don't have to understand one another in order to get along well.

She has only realized this since Adam is gone. *No,* it strikes her, *I have come to realize this right now.* Today seems to be a day of insights. She hopes this also applies to the secrets of the strange object out there. "Well, I will be going," she says.

"Don't wander beyond the range of your helmet lamp."

"I promise. And thanks for keeping your promise." Then she jumps from the sled. It is only about a hundred steps. She listens to the sounds her boots make when hitting the ground. It changes the closer she gets to the thing. *'Thing,' what a vague word.*

She calls Marchenko via helmet radio. "We should give the thing a name."

"Okay, but what?"

"How about calling it a tower?"

"We don't know yet whether it is a tower."

"That doesn't matter. Let's call it that." *Adam certainly would have liked it.*

"As you wish."

Now she is standing in front of the 'tower,' although only its top appears to be visible. What she can see looks like a cuboid structure with all kinds of additional elements attached. Perhaps those are later modifications?

She walks slowly around the tower. It looks slightly different from each side. Symmetry must not have been very important to the inhabitants of this planet when building the tower. Maybe they had different things to worry about while constructing the edifice. Eve turns fully around once. If the tower had been built from here downward, they would have had to dig a pit first. But then there should be piles of debris nearby.

"Marchenko," she says, "do you see any mountains or at least hills near us that are newer than their surroundings?"

"Sorry, there is nothing like that."

Eve nods. That is only logical. She still thinks too much in terrestrial terms, even though she only knows Earth from movies. All around her is eternal ice. How do you dig a hole into ice? With heat. Then the ice turns into water, but the water must have to go somewhere.

"Marchenko, I have to bother you again. Imagine a spring of water, at about the height of the tower, from which water flows for a long time, following the natural slope. Would the current elevation profile of the surroundings fit this idea?"

She does not receive an immediate answer. She patiently continues walking around the tower.

"Yes, that would fit," Marchenko says five minutes later.

"The spring would have to be on the opposite side of the cuboid. Meaning the other side of the tower."

"Thanks," Eve says. Marchenko is still standing by the side of the sled, so she has to turn around one more corner to be opposite him. She shines her light at the area. On the rear wall of the tower, which is invisible from the sled, she discovers a kind of barrel. It does not look like it poses any danger. She gets closer and uses the camera. Then she sends the images to Marchenko.

"What do you think?"

"I will have to take a closer look."

Eve reaches for the edge of the barrel and tries to move it, but in vain. "It's frozen in place," she says. Then she leans over its opening, which has a diameter of approximately one meter. She only sees blackness, so she shines her helmet lamp into it. At a depth of about one meter, the light is reflected, probably by a layer of ice.

"It's not an entrance," she says.

"Give me a quarter of an hour," Marchenko asks. "I am still dealing with the scans."

Eve glances up. From a close distance the tower looks rather improvised. It looms considerably above her. She touches the material with her gloved hand. It is rough. Her glove does not glide across it, so she has to exert some force. Perhaps this is an effect of the continual soft winds moving ice crystals over the surface?

Eve wonders how old the tower can be, but cannot find any clues to help answer her question. She slowly continues walking around the tower. When she sees indentations, she reaches inside, always hoping to trigger some mechanism. *Shouldn't there be a way leading inside?*

"Eve? I am finished now," she hears in her helmet.

She turns around and walks back to the side where she saw the barrel. Marchenko is already there. He is leaning over the structure. Eve waits patiently.

"That is no barrel," he says, "but you probably realized that already."

"What is it then?"

"A pipe. It is almost completely filled with ice. If I see correctly, it leads down several hundred meters."

"Very clever. They built from here downward. The tower in fact drilled its own foundation, and they pressed the wastewater upward through the pipe."

"I agree with your interpretation," Marchenko says while he nods knowingly with his large head.

"But you found out more, didn't you?"

"I did. It's actually all good news, except for one aspect."

"Then tell me."

"The area up here is hollow. But it is not completely empty. More like a walnut, so there must be cavities, but also sections filled with light materials."

Marchenko sends the diagrams to her universal device. She looks at them while he continues.

"I cannot tell for certain what kind of materials these are, only that the atomic mass values are much lower than in the walls. The walls are made of an alloy containing iron, nickel, titanium, and magnesium, among other things. Nothing unusual here. Iron has the highest percentage, so it is doped steel. The stuff is extremely impact-resistant and tough, and does not become brittle, even at low temperatures. I tried to scrape off a bit, but it took me several minutes to get a few micrograms for an analysis. I estimate that the walls have a thickness of 50 centimeters. So the tower is very stable."

"Built to last for millennia," Eve says.

"Certainly. This cuboid up here is the end piece. It reaches into the ice for another 40 meters. Then the building widens to a square shape with an edge length of 200 meters. I was surprised the tower only reaches down 400 meters into the ice. Based on the gravitational field analysis I would have estimated it to be much bigger."

Eve calculates the volume in her head. "Almost 15 million cubic meters—that is a lot of storage space."

"Yes, in principle. But even if it was all filled with lead, which according to my measurements it is not, this does not explain the spike in the gravitational field. The thing—sorry, the tower—would have to weigh three times as much for that. To put it differently, two-thirds of the mass of the tower is missing."

"Is that a problem?"

"Yes and no. Without this phenomenon we would not have discovered the tower. We would have never put all this effort into it."

And we would not have lost Adam, Eve thinks wistfully. *But that is not the fault of the tower.*

"I can't stand puzzles that can't be solved," Marchenko continues. "How can I protect you against potential dangers if I don't know their nature? There is something in this tower we still don't understand. It scares me."

Eve has never considered that Marchenko might be scared. To her, he seems invincible. Yet it is true that he has weak beings of flesh and blood with him, for whom he is responsible. And he already lost Adam. That must be tough.

"But that wasn't the bad news, was it?"

"The bad news is that there really *is* no entrance up here."

"Up here?"

"The tower must have stood for a long, long time. I suspect the base of the cuboid, where the tower gets wider, was originally on the surface. As time passed, the ice grew over it."

"So the entrances were planned to be down there? Why did the builders not take this into account?"

"I don't know whether there are entrances down there. But if they designed entrances, they would be there. I'm sure they never expected there would be such a long time without visitors."

"Then we just have to dig our way into it."

"As I said, there is still a piece of bad news. We simply don't have enough energy to melt our way through 40 meters of ice."

"And what if we drill a hole into this cuboid up here?"

"That requires even more effort."

"So we suffered Adam's death, 40 days of darkness, ice, and snow, just to stand here in front of a locked door?"

"We haven't even achieved that much."

Eve uses her fist to hit against the wall, of which she knows nothing but that it is made of very tough steel.

"I cannot accept this," she whispers, and hits the wall again. For a moment she hopes that a hatch is going to open somewhere, like in a fairy tale. But, except for a dull sound, her blow has no effect except to hurt her hand. She will have to accept it.

April 30, 19

WE AGREED TO SLEEP ON THE PROBLEM. THIS MEANS EVE SLEEPS as well as she can, while I try to find a solution. Just like Eve, I cannot imagine us leaving completely empty-handed.

So what is the problem? Our path is blocked by a thick ice layer, or alternatively, by a steel wall. We basically have a technical solution. Ice melts when you apply heat, and you can use mechanical energy to drill a hole. The heart of the problem is the same in both cases. We don't have adequate energy! I can generate energy to a limited extent, but not enough. What energy I could generate every day would only melt a little bit of ice, and we would be at it for three months. Drilling an opening large enough for us would take six months. Our supplies will not last that long.

One option would be that I return Eve to the undersea station. There she could recuperate for half a year, while I open a path for us. I am afraid she might not like this solution. It could be a kind of last resort, though.

What else is possible? We need an alternative source of energy. Unfortunately, I have no solution. Here, in the center of the hemisphere facing away from the sun, it is dark, dry, and almost windless. While there are temperature differences within the atmosphere, it would be cumbersome to generate electricity from them. The only resource available is ice, and lots of it. I imagine the giant valley formed by a meteorite strike a very long time ago. Back then there was lots of energy available here, so much that a thick part of the ice layer melted. I quickly calculate the chance of such an impact repeating itself. On average we would have to wait a million years before a larger rock once again hits Proxima b.

That is no option at all. But... could we get a meteorite to do this sooner? During our approach to Proxima b we crossed an asteroid belt, from which we managed to borrow a boulder. I start a comprehensive simulation. Indeed, even a rock with a diameter of two meters would generate enough kinetic energy to melt away more than 50 meters of ice. Due to its thick steel walls, the tower is sturdy enough not to be destroyed during impact. However, we would have to aim very precisely. During my calculations, this turns out to be a real issue. There are so many factors influencing the meteorite's trajectory that I cannot account for all of them simultaneously. We would need someone to sit on the rock and direct it. While we could get the rock on a collision course, with the help of *Messenger,* the final flight phase would not allow for any corrections.

What about *Messenger* itself? It could use its engines for last-second corrections. We managed a precision landing with the lander module. The orbiter should be able to do this as well, even if we do not decelerate. In addition, we can control the released energy very exactly. *Messenger* is larger and heavier than needed, but then we simply have it crash more slowly. Thanks to its engines we are not completely at the mercy of gravity. Using *Messenger* to clear away the ice would be much less risky than dropping a rock from the sky.

On the other hand, this would deprive us of a quick means of escape. Without *Messenger,* which would certainly be destroyed in the crash, we would be stuck on this planet for a long time. Moreover, we would lose our eyes and ears in orbit. It would no longer be possible to have *Messenger* measure the gravitational field variances for us. The orbiter also could no longer warn us of surprise flares. *Should we give up all that for the chance of still finding an entrance to the tower?*

I wake Eve. "I am sorry, but we have to discuss something," I tell her.

"What's up?" Her voice sounds as if she had been lying awake.

"There is an option to get rid of the ice," I explain, "one single option. I ran all the calculations."

"Yes?"

"We could deliberately crash *Messenger*."

"That... just a moment." I hear a rustling sound inside the tent. Eve is probably sitting up, thinking about this.

"It would make us prisoners of this planet for a long time," I say.

"Do you really think we will ever get away from here?"

That is true, of course. *Messenger* is much too slow to reach any destination during Eve's lifetime. That does not apply to me, though. "You certainly won't," I answer.

"I understand," Eve says. "Then I must let you decide."

I have a very good idea what Eve would like. It is on rare occasions such this one that I realize my consciousness is immortal. In light of these facts, priorities would change. I will no longer be able to travel through the universe using *Messenger*. But in that case I will wait. If no other spaceship appears, I will build one. It poses no problem to generate energy on the bright side of the planet. Given enough time I can build anything I find raw materials for, and there is no shortage of those here.

"Well, then let's try it with *Messenger*. Let's give it three more orbital revolutions so I have plenty of time to calculate everything."

"I will get dressed now," Eve says. "And I thank you."

IT TAKES ALMOST ANOTHER 12 HOURS BEFORE EVERYTHING IS ready. The trajectory I calculated only strikes the tower tangentially. The goal is to create a valley with its lateral boundary approximately at the tower. When the kinetic energy of the strike melts the ice, which has a temperature of minus 80 degrees, this will reduce its volume. The advantage of our decision to use *Messenger* is that I can calculate everything very accurately. I know its mass and can regulate its speed precisely. The speed, in turn, determines the kinetic energy which will be turned into heat during impact. How much heat do we need? I start out with the desired effect—access to a platform 40 meters below—and then calculate backward. If everything works well, there will be a bubbling lake next to the tower after the crash. We have to hurry, then, because the volume of the water will increase as it refreezes.

"Eve? We should start moving away."

I know that she is still examining the cuboid. She is really very patient. "On my way," she says.

I can see the light from her helmet lamp. Eve climbs onto the sled and then we move away, perpendicular to the planned trajectory of the impact. I stop after half an hour.

"Ten kilometers,' I say, "that should be enough."

Eve gets out. I turn the sled so that the transport deck protects her. I will sit down in front of it, in order to give her additional protection. The majority of the material should be thrown forward and backward, at least according to my calculations. But it is better to be safe than sorry.

"Are you ready?" *Messenger* is already on its way. Right now, I could still send it back into orbit. I will be able to abandon the plan until shortly before impact. However, during the last few seconds *Messenger* will be unable to make it back into space and would crash elsewhere on the planet.

"Let's get started," Eve says.

I send the decisive signal. Then I remember something we forgot. "Please tell me Adam is not wandering aimlessly through the crash area right now."

"Certainly not. How could he have reached it? Adam is dead," Eve says, quite calmly.

I hesitate. And what if he has somehow managed to survive? But that is nonsense. There was nothing in the vicinity that could have saved Adam. I don't believe in miracles.

"Thanks, Eve," I say. The approach vector of *Messenger* remains unchanged. The spaceship that brought us so far is currently experiencing its last minutes. With it, Eve's hope of ever leaving Proxima b will die.

But that's not all. The last tardigrades containing Adam and Eve's DNA will also perish. While they could have continued to survive in space, they certainly won't be able to withstand the heat of the impact. *What if they do, though?* Perhaps I just made a mistake and contaminated this planet with terrestrial life forms. On the other hand, in the strictest sense, this contamination already occurred when we landed. Together with the tardigrades, the sophisticated machinery—that which can create human embryos from the human DNA in their genome and can raise them—will be destroyed. I will not be able to create a third Eve or a third Adam. I never told the two of them they were the second human generation on board *Messenger.*

My memory plays strange tricks. The last few minutes of the spaceship are at hand, and I keep remembering things that will be lost forever. The Creator had set up a protected memory sector I suspect contains details about me and my fate. No matter. I haven't needed it so far, so I will be able to make it in the future without this knowledge.

"What does it look like?" Eve asks.

"Eighty seconds. You are so calm."

"Well, this time it feels odd. There is some insulating layer between me and reality. Maybe I got excited too often in the past."

"Sixty seconds," the system warns. Then it continues the countdown.

"Are we going to see *Messenger*?"

I briefly think about this question. "No, Eve," I say then. "Only if there is a course correction using the engines. Doesn't look like it, though."

"Won't the ship glow due to the quick descent?"

"It is not going that fast. It only will gain real speed during its final phase."

"Twenty seconds," the automatic system reports.

A roar approaches. It sounds like an airplane that is landing. The noise becomes louder and louder. I am controlling the trajectory. Everything is fine.

"Don't worry, everything is according to plan," I call out.

The roar is overlaid by a hissing sound. I hope Eve's helmet keeps out the noise. The impact is about to happen. *Messenger* will first touch the ground a few hundred meters away from the tower. Now the ground is shaking. I experienced earthquakes back on Earth, but this feels quite different. It must be because of the ice. The ice makes a clinking sound. Fissures crackle through the surface. My calculations definitely showed there shouldn't be any deep crevasses forming. Despite this I am still afraid. In my inner eye, I see a fissure opening and swallowing Eve.

The roar is gone. We only hear the hissing, mixed with a squeak. A strong gust of wind pushes the sled sideways. Just to be safe I hold on to the sled. The hissing turns into a bubbling noise that soon fades away. It is over. *Messenger* has landed. We have to hurry.

"I am turning the sled back to its original position," I say.

"Please do," Eve replies. She stands a few steps away. She quickly jumps aboard, and we race back the ten kilometers.

WHEN WE ARE BACK, EVE ASKS, "WHAT HAPPENS IF WE GET IN, and later want to go out again?"

"The ice has been distributed in various directions," I explain. "It is unlikely that the tower would once more completely disappear below the ice. But we don't know how much of it will be covered."

HERE WE ARE. EVEN IF I HAD NOT SAVED THE LOCATION, I WOULD have recognized it by the sloping ice floor. It has worked even better than I expected. I shine my light downward. At the bottom of the valley I see a platform about 100 meters wide, with a rectangular structure on top. I trace the structure with my lamp and point it out to Eve.

"Up there is the cuboid we saw," I inform her via the helmet radio.

"Yes, and do you see the pipe running down next to it?"

"Your barrel."

Eve laughs. "It bends before reaching the platform and continues over there." She points to the right.

"But I don't see any doors," I say.

"Let's move closer."

I hold on to Eve. "Just a moment, I am going to check the temperatures." Everything looks fine in infrared. "Perfect, we can go."

Eve races ahead. I want to ask her to be careful, but I suppress the impulse. I reach the bottom half a minute after her. I check the ice, but it seems to be stable. A dark wall looms in front of us. I examine its structure. "The same material as the cuboid."

Eve moves toward the right. It is 150 meters in a straight line. Then she reaches the first corner. Eve stops. "From here on it slopes downward," she says.

I see that the lake starts approximately halfway down. Cold fog rises in the light of my lamp. The lake is already starting to freeze again. "We can't go on from here, Eve." I am surprised she does not contradict me.

She seems to ponder this for a while. Then she says, "Please lift me up."

"What do you want to do?"

"Did you see anything on the front side that could serve as an entrance?"

"No," I admit.

"You see? Therefore the doors must be on top."

"And if not?"

"What does it matter, Marchenko?"

Eve is right. I lift her so she can reach the platform. That is the next logical step. I use my third arm to pull myself up. Eve just stands there. She has taken off her helmet so she can better move the light of her lamp across the surface. I immediately notice her reason for doing so. On this surface, there is a grid of raised areas that remind me of trapdoors. Do they open? The rectangular structure, which we called the cuboid, sits a bit off to the side. It looks as if it had been added later.

"That really looks good," I say.

Eve shakes her head. "I don't know. There are too many of them."

"Perhaps they were escape doors in case of emergency? Then you can never have too many exits."

"But how many creatures would there be inside the tower, if they were to need that many doors?"

"We are going to see," I reply. I already envision some kind of insect colony.

Eve slowly walks out on the platform. She stops in front of the first door. I follow her. "What now?" she asks.

I look around. "There must be an opening mechanism somewhere."

"In a VR simulation we would now have to solve a puzzle, by combining patterns or something," Eve says.

"That is nonsense. If I built a tower, I wouldn't put puzzles on the outside. Something more like a door handle or a keyhole."

"Yes, I always found that unrealistic in those games. But it would be practical. We simply solve the puzzle and we are inside."

"Let's start by looking for some mechanisms, Eve. Or electronic devices. Or... whatever thingamajigs these creatures had."

"I bet it is a mechanism. A lock that only works when energy is supplied would be useless in an emergency."

I agree with Eve. "Perhaps the doors can only be opened from the inside."

"That would not be very smart either," she says as she continues walking toward the center of the platform. "What if you were outside and in danger?"

I focus on the door in front of me. It is a massive metal plate, about five centimeters thick. "We could use a drill if we have to."

"That won't be necessary," Eve replies. "Come on over."

I follow her request. Eve is located about three meters from the center of the platform, and she is pointing down. Some kind of circle has been etched into the floor here.

"What do you see in the circle?" I ask.

"The circle is actually a disc. Take a look at the material. It sits flush on the ground. I bet it can be turned."

"How did you get that idea?"

"The hole there," she says, pointing at a hole close to the outer edge with a diameter of about five centimeters.

I examine it. It is deeper than the thickness of the disk. Too primitive to be a keyhole.

"I think this is simpler than we think," Eve says. "Do you have anything you can stick into the hole? We can probably use it to move the disk."

I take a look at my body. The third arm! It should work if I use three fingers simultaneously. I try to move the disk this way, but it won't budge.

Eve laughs. "You have to step off the disk first."

Oh, Marchenko, it has been a long day. I move to the side, stick my fingers into the opening, and try to turn the disk. It does not turn counter-clockwise, but when I push it clockwise, something happens. I hear a scraping sound spreading across the entire surface. What could this mean?

"Go on, Marchenko."

Great, I think, and continue to turn the disk. *30 degrees, 60 degrees, 80 degrees.* As I am approaching 90 degrees, the scraping sound is supplemented by a clicking noise. It sounds as if something is being released. I imagine a crossbow that soon will be fired.

"Just a little bit more," Eve says. I turn the disk to 90 degrees. Behind me I can hear a crack. I see Eve flinch. The next crack. I throw her to the ground and place myself protectively above her, being careful not to crush her. One more crack, then another. I continue to count but stop at 100. Besides the loud noises, nothing happens. From below, Eve knocks against my chest. I let her get up.

"Just look!" she cries, starting to jump up and down. "We made it, we were successful, finally!" I haven't seen Eve this happy for a long time. Every door in three of the four quadrants has opened. We can finally enter this alien building. I take a look at the disk. Turning it probably moved a number of connecting rods that released the springs of the doors, a clever device for an emergency, as it can be triggered centrally without electricity.

Eve walks to one of the doors. I worry she might try to climb down immediately, but she stops and bends down. I aim both searchlights into the opening. A spiral path leads downward, like a staircase, but without stairs.

"Can you smell that?" Eve asks. She briefly takes off her helmet to be totally sure.

"I could analyze it," I say.

"That's not necessary," Eve replies. "It stinks horribly of dirt and decay."

"Probably hasn't been cleaned in a long time," I say.

"No, I don't think simple lack of cleaning would produce such a stench. Something much worse must have happened here."

Now Eve is about to use the entrance in front of her. I grab her arm. "Let's think about this first."

"I thought we were in a hurry."

"The doors are open, so this is the perfect opportunity to take a break and think things over."

"Fine. What is your problem?"

"We don't know what awaits us in there. Take a look at this kind of staircase. Perhaps it is a slide. You climb inside and you are gone. It contains 15 million cubic meters, don't forget that! I would never find you again."

I can see my words bother her.

"We are going to descend, linked by a rope. But we also will need some rules in case we get separated."

"And what would those be?" asks Eve.

"There is an unknown labyrinth below us, even if it might look less confusing later on. You don't know the logic the builders used. If we get separated, we will always turn left. That is important. If you have the choice between up and down, always choose down."

"Why not up? Then we'll never find the exit again."

"We don't know anything about the builder. Perhaps you are not even big enough to take the way leading upward."

"Sure, I can always get down."

"I would also like to pack you some food and water. Water can be very important. We are no longer on the ice shelf. Who knows whether we can find water in there?"

"Sounds very reasonable," Eve says.

"So you will wait here, while I get supplies from the sled?"

"I promise not to move a single centimeter."

I turn around. It is going to take me ten minutes to reach the sled. "I will be back in 20 minutes. Don't—"

"... go anywhere, I know," Eve says. I hurry across the platform at top speed and race up the slope. The sled stands where I left it. I pack the necessary things. I put some of it in a small pack Eve can carry, and pack another one three times its size to put on my back. I really hope we won't get separated inside that building.

It takes me 16 minutes, then I climb the platform again. Eve is nowhere to be seen. I call her via my helmet radio. She appears behind one of the doors.

"Sorry," she says. "I just tried to press the latch down. Not a chance."

"The springs must be very strong. They were probably built for eternity."

"I would like to know whether the inhabitants would have had a chance to get out of the tower while it was covered by ice," Eve says.

"If they thought of heating the surface, then they definitely could."

I hand her the backpack and Eve puts it on. "Let me guess what you have in your backpack," she says.

"More food and water for you, that's obvious."

"Marchenko, in case we lose sight of each other and

cannot meet again, I really appreciate everything you have done for me. I am sorry if I did not always express this clearly."

That is nice of her. Suddenly I feel all warm. "It is much too early for a farewell," I say.

May 1, 19

RIGHT AFTER MARCHENKO HAD GIVEN HER THE BACKPACK yesterday, Eve yawned loudly. Almost simultaneously they had checked the time and determined that a break was a necessity.

"One night in the tent, okay?" Eve had asked, and Marchenko nodded. She could see he was relieved. To be on the safe side, they had placed the tent on the platform, so that they could jump into the entrances in case of emergency.

THE GRACE PERIOD IS OVER. EVE FEELS WELL-RESTED AND EAGER for adventure. She has no clue how Marchenko is feeling. Sometimes it bothers her that she knows so little about him, while at other times she does not care. After all, he is old enough to start a conversation with her if he wants to talk about himself. She is not his nanny.

Eve crawls out of the tent. Marchenko is walking around between the rows of rectangular entrances. He has placed three spotlights covering the entire platform.

"Are you looking for something?" she asks via helmet radio.

"The ideal entrance."

"Did you find it?"

"Sadly, no. Each ramp looks just the same as the others. I cannot detect any differences."

"So we just go down somewhere?"

"In terms of strategy, I thought we should use an entrance in the middle."

"Why, Marchenko?"

"The most important structures are often located in the center of buildings. That way they are better protected. I assume that the entrances will lead to different parts of the tower."

"Of course that might be true... or not."

"Yes, Eve, perhaps all paths somehow lead to a central chamber."

"So you might say you made a decision based on emotion."

"I rather prefer 'strategy' as the term to use."

Eve laughs, takes the backpack from the tent entrance, puts it on and walks toward Marchenko. "Then let's get started," she says.

"Did you have a hearty breakfast?"

"Just stop it, Marchenko, I want to get going."

"Okay, let me attach the cord." Marchenko takes a rope he has wrapped loosely around his waist and uses a snap hook to attach it to Eve's tool belt. Then he points at a relatively central entrance. "Let's go down there!"

Eve stands in front of the central entrance. A fixed spotlight shines into the rectangular hole. A spiral ramp starts leading downward about a meter below her, similar to the one she saw at the other door. She casts a glance at Marchenko and jumps down. She lands with a thud.

Eve looks around and scrapes the ground with her right

foot. The path is covered with a non-slip surface. The passage leading down is so high that even Marchenko, with his height of more than two meters, won't bump his head. The creatures for whom this path was designed must not have been much smaller than is J the Robot. That is the first piece of good news. But the idea of having to crawl through narrow corridors for days still makes a shiver run down her spine.

Neither the ceilings nor the walls show any sign of technology. How had this area been lit while the door was still closed? Perhaps these creatures don't need any light. On the other hand, the symbols they had found were only legible in bright light. She'd better stop speculating too much right now. These creatures might have had helmet lamps, or the ceiling might have glowed when energy was supplied.

The stench is not as intensive as it was yesterday. *Hard to believe how useful airing out extraterrestrial towers for one night can be,* she thinks with a laugh. "It doesn't stink as much," she informs Marchenko.

"Could you go a few steps forward? Then I might be able to follow you," he says in a whiny tone of voice.

Eve complies. The slope is steep. She aims her lamp downward. Then she slowly walks ahead. Judging by the sound of her own footsteps, the ramp does not seem to be made of metal. She walks until the rope tightens. "Are you finally coming?"

The rope goes slack again, telling her that Marchenko has come down. She begins moving downward and he follows.

Now and then Marchenko stops. She only notices that when the rope stops her from going forward.

"What are you doing, stopping like that all the time?" she asks in an annoyed tone.

"I am determining our position in the tower."

"We are approximately 40 meters below the surface," she says.

"Good estimate—it is 35 meters. We have moved down vertically."

"I could have told you that, Marchenko."

"You can do that now," he replies, "but later on you will be grateful for it."

Five minutes later the corridor ends. It leads to a small, square room. Eve stops at the entrance to the room. Marchenko stands behind her.

"Well, that's it," Eve says.

"That can't be true. There are still many cavities below us."

"Perhaps it is a fake corridor, like in Egyptian pyramids, meant to confuse unwanted visitors. Let's go back."

"I have to check it out first," Marchenko says. "Let me go past you."

Eve presses herself against the wall to let him through. Suddenly the floor in front of her disappeared. Eve has the impression that Marchenko is floating over a dark hole for a moment, then gravity pulls him down. She tries to get a grip on the smooth wall, but she knows what is about to happen. The rope tightens. She doesn't stand a chance. Marchenko's mass pulls her into the abyss.

A moment later she feels mud against her face, filthy stinking mud. Disgusted, she tears off her helmet. The stuff must have somehow seeped inside.

"Calm down, Eve, I am here. It is just some kind of dirt."

Easy for you to say, you darned robot, she thinks.

Marchenko shines his helmet lamp at her. She tries to activate her own lamp, but it doesn't work. Marchenko hands her a flashlight. In its glow she sees that his body is splattered with mud. She probably looks just the same. She tries to clean her face with her bare fingers. That only works after a fashion. She is glad not to have a mirror with her right now.

"Where are we?" she asks, choosing to ignore the mud.

"This is a large room, at least 100 meters long and wide.

The ceiling is three meters above us." He aims his spotlight upward. "We fell through that hole. The floor must have reacted to my weight."

"I would be worried about this," Eve says. "No, 'I *am* worried about this,' I should have said." Now that Marchenko is talking to her, she almost feels normal again. *If only that acrid stench would go away!* Will they find a way back?

Marchenko concurs. "I am worried, too. It tells me that the creatures this mechanism was meant for are considerably heavier than you."

The echoing sound of Marchenko's words shows Eve that they are in some kind of hall. She aims the flashlight toward her helmet. The lamp on the forehead is cracked. "Lousy quality," she says.

"You should complain to the manufacturer."

The irony is not lost on Eve. "Haha, very funny. Do you at least have something I can use to clean the visor? Stuff got inside."

Marchenko steps closer and hands her something that feels like paper. Eve squeezes the flashlight under her right arm, picks up the helmet with her left hand, and wipes the visor. Then she looks at the dirty piece of paper. It is covered with dark green slime that seems to glow in the shine of the flashlight.

"Show me," Marchenko says. She gives him the paper and he holds it close to his head. "Organic material. Medium-chain fats, carbohydrates, something like cellulose," he analyzes.

"Sounds tasty."

"Unfortunately it has almost decayed."

"So did we land on a kind of garbage dump? Perhaps a food storage silo for hard times?"

"It might be that this grew all over here. Perhaps this was a public park. The air is very humid, do you notice? In times when it was just 20 degrees warmer, there might have been abundant vegetation here."

Eve nods. Marchenko is right. A simple food depot makes no sense, but a habitat for the survivors seems more likely. *But where have they gone?*

"If this was a public park," she asks, "then where did the public disappear to?"

Marchenko does not answer. Instead, he turns around and points with one arm into the distance. "Let's check," he says and starts walking.

Eve slowly follows him. With each step she shines her flashlight toward the ceiling, the floor, the sides. She does not want another surprise just like moments ago. Now the hall starts to make her feel scared. It was just as dark on the surface, but she never felt this kind of fear up there.

After about 30 steps, the flashlight shows an obstacle on the left side—perhaps a wall? The hall seems to narrow there. Shouldn't she take a closer look? Yet Marchenko keeps marching on steadily, as if he is already aiming for a specific destination.

Eve shakes her head. Stopping means she might lose sight of him, but... She aims her flashlight toward the left again. The wall is still there. At about waist height she sees a narrow, more-reflective stripe. Otherwise, no embellishment can be detected.

Then she notices a cavity heading into the wall. She wonders whether to call Marchenko. He is already 15 steps ahead of her. He probably will be grouchy and will try to dissuade her from this detour. Eve stops anyway. She can clearly see the light on Marchenko's head, even though he is moving away step by step.

What can happen, after all? She once read that the human eye can detect a candle flame in the dark at a distance of one kilometer. She cannot lose sight of Marchenko down here. Eve nods and slowly moves toward the side. The cavity turns out to be a corridor that starts beyond an opening in the shape of an inverted 'U.' The smell around her is getting stronger, so this path definitely does not lead to the outside.

Eve turns around again. Marchenko is still moving in the same direction. While she can no longer see J's body, the light shows her his location. She is relieved and shines her flashlight into the corridor. She imagines that there might be a light switch right inside the opening. Unfortunately, the extraterrestrial architects were not so obliging. The only thing she sees on the wall is the luminescent stripe at waist height.

Eve walks one meter into the corridor. There is something approximately ten meters beyond the portal. Several objects reach upward from the ground to slightly above knee level. She scans a full 360 degrees. Everything appears to be safe. The hall behind her is only a few steps away. *If I yell, Marchenko will be here in a few seconds*, she tells herself.

Eve cautiously approaches the objects. The flashlight reveals ten of them. At first sight they resemble rounded vases. The mud on the ground is getting thicker. When Eve walks, her boots make a smacking sound. She crouches in front of the first vase. She shines her light at the outside of the vessel. The wall seems to be transparent and must be very thin. The vase tapers considerably from its not-very-wide belly to its top and could be compared to a very slim egg. In the cone of her light, the thing—whatever it is—looks celestially beautiful, as if it had not been manufactured, but had grown naturally. It might be connected to the slowly decaying mud, but then why would it look so clean and bright?

Eve kneels to get a better look at the vessel. Her knees sink into the mud, but she does not mind because her suit is already splattered all over. She places her hands on the slightly-bulging sides of the vase. The area feels surprisingly warm. Eve is startled for a moment, but then she remembers they are no longer on the icy surface. She leans forward to look inside the vessel. The opening of the vase has a diameter of approximately ten centimeters. It is too dark to see anything inside. Eve moves the flashlight across the outside, but even though the wall of the vase seems transparent, the interior remains black.

She lifts her right hand to shine the flashlight directly into the opening. *What might I see inside?* Eve bends forward a bit more. Her heart is beating faster. She feels like she is about to open a treasure chest. Soon she will see it. The beam of the flashlight touches the edge of the vessel.

Suddenly she is yanked backward. She shrieks. Just as quickly, she recognizes the hard robot hand on her shoulder. "Are you insane, Marchenko? You could have said something first!"

"What are you doing here? Why didn't you notify me? We must not allow ourselves to get separated. Eve, that is much too dangerous!"

"Come on, we are all alone down here, or haven't you noticed? Everything here is dead and decaying." Eve conspicuously leans over the vase-like thing and shines her flashlight into it. "You see? It is all empty." There is only a black layer on the bottom of the vessel, which probably resembles the ubiquitous mud here.

"That might be true," Marchenko says in an angry voice, "but you are being reckless if you impose your own ideas on everything you see here."

"Are you trying to say that not everything down here is dead?"

"I don't know. We have far too little information yet. What do you think you are dealing with here?"

"A vase... a trash can... a flower pot... I have no idea." Eve says.

"Then try to lift it."

Eve snorts. *What is that supposed to mean?* She once again carefully puts her two hands on opposite sides just below the bulge of the vase. The vessel weighs less than a kilogram, she estimates. And she has already seen that it is empty.

"Go on!" Marchenko encourages her.

Eve tries to lift it, but the thing resists. Her gloves keep sliding over the surface. "It is simply too smooth," she says. She does not want to admit defeat.

"As if!" Marchenko stands next to another vessel and holds it with all three of his hands. Then he tries to lift it. The vase does not budge.

"You are not really trying," Eve complains. Yes, she knows it isn't true, and yes, she knows that Marchenko is reading her like an open book.

"We have to be really careful here," the robot says. "Nothing is what it seems. And now, come with me. I found an exit at the end of the hall."

MARCHENKO LEADS HER OUT OF THE SIDE CORRIDOR. THEY CROSS the hall in silence. The wall they are approaching looks different from the side walls. There are vertical lines at regular intervals.

"It almost looks like pleats," Eve says.

"If I am not mistaken, those are pleats."

"You think—"

"Yes," Marchenko interrupts, "this is not a wall, but a curtain."

"It's not made of fabric," Eve determines once they reach the wall. "The material feels amazingly hard."

Marchenko starts an analysis. "A mixture of asbestos, tar, and carbon nanotubes," he finally says.

"A strange mixture."

"Yes, and I suspect the tar represents a decayed form of the nanotubes."

"Why?"

"Just a hunch. Perhaps it is also a precursor material. But it doesn't matter." Marchenko tries to jostle the curtain, but it is rigid, immovable. "I am sure there is a switch somewhere around here," he says.

"So far we have not noticed any energy emissions," Eve says. "If the switch is not supplied with electricity, it won't be any use to us."

"And what about the warm temperature in here? If this building has stood empty for a thousand years or longer, it should have cooled down to the ambient temperature a long time ago."

A good argument, Eve decides. While it is not exactly warm here, there must be an energy source somewhere further down that still supplies heat. "Then we should find the energy source," she says.

"No we shouldn't, or at least not until later. Imagine if we examined a gigantic car. What good would it do us to find the engine?"

Eve nods. "We would certainly learn something… but you're thinking we need the command center, the steering wheel."

She slowly walks to the left alongside the odd curtain. It is definitely not a normal wall. So... the builders must have designed it this way for a reason. A curtain is meant to be opened. Therefore there must be a mechanism that triggers the opening process. And it should be at the left side or the right side of the wall. Or is she still thinking too much in human terms? *What if the mechanism is hidden on the floor or the ceiling?* She carefully shines her light at every square centimeter. She briefly turns around and feels gratified as she observes Marchenko currently walking toward the other edge of the wall. So, her idea was not that bad.

Eve finds something indeed. She can see it from three meters away, when her flashlight shines on the luminescent stripe. At the end of the stripe there is a fist-sized, egg-shaped object. It has three indentations on top and one on the bottom. Eve looks at her hand. The egg is slightly larger than her palm. If this object is meant to be used with an extremity, the aliens should have three fingers and an opposable thumb.

"I found something," Eve calls out via the helmet radio.

"Me, too," Marchenko replies. He sends her an image. It shows a matching egg-shaped object at the end of a matching luminescent stripe.

"I have the same thing on this side. What now?"

"We have to find out how it works."

"Shouldn't we be more cautious? Nothing is what it seems, you know." Eve gets a kick out of teasing Marchenko with his own words.

"That is a different situation. We can't go on from here. Or should we turn around?" A rhetorical question.

Eve is not against learning more about the egg-shaped object. She places her left hand around it for a moment, lets go and switches her flashlight to her left hand, and feels the object with her right. She does not feel any difference. The intended users must have symmetrical extremities. She tries to turn the egg, but no matter the effort she cannot get it to move. Instead, she hears a loud cracking sound in her helmet radio.

"Damn," Marchenko says, groaning in frustration.

"What's going on?"

"It broke off. I must have turned it a bit too forcefully."

"We still have one left."

"And what if both have to be used at the same time?"

"They are so far apart from each other that it would make no sense. One has to be enough."

"Hopefully! But wait a moment," Marchenko says, "at the back of the egg-shaped object there is a kind of pin."

"How do you know that?"

"I have it in my hand. Before that, the pin was inside the wall. Now there is a hole there."

"About where?"

"Exactly in the center of the luminescent stripe."

"Hmmm." Eve is not sure what she can do with the piece of information Marchenko just gave her.

"I am coming over," Marchenko says.

"Take your time. I'll come up with an idea." She reaches for the egg with her left hand and tries to push it carefully upward and downward. She must not damage hers as well. She pulls on it, but nothing happens. Eve bends down a bit. Why is this object directly on the luminescent stripe? Only because it looks pretty there?

She takes off her glove and feels the stripe with her index finger. In the middle she can feel an indentation invisible to the naked eye. If the egg has a pin on its back, as Marchenko said, that might be the decisive element. The egg would then only be the handle for it. She gently pulls the object away from the curtain and to the left, in the direction of the luminescent stripe. She has to overcome a slight resistance, then it feels as if she were tearing a piece of paper. She does not need a lot of force, because the egg in her hand moves almost by itself. It moves along the stripe in the direction away from the curtain, obviously held on track by the pin. Yet her hope that the curtain would now open does not become reality. Eve has moved the strange egg two meters toward the center of the room, but the curtain stands rigid, unmoving.

"Nothing is happening," she says via radio. "I am already two meters away from the curtain."

"And the egg?"

"You were right. It sits on a pin that runs inside a notch inside the luminescent stripe."

"Let's try for another meter or two."

Eve nods. It could not hurt, pulling the egg-shaped handle a bit farther back. She walks one step, two steps, three steps along the wall. The farther she gets, the less force she needs to apply. And then comes the moment in which the egg definitely starts moving by itself. She has to push against it with her hand to stop it.

"Um, Marchenko."

"Yes?"

"The egg is sliding along by itself."

"What do you mean?"

"If I let go of it, it moves backwards, farther into the room."

"Just a second," Marchenko says. "I am locating you. Now let it go for a moment."

Eve lets go of the egg. It slides along the wall hesitantly. She walks with it. Could it be increasing its speed?

"Stop the egg now," Marchenko says. "I don't want to worry you, but I think we've got a problem."

"Really? You mean because the curtain is still not opening? What a bummer."

"No. While you were walking along next to the egg, the hall narrowed, according to my measurements."

"What do you mean? Isn't that impossible?"

"It looks like the curtain has moved. In our direction."

"And is that dangerous?" Eve immediately realizes the answer to her own question: *Of course it is.* After all, the curtain is not made of soft cloth. "Can you stop it?" she asks.

"It is worth a try. Let the egg move another two meters, while I will stand right in front of the curtain."

Eve lets go of the egg. It starts moving along the luminescent stripe again. After another meter she hears a metallic creak.

"Stop," Marchenko orders. Eve has an idea of what is about to happen. She holds on to the egg, but now she has to use a surprising amount of force.

"The curtain is simply pushing me along."

"You can't stop it?"

"Not in the least. It is not even slowing down."

"Then I better never let go of the egg."

"That is not possible," Marchenko says.

"Oh," Eve says, "do you have a better idea?"

"We still know too little."

"A nice excuse. What would happen if I let go?"

"Then the curtain will sweep us to the end of the hall."

"And what will happen there, Marchenko?"

"No idea. Maybe it will squash us."

"But why?" Eve asks.

"Perhaps we activated a defense mechanism."

"So they would let us get here, to a place where we can't go on, only to then crush us? It makes no sense. They could just wait for us to die of old age."

"Maybe that would take too long for them."

"No, Marchenko. I rather think it is a kind of cleaning device. This place definitely needs a thorough cleaning. Could there be a chute at the end of the hall, where things are disposed of?"

"It is hard for me to tell that from here. If so, the chute would have to be very narrow. Less than ten centimeters."

"Then it looks like death by being crushed."

"You might have a chance, Eve. The curtain can push me to the end of the hall, but I don't think it can deform my body."

"So I am going to spend the remaining years of my life in a gap with a width of 80 centimeters."

"120 centimeters, if I stand sideways."

"Very funny, Marchenko."

For a while there is silence. Eve is letting her thoughts wander. She is surprised about not feeling panic. *Shouldn't I be afraid of death?* She remembers her long journey. She had been close to death several times. So perhaps she was getting used to it to some extent.

She is startled when something taps her on the left shoulder. She turns to the left, but there is nobody there.

"Marchenko, you're such an idiot." The robot had silently

come up right behind her. He is standing to her right. Adam sometimes teased her by tapping on her shoulder like this. Then she slaps her hand against her forehead.

"Marchenko, the corridor." She sees how the big robot smacks one of his steel arms against this head.

"Of course, the corridor," he says.

"Let's count to three and run."

"Wait, Eve, you don't know how fast the wall will be moving. I definitely can run faster than you, particularly in the dark. I will hold the egg, and you will have all the time in the world to walk ahead to the corridor. Let me know once you are safe, and I will come running."

Eve does not like this, but she knows Marchenko's suggestion makes sense. Once again he puts himself in danger for her. How often has he already saved Adam or herself? She hopes his plan works out.

"Okay, I am going now," she says. This isn't the moment for farewells. Marchenko will meet her in the corridor. Touching the wall with her right hand, she moves quickly in the direction where they found the corridor. She is relieved to find it is still there. Everything is going as planned.

"I am safe," she communicates to him via radio.

"Okay, I am going to let the curtain slide now."

Eve hears footsteps from afar. The helmet radio remains silent. She can feel a scraping sensation transmitted via the floor. That must be the curtain, which is now cleaning the hall.

"Damn, too fast," Marchenko says. "I am going to stop the egg." There is silence for three seconds. "Not a chance, the mechanism is too strong," he says. He seems to be completely calm.

Eve hears a dull knocking sound. Then she realizes it is her own heart. The patter of steps is getting faster, then it is mixed with a squeak. The scraping noise comes closer and becomes so loud she can no longer hear the pattering sound.

Eve retreats a few steps into the corridor and shines her flashlight into the entrance. She notices mud seeping in, which apparently is being pushed forward by the curtain.

She sees an iron hand appear briefly at the right side of the portal and recognizes the grasping part of Marchenko's third arm, which is located on his back. He must be trying to hold on, but then the hand disappears, while a dark shadow zooms by the entrance with enormous speed. Mud splatters in her direction. Then the eerie scraping sound fades away. A squeal, a heavy thud, and now it is as quiet as before.

"Marchenko?"

She receives no answer. She did not expect anything else, but she still calls out his name three more times. Then the realization hits her. She feels as if it were climbing her sleeve and she could watch it. Now it crawls across her chest. Breathing becomes difficult. It enters the side of her neck and follows blood vessels into the brain, where it manifests itself as a stabbing pain.

Eve slowly sinks down against the wall of the corridor. Here the mud reaches the top of her boots, but she does not care. She knows she is alone.

Darkness rises in front of her eyes. This is more than the absence of light. Eve notices that she is sliding into unconsciousness. She is swimming through the waves of a black sea. Pain appears when she reaches the surface. Marchenko is dead. Adam is dead. She is alone. Then she goes under. The water surrounds her. She feels a salty taste on her lips. The pain dissolves. She would like to sink to the bottom, be buried in the soft sand, and finally stop breathing and thinking. But then the next wave comes and lifts her up mercilessly, into the pain and into life, and she finally understands why there is no difference between those two things. Most of all she realizes she lacks free will. The ocean won't let her sink into the depths. She has to withstand the pain, again and again. She has to live.

A GROWLING SOUND WAKES EVE THREE HOURS LATER. SHE flinches. She must have actually slept. And besides that, all of her body's vital functions are still working. Her stomach complained because she is hungry. She stands up and almost falls back down. Her right leg has become numb.

She takes off her backpack and uses her flashlight to check its contents. Luckily, Marchenko put some food in there for her. If she rations it carefully, she might feed herself for three or four days. The air down here is so humid she should certainly be able to extract drinking water from it. This leaves her a few weeks before she is going to starve.

This realization does not shock her. Quite the opposite, it feels like relief. Now she knows she won't have to hold out forever down here, all by herself. Her time will be over at some point. Eternity would have been frightening, while death isn't. There is a big bubble in her mind, and she must not touch it. It has to do with Marchenko leaving her, and with Adam. But if she leaves this sensitive bubble alone, if she does not poke it, she will be fine. She even feels her spirit of adventure reviving.

The curtain, which until now had blocked any further advance, is gone. At least for the moment. Does the cleaning mechanism have a kind of reset function? She should hurry before the curtain returns to its old position. It is still quiet out there, and the only sound she hears is her own growling stomach.

Eve decides food will have to wait. First she has to get out of the corridor, then go to the left, and past the spot where the curtain used to be. She aims the flashlight forward. The beam is getting weaker. That could turn into a problem soon. Only Marchenko would be able to recharge the battery. No, she must not think of him. She only has to find a light switch, then the problem is solved.

She walks ahead slowly. A little bit of the mud has flowed back into the hall. She turns toward the left. After three meters it already gets noticeably drier. The curtain has fulfilled its purpose. Now the air also seems to be slightly warmer. Had she and Marchenko started some kind of process? Or was the air on the other side simply warmer, and now it is flowing to her side?

Eve keeps shining her light at the wall next to herself. She follows the luminescent stripe. Its end is her destination. She walks and walks, and suddenly she is there. This is where she had found the egg. Had it been a mistake to move it? No, they had no choice. They simply acted as human beings would, even though this drastically shortened their lives. *Oh well, humans are not made for infinity.*

Eve keeps on walking. The hall is gradually changing. The wall next to her recedes and the room is getting wider. She shines her light upward. Even the ceiling is much higher here. She now notices there is no mud on the floor, even though the curtain did not sweep through this area.

Her flashlight blinks twice and then shuts itself off. Eve stands in darkness. She should be experiencing fear now, but she isn't. She wonders what to do with the flashlight. It could be used as a striking tool or a weapon. Eve has to laugh at this idea. Then she drops the useless flashlight. The echo of its clinking sound tells her that the hall she is in must be very large.

She just plain stands there, while her eyes attempt to adapt to the darkness. She has never stood so long in the dark with her eyes open. *What else should I do?* Eve waits for something to happen. First she sees sparkly flashes in her visual perception. Could that be a side effect of being cut off from all optical-sense inputs? Is her brain starting to create its own images?

Eve does not know how much time has passed when a dark red glow slowly emerges from the blackness. It is still far away, but it gradually approaches. The contrasts become more defined, then weaker, and then once again defined. It seems as if her brain is busy calibrating this new perception and integrating it into her view of the world. Her brain appears to integrate this dark red glow, just as it would connect the source of a sound with a change in the field of view of her eyes. It is not a true red—she perceives the color red as bright, but this one is dark. In fact, almost a shade of black.

Eve starts to suspect what she is perceiving here, but she still cannot believe it. She does not dare give it a name—which would have to be 'infrared'—but the heat she sees at the end of the hall lures her on, nevertheless. She marches toward it and then adjusts the strap of her backpack. As she looks at her extended hand, there is something out there in the ultimate blackness of the lightless hall that she never would have expected—a warm outline that moves whenever she flexes her muscles.

A shiver runs down her spine. Why isn't Marchenko here? She misses him. Could he perhaps have managed to save himself? She would like to tell him about it, that her genome just gave her a new gift.

May 2, 19

THE GAP BETWEEN THE WALL AND WHAT WE MISTOOK FOR A curtain is exactly eight centimeters wide. So my estimate of ten centimeters was not far off. Unfortunately, the gap is also decreased by the 'pleats' sticking out. The metal front smashed me against the back wall at 120 kilometers per hour. Then the pleats cut my body into pieces. I was exceedingly lucky that large parts of my central computer and a significant section of my memory remained intact. My body is gone. While I cannot move or communicate, I can still think. And I have access to two-thirds of my nano-fabricators. I hope those little things will work a miracle and get me out of here.

I cannot get back through the wall, where Eve must be somewhere. My escape route must be downward. Below me there is another room, probably some kind of garbage dump, because the cleaning mechanism squeezed all the mud there. I am looking forward to dropping down there, because there is likely no better place for me to stock up on my resources.

First the fabricators will have to change my shape. I will turn into a reptile that can crawl through cracks eight centimeters wide. My body will have six legs and a flexible tail that I can use as a weapon. While I don't think I will need a weapon down here, it is better to be safe than sorry. Besides, the tail will help me climb. After all, I have to move through the room below me and then somehow get back up. Eve needs me.

However, my modifications will take time. During the past 24 hours my fabricators finished about half of the job. I follow each of the steps of their project, for the simple reason that it keeps me from imagining the dangers Eve might be in right now. She is all on her own. Her resources will barely last longer than two weeks. First she is going to run out of energy, so she will have to make her way blindly through a potentially hostile environment. It might have been better not to bring her into this extraterrestrial labyrinth. Yet I know quite well she would never have agreed to waiting on the surface.

I have come up with something to keep me from being bored for the next 24 hours: All my extremities must be able to separate from my body. They will have their own sensors, so they can transmit their observations to me. That way I can explore areas not accessible to my whole body.

The two lower extremities are already finished. I check them once more, then I drop them down. To keep with tradition I named them ISU 1 and ISU 2, after the Independent Sensor Units. Sure, I could have called them Foot 1 and Foot 2, but talking to my independently-acting feet would have seemed a bit schizophrenic to me.

The ISUs move using the wriggling movements of terrestrial serpents. Once they reconnect to my body, they stiffen at the right spots and become real feet again. Right now, they take to exploring like a duck takes to water. Both of them report falling to the floor at the end of an unknown room without suffering any damage. I have them send me radar scans. The ISUs are close to the rear wall of a room that is only one and a half meters high. If I compare that to the height of stairs and passages, this area could not have been designed to house inhabitants.

The fresh piles of mud that the cleaning process swept down there indicate this to be an in-between floor. However, the ground is uneven. ISU 1 shows me it contains ditches and pools. I launch a quick simulation. These might be canals carrying away refuse. Perhaps it is being processed down here. Further in front I detect structures that might be machines. Were they used for garbage processing? Suddenly I realize we have been wrong concerning the hall up here. Who would build such an aggressive cleaning device?

Yet if the inhabitants grew food there, it would make sense. The 'curtain' then would be a harvester moving all the organic matter that would next be separated into usable components down here. It would be a very advanced form of agriculture, wasting not a single gram of biomass. I will never find out whether I am right, though, because the machinery down here seems to have been inactive for a very long time.

I have the two ISUs crawl forward along opposite walls. Their task is to find paths leading upward. However, the paths obviously do not exist. After half an hour they have searched the entire room. I won't find the way to Eve so easily. The ISUs marked two promising entrances to other floors below me, though. One of them is an air duct that must have drawn off waste air, judging from the shape of the rotors. The other might be a water pipe, by now dried out. The limestone deposits show water once flowed here. Both paths are large enough for my new body to squeeze through.

Which one should I select? If I use the water pipe, I probably will reach all rooms connected to the water and wastewater system. I do not know how many rooms that would be, but certainly fewer than the number of rooms requiring air. Therefore, the decision is not difficult. Now I only have to wait until the modification of my body is complete. *Eve, I implore you, hang in there!*

May 2, 19

Discovering a new sense seems to be exhausting. After Eve had found herself yawning repeatedly, she listened to what her body was trying to tell her. She lay down with her head on the backpack and slept for six and a half hours, as the screen of her universal device indicates. When Eve activates it in the dark, the glow almost blinds her. She immediately sets it to the lowest brightness in order to conserve energy. The device with its many functions is too valuable to waste as a mere flashlight.

If Marchenko has somehow survived, this would offer the only method for him to contact her. When she turns the universal device around she sees a dark spot on the back, in the infrared spectrum. That must be the battery warming up.

Eve sits down. Her butt hurts and she feels sweaty. Apparently it has become even warmer during the past few hours. The temperature is 12 degrees according to the universal device. That's seven degrees warmer than yesterday. Does a day cycle exist in here, or did they trigger something by launching the cleaning process?

She turns around. The place from which she came is still dark. Yet the opposite direction seems to have brightened.

The heat must be coming from there. Eve opens the upper part of her suit and slips out of one of the shirts she has been layering, like the skins of an onion. She hopes it won't get too warm. *What would the inhabitants of this planet have liked?* Eve laughs. She is thinking about a non-issue. No matter how cold or warm it is, she needs food and water to survive.

One step after the other. It is difficult for her to get up. After sleeping on the hard ground all her joints and muscles protest against her cautious movements. That will disappear once she gets going. Eve turns around again. All of a sudden she feels the slight hope that Marchenko will surprise her by stepping out from the darkness, placing a hand on her shoulder, and saying, 'Let's go, the aliens are already waiting.'

"Easy for you to say," she replies aloud. Her voice echoes in the tall room. Then she starts walking, her view aimed forward at the wall shimmering in reddish tones. During the walk she estimates the size of her environment. What can be seen from the outside of the building in which she now finds herself does not match the long distances she has to cover inside. The inside of the building seems to be larger than its outside. *Would Marchenko have an explanation for this?*

The reddish gleam on the wall in front of her gains more detail by the minute. Soon she recognizes lines, then shapes. They are regular hexagons, honeycombs distributed across the entire wall. Some are additionally crossed by a dark line that seems to stretch over the whole wall. The honeycombs still don't emit visible light, she can only see them in infrared.

Eve's chest abruptly collides with an obstacle. "Whoa!" she utters in surprise. She stumbles but manages to stay upright. *What was that?* Standing up, she feels her way forward. Her right hand finds a bar about five centimeters thick that seems to run parallel to the wall. She feels her way along it for a little while, until she encounters a pole of the same diameter. She checks the area below the bar, but there is nothing there.

This must be some kind of railing, designed to stop the movement of persons of a size similar to hers. Therefore there must be something the railing is meant to protect them from. Eve cautiously moves her foot below the bar and feels around with it. At a distance of about 20 centimeters, her foot reaches empty space. *Thanks, railing.*

She sits down and nervously pulls the universal device from her pocket. She turns up the brightness of the screen, leans forward, and tries to see something in the light of the display. Her foot was right. There is a shaft, and it is so deep she cannot see its bottom. It seems to reach all the way to the wall, and it is about ten meters wide.

The honeycomb structures continue downward. Now Eve can estimate the size of the honeycombs. They are approximately two meters tall and wide. Now she counts how many rows there are. She has to stop at 90 because the view gets blurry. This means the shaft is at least 90 meters deep. However, she estimates the depth to be much greater, maybe something like 500 meters.

Eve stands up carefully. Now she is really glad she can hold onto the railing. On the other hand, she would like to investigate the honeycomb structures. Might there be a way leading into the shaft? She follows the railing to the right. Here she can almost touch the honeycombs, yet they are out of her reach. If she had not suddenly learned to perceive infrared radiation, she would see only blackness in front of her the whole time. Isn't that a strange coincidence?

She remembers how her gills became noticeable shortly before she would have drowned. Her body seems to be programmed to reveal its special abilities only under extreme stress. Technically it should be no problem to have it react to the increased release of stress hormones. When she thinks of being alone in the dark without any light, the idea still makes a shiver run down her spine. Could there be more abilities hidden inside her? It is an odd feeling—she always thought of knowing every aspect of her body, but then it suddenly reveals surprising capabilities. Eve feels estranged from herself, which is an unpleasant feeling.

She stops her musings. Right now, there are more important problems to solve. She shakes the bar of the railing with all her strength. The metal does not move. It is strange how such an object can give her a sense of security. Then she sees that the honeycombs end a few meters away. The side wall of the hall must be there.

Just as if on cue the railing now ends. The bar she is holding onto makes a 90-degree turn and then points downward at an angle. There is probably a slow descent waiting for her, but Eve does not want to rely on that. She kneels down, takes out her universal device, and shines it at the floor ahead. And indeed she has a broad path in front of her, that—as far as the weak light of the display reaches—leads past the honeycomb-covered wall into the abyss. This must be—as seen from the side—the thin line she noticed earlier. The path down seems to be made from a very thin material.

Eve slowly pulls herself up on the railing. She adjusts the backpack that had slid to one side when she knelt down, and then she starts walking. Her path first leads toward the wall with the honeycomb-like structures and then once again makes a 90-degree turn to the left. This time Eve does not bother to check whether there is an abyss in front of her. She trusts in the function of the railing. The descent leads her directly past the honeycomb-like structures.

Eve lets go of the railing in order to take a closer look at the honeycombs. She stands directly in front of the wall and moves her hand over it. She can feel the temperature differences with her fingers. The walls outlining the structures are significantly warmer than the hexagonal surfaces within them. The surface she touches is smooth, but there is a round bump where she sees warm lines. She traces the lines with her fingernail. Could there be a hairline crack in the middle of the line?

In the center of each structure, though, the surface feels surprisingly cool. She exhales toward it and the moisture in her breath promptly condenses. There is a squeaking sound when she wipes away the water. Then she walks down a few more meters, to investigate another honeycomb. She is not surprised when she notices no differences. Yet this does not solve the mystery. *What is the function of this design? Is it purely ornamental, as a geometric pattern? Or is there some technology behind it?* If there is a technical background, then there must be some way to influence it: a control panel or another kind of interface.

How might the inhabitants have seen their environment? A control panel for bats would look different from an interface for hippos, or one for flounders. All she knows of the inhabitants of Proxima b is that they were slightly taller than most humans, at least if the corridors were designed for them. She can only hope they had a visual sense and extremities. Otherwise, she might not even recognize a control panel for the local technology.

Eve leans against the wall and briefly closes her eyes in order to think. There is a dripping sound somewhere. She opens her eyes again. She carefully moves away from the honeycomb-like structure until her hands feel the railing at the edge of the path down. Once again she counts the honeycombs. The area is so large that its operation must be centralized. Otherwise one would need hundreds of individuals to push all of the possible buttons. So far, she has not encountered a single one. She is already assuming that the honeycombs fulfill some function. But what if they just serve as decorations or lighting elements? Perhaps she will never find out.

Eve ventures into the depths, holding onto the railing with one hand. Whenever the walkway has covered the entire width of the wall it makes a 180-degree turn and follows the wall closely again afterward. The deeper she gets, the warmer and more humid the air becomes. This does not seem logical to her, since she knows warm air should rise, and the warmer it gets, the drier it should feel, as it can absorb more water. This means the source of heat and moisture must be located at the bottom of the abyss. Now and then Eve glances down over the railing. At some distance down below she clearly detects a reddish glow. She repeatedly examines the honeycombs, always with the same result.

After a while it gets noticeably brighter. So far, it is purely radiated heat, no visible light, but she can already discern the outlines of the entire shaft. The bottom is covered with dark spots. Eve suspects they are puddles of water that evaporates from the surface, thus cooling the remaining liquid.

The path ends in an unspectacular manner. In the glow of thermal radiation down here she can even detect the metal railing, which appears to be a good thermal conductor. The bar of the railing sinks into the floor, which is hard and without a discernible structure. How could she manage here without her new sense? The one important disadvantage is she can only recognize things associated with temperature differences. She is not like a bat that can use echolocation to map the world all around it. Where there are no honeycomb structures to be seen, the walls of the shaft look completely uniform to her. This doesn't mean, though, that there is nothing to find here. There is only one possibility. She must continue feeling the areas with her hands. She hopes she won't once again activate some dangerous mechanism while doing so.

Eve starts her tactile investigation at the wall on the opposite side, at the base of the ramp. To her, that would be the most logical place for installing a control panel. She raises her arms to head height and cautiously touches the surface with her hands. Then she systematically brushes across the area, from left to right and then, slightly lower, from right to left. Eve is startled when, at about chest height, her fingers come across a horizontal bumped-out line, the edge of something protruding perhaps five millimeters from the otherwise-flat wall.

She had *hoped* to find something... but not really *expected* it. She feels around the edge, following it to the left first, then to the right. It seems to be approximately two meters wide. Moving back to her left, and then again to the right, Eve feels a right-angle bend, a corner, at either side. The edge then continues down to the floor. *Is this some kind of door?* But how can she open it? She tries pushing against the right side, but nothing happens. Then she uses more force, now pushing on the left, top, and bottom—each time without success.

She investigates the edge again. Is there a groove she can open with a sharp object? She doesn't find anything. What now? Eve takes a deep breath. Then she places her ear against the wall and starts tapping the area. The sound is not the same everywhere, but that doesn't help her. The door, or whatever it is, does not reveal its secret. Would Marchenko be able to help her by finding the lock with his X-ray vision? She knows the question is irrelevant. She is all alone.

She pushes harder still. Her muscles cramp and protest against the growing pain. Perhaps she simply needs more strength. If the inhabitants are significantly taller and heavier than she is, the door would be adapted to that fact. She kicks the door with her boots, but except for dull echoes there is no reaction. Then she walks a short distance up the path, gets a running start, and hits the wall at full speed.

Nothing. *Ouch!*

She can't do anything else. She has failed.

Either she has overlooked something obvious, or the door—if it is a door—can only be opened by a very different method. Perhaps she has to say 'open sesame' in the Proximan language, or her body has to emit a specific scent, or she must tap a certain rhythm. She could accept something like that, as it means she never had a chance to begin with. It would also be okay if this door really isn't a door and therefore cannot be opened. That would be okay. It would be annoying, though, if she were to find out later that she had just overlooked an obvious switch, even if she might never know because she will starve to death down here in the shaft.

Eve puts her backpack on the ground, then takes off the upper part of her suit and carefully places it on top of the backpack. Nevertheless, she continues to sweat. She leans with her back against the wall and feels how wet her T-shirt is.

Searching for an opening mechanism has tired her out. She slowly slides down to her knees. Just as she is about to close her eyes, a feeling pops up. *Something is wrong here.* It is not even a thought, just a slight hunch. Suddenly she is wide awake. What is bothering her about this situation? Had she overlooked something she'd briefly glimpsed from the corner of her eye?

She slaps her hand against her knee. How could she be so stupid? The answer is right behind her. She slid down the wall without feeling any friction. That part of the wall must have moved downward with her. The door is open! Or there must at least be an opening on top. Eve moves away from the wall, gets up, and turns around. There is nothing to see. The area is as jet black as before. She does not dare extend her hand. What a disappointment it would be if she felt a wall again!

Eve has to force herself and command the muscles of her right arm to move her forearm, centimeter by centimeter, until her fingers meet cool steel. An electric shock hits her, or at least it feels like that, though not a single electron flowed. She has found something! She frantically searches for an edge. The door must be halfway closed, because she only slid down to her knees. And she indeed finds a border extending across the space in the wall and it can be pushed down with little effort. She lowers the entire door into the floor. *Ha!*

Her fingers move over the floor. What she feels is not a passageway, but neither is it a simple wall. With her fingertips she senses patterns, symbols, signs. The entire area beyond the door appears to be covered by something like braille. Eve's fingers move over the small raised spots. She does not understand anything, but she is excited. Then she notices tiny crevices between the symbols. This could mean that each symbol is a button of its own. She tries to concentrate on one of them. The symbols are small, a fact that does not match the large, four-fingered hands of the Proxima b inhabitants she imagined based on the indentations in the egg. The icon on which her right index finger rests consists of a circle, with a dot in the middle. If that isn't an invitation! She slightly presses her fingertip against it, and the icon briefly moves inward, before moving back out, as if pushed by a spring mechanism.

Eve is shocked to suddenly see her own shadow. She spins around. She has to hold her hand up to shield her eyes, which are now adapted to the darkness. A yellow light is visible about 30 meters above her. She turns around again. In the glow of the new light she discovers a large control panel in front of her. The number of symbols is impressive. If each symbol has a key of its own, then there are significantly more keys than honeycomb structures on the wall.

She takes a closer look at the icons. There is a kind of frame that contains something almost like continuous text, though it is only five centimeters wide. The largest part of the control panel consists of repetitious sets. Three keys. She has already tried out the first one in a triad—the circle with the dot. The second in each set looks like two equilateral triangles connected at their tips. The third one resembles a reversed S.

Eve once more turns toward the wall with the honeycomb cells. The lamp she had activated with that first key now seems rather dim. It only seemed so brilliant at first because her eyes were so used to darkness. It shines with a warm, yellow light. Eve runs up the path until she reaches the lamp. It is located in the upper part of the honeycomb and cannot be distinguished from the rest of the surface. Here the wall shines with a yellow light, that's all. Nothing else has changed. Eve walks back down to the control panel. Unfortunately she does not remember which specific key she pressed. Therefore she tries another circle but keeps her finger on the key. Once again a light is turned on. This time it is considerably higher up. It is blue, with a violet tinge. Then she presses the same key again. The light goes out. On-Off. A very practical method. It is only logical that other intelligent beings would use this.

But what do the two other keys mean? Eve is afraid of triggering something she cannot control. Yet she has nothing to lose. Being able to turn lamps on and switch them off again won't get her any further. She wants something to happen. Therefore she presses another circle symbol. It also activates a lamp, one with a more truly-violet hue than the second one. Now the coordinate system used by the panel becomes clear. Up is down and left is right. The visual perception of the Proxima b inhabitants must, for some reason, switch directions. It shouldn't be a problem for her brain, as humans can adapt to a mirror showing the sides of the body reversed. It would have been practical, though, if she could find out which keys she had already pressed. There are probably charts at the side of the panel that could provide this information, if she could only understand them.

Time for the second type of key, the one with the two triangles. Eve selects a position on the upper right, so something should be happening at the bottom left—near her. She presses the key and tries to remember its location. The key follows the impulse provided by her fingertip and then moves toward her again. Eve lets her finger rest on it. That was a wise decision, because at first glance nothing seems to have changed. Therefore she also activates the respective lamp by pressing the circle key. She turns toward the wall with the honeycombs. Now a new yellow light shines there, in approximately the fourth row from the floor.

Eve has to walk up the twisting path to reach the level of this honeycomb. When she turns around the corner she can see what happened—the surface of the honeycomb is now translucent. From inside, white light with a strong blueish tinge falls on the path in front of it. She slowly approaches, torn between fear and curiosity. From a distance of two meters she notices a kind of chamber behind the transparent surface. She is hurrying now, because she has a hunch about what to expect.

Inside the chamber is a flat couch covered by a white material. On it lies an alien creature. It can only be one of the inhabitants of Proxima b. Eve is fascinated and repelled at the same time. The creature, whatever gender it may be, looks horribly ugly at first glance. As she suspected, the being is larger than a human. She estimates the body length to be 220 centimeters. It is hard to say, though, because the creature has tucked its legs close up against the body.

The body is ungainly and sack-like, with green skin dotted by brown spots. It must be heavy, as the legs look extremely muscular. Their shape indicates they are perfect for jumping. Perhaps the creature is remotely related to the mini-frogs that attacked them when they crossed the mountains. Eve knows the term 'frog' is misleading, because the being certainly has much less in common with Earth's frogs than humans do.

It possesses four arms. Two of them look strong but short. They consist of only one joint each and end in four-fingered claws. The other two arms are long and thin. These arms don't seem to be very strong, but they appear quite flexible. They consist of the upper arm—a humerus—and a joint leading to a section with what looks like an ulna. Then there is an additional forearm that culminates in a wrist-like joint, and a hand displaying seven extremely slender fingers. Eve counts again. The number of fingers might be reflected in the numbering system of a species, so she wouldn't be surprised if a mathematical system based on 7 or 14 was used here. The arms are located on the sides of the squat body, with the thinner ones starting at joints further up.

The creature does not seem to have a *real* head. The body tapers toward the top, where it measures maybe 20 centimeters across. Eve detects four eyes. At least these organs—each covered by a palm-sized transparent lens—appear to be suitable for seeing. At the top of each eye is a skin fold that might serve as a lid to cover and protect the visual organ. At the moment, the creature's eyes are open. Eve feels like she is being watched, but there is no reaction to whatever she does.

The extraterrestrial is either dead or asleep. The chamber is well insulated from the outside so that Eve notices no temperature difference. But even cooling systems generate heat. Maybe the infrared lines she can see, which outline the shape of the honeycomb, dissipate the generated heat.

Eve feels nauseated and has to sit down. She is angry at herself. She gets to see her first extraterrestrial, and then she finds its shape ugly and repulsive? Is that normal, or is she... what might you call it? Humancentric? Will humancentrism become a negative term on this alien world? She doesn't understand her own reaction. Pictures of frogs don't scare her. Yet this creature does. However, it might be her only friend in this empty world—or, eventually, it could become her only friend.

She looks around and realizes this is not true. Above her there are thousands of honeycombs, with probably as many extraterrestrials waiting to be awoken. If she only awakens one of them it might be the same as awakening all of them, because that creature could possibly take over that task. That could turn her from a researcher into someone being examined by the planet's inhabitants, who are certainly physically and technologically superior to her. Newly discovered tribes on Earth did not fare too well when that happened. She must not make the same mistake.

On the other hand...

On the other hand...

She starts this thought—then immediately suppresses it—several times. In the end, though, she is unable to resist. It is obvious that things could hardly get worse than they are right now. She has no hope for the future. How many times has she already felt like this just today? She could sit down, use up her last food, lick water from puddles, and wait for her death. Or she could try to find help.

Adam disappeared on the ice. It hurts to even think of his name. Marchenko was crushed by the sweeping mechanism. The image of his hand trying to hold on will haunt her dreams. But in one of these honeycomb-shaped chambers there might be someone who knows a way out of this trap, or at least someone to talk to. That, she admits, is her greatest fear—going insane in solitude. She managed to go on in total darkness, she tolerated both cold and snow, heat, and excessive light. She almost drowned. But the idea of being alone forever gives her the creeps. She probably won't starve here, as the doubtlessly available organic material should solve her food supply problem. *Terrible!*

Eve slaps her hand against her face. She is ashamed of her own thoughts. It is better to just plan from day to day. What can she achieve today? The decision of whether to press the third button can wait until tomorrow. Now it is time to go to sleep. At least it is so warm down here she can use her suit as a bed. She takes off her LCVG, as she only will need it again on top of the ice sheet. Meaning never. She takes her spare T-shirt, dips it into one of the puddles, and then wrings it out over her mouth. The water does not taste too bad.

Tomorrow she will think about how she can get more of it. She already has an idea.

May 3, 19

My body is working. The modification process is not quite finished, but that involves only a few sensors I don't need right away. The fabricators can continue working while I try to find Eve. I order the ISUs to return to me, to complete my six legs. Then I let the fabricators remove the last bit of the material that still keeps me stuck in this gap in the wall.

I fall down two meters. I already know this room from the images sent by the ISUs. Over there is the air duct I selected. I crawl across the floor on my six legs, but I keep looking upward. This is an unfamiliar position. I am used to seeing a wide field of view. Now I feel like I am lying on my back. Yet I don't see less from down here. I am even surprised at how much I perceive of what is happening above my body. *Isn't that much more important for my survival?*

In order to reach the duct, I have to pull myself up with my front extremities. That is not too difficult. I might look like a crocodile, but I am more flexible in all directions. I push myself up a bit on the smooth wall. Then my front end bends at a right angle and enters the air duct. My forward optical sensors report the first surprise. The rotor, which was standing still yesterday, is now moving. Something must have been triggered inside this building. *Could it be related to Eve? Or is it the result of our failed activity?*

I flip my tail forward, stop the rotor with it, crawl through the rotor, and then quickly retract my tail before the blades start spinning again. The fact that this seemingly-dead building is coming alive is probably good news, but it won't make the search for Eve any easier. I slowly crawl through the air duct and try to determine my location. Right now I have no choice concerning my path, but that will change.

And, after half an hour I do come to a fork in the path. Two additional pipes join my duct and increase its diameter. *Should I crawl into one of the smaller pipes, which probably would lead to a room further up? Or do I choose the wider one, which might lead me to the life support center on one of the lower levels?* Option 1 might take me closer to Eve, at least with a little bit of luck, while option 2 could get me into one of the most important sectors of this building.

I choose the larger pipe. If I can find the central room, which somehow must control this huge edifice, I should be able to reach any room where a living being might be found. That sounds like a good plan. I could send small probes from the central room to independently scout all possible paths I could use to get to Eve. Trying out all these routes in this huge labyrinth by myself would take me more time than Eve has left.

I regret that I am not advancing as quickly as I had hoped. First I end up in a kind of lint trap. The designers placed a mesh in the air duct. Its openings are much too small for me. Of course I could cut a hole in the mesh, but I first examine what has already been caught here. I find plant matter and also a few scraps that hardly could have grown naturally. The structures are so regular that they appear to have been carefully woven. Are those the remnants of textiles the inhabitants wore? The DNA traces on them are interesting, as I already know them from the mini-frogs that attacked us in the mountains. *I hope Eve still has the bone knife I tossed to her back then. Or did I give it to Adam?*

The mesh material is similar to a titanium alloy known on Earth. I cut a hole of a suitable size and crawl through it. The pipe is surprisingly long. It reaches so far ahead from my location that I cannot fully light it with my searchlight. However, the radar shows me it ends after about 500 meters. This is strange, because my spotlight ought to be bright enough to light the pipe up to half a kilometer. There is either some gas which absorbs light inside the pipe, or it has a curve that cannot be seen on radar. Physically, both options should be impossible.

I try the method used by bats. I emit a loud ultrasound 'ping' and wait for its echo to reach me. The result is also 500 meters. That does not tell me anything about a curve, as the sound waves are guided by the pipe. At least the distance is correct. Ultimately, that is the only thing that counts. Therefore I simply keep on crawling and wonder what I will find at the end of the pipe.

Of course... a larger pipe. I should have known. Once more, smaller air ducts join a larger one that voraciously pulls in air. There must be a strong pump at its end. I also notice that the air from the various ducts has different temperatures. Accordingly, a fine mist has developed in the cube-shaped chamber where they meet. I don't mind, so I simply crawl into the largest pipe. According to the hierarchical principle, it is most likely to lead me to the central room. Its diameter is so large that Eve could easily accompany me.

After 30 meters I find a rotor drawing in air. Its blades are half the size of the pipe diameter, and they are moving very, very quickly. They contain a lot of kinetic energy. I won't make it past this spot so easily, and my prehensile tail is not strong enough to simply stop them. I have to work on its weak spot, the axle around which the blades rotate. If I manage to misalign the axle, the rotor will destroy itself due to its high angular momentum. However, I better not be standing too close to it when that happens.

It's no use, I simply must make my way through it. I use the tip of my tail as a file. When metal presses against rotating metal, it soon forms a groove that keeps getting deeper. If I continue this long enough, the axle will break and the rotor blades will fly away. Normally, they would each hit a random spot, but in this case the airflow will play a role, as it gives fragments a small impulse in the direction of the control center. The probability of the heavy metal pieces hitting me, of all targets, is therefore 25 percent at most.

FIVE MINUTES HAVE GONE BY, BUT THE GROOVE IS NOT NEARLY deep enough. There is an incredibly-loud squeaking sound inside the pipe. I suppose it can be heard in the entire building. If anything is awake here, it will start moving toward this disturbance. I am glad that I can regulate my sense of hearing so I don't have to suffer this noise.

AFTER HALF AN HOUR THE SQUEAKING IS STILL THERE, BUT NOW the swoosh of the rotor is changing. I can hear it is no longer running true. The unbalanced mass increases the forces acting on the hub. It shouldn't be long before everything blows up in my face. Now I am getting a bit scared. Compared to this, the wall that cut up my body the day before yesterday was rather harmless. According to my estimate, each of the rotor blades weighs 200 kilograms. Moment of inertia multiplied by the square of the angular velocity equals an amount of energy I can in no way withstand. If the fragments tear apart my body or destroy my memory units, I will not be able to repair myself again. My immortality would be gone in a few seconds.

The imbalance of the rotor increases. I even feel that in the pressure of the air being drawn in. Now it can only be a few seconds. This is the moment for me to escape to safety. I want to retract my prehensile tail from the hub, but it is stuck. What has happened? From down here I cannot see anything. I run several simulations at once. One of them gives me a possible reason: The tip of the tail, which I use as a file, might have fused with the metal of the hub due to the enormous heat.

I will never find out whether this theory is correct. My prehensile tail ties me to a rotating machine that will soon blast itself apart. I can detach my legs, but not my tail. I did not foresee such a situation. But wait... at least I can send my legs to safety. Even if I don't exist anymore they could become six ISUs with limited intelligence. They can wander through the building, search for Eve, and transmit my farewell to her. I send them, and use my rear optical sensors to watch them crawl quickly out of the pipe.

The rotor constructed by the extraterrestrials is very sturdy. My legs have now left the immediate impact zone, and I am still alive. The squeaking has stopped. The rotor blades are humming in a skewed rhythm, sounding like a broken heart. Suddenly there is a noise like ripping paper, a horrible sound that gives me the creeps. This must be the end.

I would like to close my eyes, but that would be unreasonable. I do quite the opposite and activate the high-speed camera. It shows three of the rotor blades flying off toward the control center. During their short flight they rupture the walls of the pipe. The fourth blade is hurtling toward me. In slow motion it seems to float elegantly, almost like a ballerina. It approaches me as if it wanted to ask me to dance. I try to modify the cross-section of my body in order to minimize damage. The steel blade sweeps me off the ground, cutting off the rear part of my body. I don't experience any pain, something more like elation. The blade whirls me through the air as if I were weightless, and it possesses an overwhelming, fervent energy that sweeps me along. I become part of a strange choreography the universe has never experienced.

The metal of the pipe bursts under the impact of the rotor blade. My dance is accompanied by a cacophony. Somehow I manage to hold on somewhere. I still can think and remember things. I wait for that to end. Only a few seconds have gone by, but time seems to stretch eternally. This is one of the moments when I notice I am no longer a human being, but I have still retained something essentially human—the strong urge to survive such chaos as this.

May 3, 19

Suddenly there is a loud screeching sound. Eve is startled and wakes up. Her heart is beating faster. She looks around frantically but cannot see any immediate danger. The noise reverberates through her entire body. It sounds... existential, as if two machines are engaged in a life-or-death struggle. She thinks of combat robots from videos Adam used to watch. Would this station be equipped with such security measures?

Eve places an ear to the ground. The noise definitely comes from below, but that is not the only direction. She gets up and looks around, then turns around several times. Over there, on the right, the wall across from the honeycombs, the shaft is still lit by the lamps she activated yesterday. Is she mistaken, or did the yellow light become a bit more reddish?

She walks toward the source of the noise. It must be inside the wall. She carefully touches the wall. There is something, quite a ways above her head. She can only reach the lower part of what might be a circular structure. Eve wets her finger, reaches up to the bottom edge of the structure, and notes that she can feel a breeze. It seems to be a vent of the life-support system.

The air carries the screeching sound with it. It is a bit more muffled than what she can hear through the floor, but it definitely comes from the same source. Eve is startled when there is suddenly a humming sound as well. One of the opponents seems to have drawn a new weapon. In her imagination he has forced his enemy down and now hits him with enormous force. She shakes her head. All kinds of things could cause the noise. Perhaps it's just a defect somewhere.

Of course it is odd the cacophony should occur now, shortly after her arrival. Or is someone trying to tell her something? She listens to the rhythm, but it almost certainly does not contain a signal. She should not get worried now. What else can happen to her, after all? She has nothing to lose. The universal device tells her that it is 5 a.m. What does it matter?

She feels the pressure of her bladder. Eve walks to the opposite corner of the shaft, pulls down her panties, squats and relieves herself. Her urine splatters forward between her legs. The floor must be slanted slightly downward. She notices she has not washed in a long time. She raises her arm and sniffs her armpit, but she cannot smell anything. Could her sense of smell have adapted to the current hygiene conditions? Eve rises, pulls up her panties, and walks back to the other corner, where her suit and her backpack are awaiting. She is actually walking around in her underwear... imagine that!

But who cares? "I don't think anyone will complain." She flinches when she notices that she has answered herself out loud. That was fast. Now she is already talking to herself.

She pulls her suit into the corner, sits on it, and leans against the wall. *What's on the agenda for today?* Her first idea, which was about to enter her consciousness, quickly retreats when there is another loud bang. After that, the noise is gone.

Eve looks at her universal device. The fight, or whatever it was, lasted for more than half an hour. *Please come back, dear idea,* she thinks. She knows it was an important one. Now the idea is hiding behind the door of her subconscious. How could she lure it out again? Perhaps with a reward? *Eve, you are slowly turning schizophrenic,* she thinks. There it is, the idea. It stands right in the center of her consciousness, spreading its hands in apology. The idea did not want to criticize her, but Eve—first talking to herself and then to the idea—might have cause for concern. She slaps her cheeks because she realizes she is about to slide into a weird dream. What she needs now is reality, not an escape from it.

Good. Problem number 1: She needs water and, at some point, food as well. Eve remembers her training. The air holds enough moisture. Producing potable water through condensation should not be too difficult. Finding food might be tougher. But does she really want to solve this problem? Does it make any sense to survive down here any longer than her reserves will last? She can't make up her mind right now.

On to problem number 2: Loneliness. She never would have expected that it would be so hard to bear. Up to now she had considered herself a woman who could quite well get along on her own. On the voyage across the ice sheet there were days when she barely exchanged five words with Adam or Marchenko. But now she misses them both so much. The alternative is hoping to awaken one of the creatures sleeping here in one of the honeycomb-shaped chambers. She must be getting really desperate.

She remembers the first impression she had when she saw one of the inhabitants of Proxima b, the disgust she felt. Yet she would prefer the company of such a creature to eternal solitude. However, she does not even know whether she could find a basis for communication. Or if one of the giant frogs might regard her as food.

Eve turns sideways and looks at the control panel. It is probably quite simple. Three symbols, three functions: First, a light that most likely informs about the status of the cell, then the second key, which allows for a more precise diagnosis. The third symbol, the third key, can only have one function—

to start the hibernation process, or to reverse it later. She only has to press the key once.

It would be better, of course, if Marchenko could be beside her. He would be able to handle the recently-revived creature, even if it showed hostile intentions. Eve is not so sure she would be able to do that. Shortly after awakening, the creature might be relatively weak, but what about later? Should she try to acquire some weapon? Then again, the very fact that she would be holding something threatening could trigger the hostile intentions she wants to avoid. No, she does not need a weapon. However, she is going to put something on. How strange, the idea of facing an extraterrestrial makes her feel prudish. After all, these creatures appear to be naked in their sleeping chambers.

Eve rises and puts on pants and also the jacket of her suit. She decides to not put the LCVG back on. Then she stands in front of the control panel. The number of options is huge. Her gut feeling tells her she should ensure some distance from the place where she is standing. That seems silly, but as she has no other selection criteria, she might as well follow her instinct. She looks for a position on the bottom left of the control panel that corresponds to a honeycomb close to the ceiling. Yet she hesitates. From here she could not even recognize the color of the light. And she does not know how long the awakening takes. It would take her several minutes to go up there. If she is unlucky, she might be too late.

So she selects a honeycomb further down. She moves her finger around in a circle a few times and then chooses a sequence of symbols in the lower third. First the circle with the dot. She presses it and shortly afterward sees a light go on about two meters above the ground. During the first seconds it flickers, as if it could not make up its mind, but then it glows a steady red. She already knows yellow, blue, violet—but red is something new. What might the different colors mean? Do they indicate the rank or sex of the sleeper? Or are they related to the state of the chamber?

The alien in the only honeycomb whose interior she saw seemed healthy, as if just taking a little nap. The associated lamp had been yellow. She activates the next symbol, the two triangles. She does not wait long but goes directly to the honeycomb that by now should have become transparent. Yes, she can look inside. The revulsion she feels when seeing this alien is not as pronounced, even though this creature looks just as strange.

Eve tries to notice possible differences. The condition of the sleeper appears to be good, as far as she can tell. The creature is naked. At least she doesn't detect any clothing. Could the eyes be a different shade? She walks to the other transparent honeycomb to make sure. Yes, she was right. The iris of the first alien seemed almost black, while that of this new candidate is dark blue. The new guy also has fewer muscles on his load arms. That's what she is calling the shorter arms that are obviously intended for harder tasks.

How does this creature consume food? Eve cannot discover a mouth. At the belly the leathery skin forms some wrinkles, though. Perhaps there is an opening hidden below. She does not notice any sexual differentiation. She sees a few pointed appendages between the legs of the creature, but these could be either genitals or excretory organs, or teats for feeding offspring. Eve wonders whether she should turn a few more honeycombs transparent. Then she might find children or other variants of this life form. She does not even know whether this species is oviparous or viviparous, or how many sexes it has. In the end, though, she can only conjecture.

Would that help her? She shakes her head. Only one of the aliens could provide her with reliable information. Eve imagines how the awakened sleeper hops toward her and stretches out a seven-fingered, slender hand. Then she would have to control herself and not flinch. She turns around to the control panel. This time she remembers the two keys belonging to the selected honeycomb. But why did the builders not integrate any status light into the control panel? Do aliens have a perfect memory?

She is once more veering off from her actual task. A key with a reversed S is waiting for her. Is this a letter of the extraterrestrial script, or rather a pictogram? She places a finger on it. The pattern has a soft feel to it, without sharp edges, as if thousands of fingers had already touched it before. Hers definitely is not the first one. She just has to push it briefly into the control panel, and then the event she both fears and desires will happen.

Eve presses the button. The metal vibrates slightly. That's new. She turns around and walks to the selected honeycomb. For half a minute nothing happens. Then the lamp starts to blink. The infrared glow around the honeycomb increases, as energy is apparently supplied. Fog appears inside the chamber. At first she can discern the outline of the alien, but then the vapor gets too thick. Eve stands right in front of the chamber. The fog is pulsating, as something is probably being blown into the honeycomb.

Suddenly something slaps against the pane from the inside. Eve jerks back. It must be the sole of one of the two feet. It seems to suction itself against the transparent wall. These frogs can probably climb walls. The fog is getting thicker and now almost resembles cottony clouds. The foot falls down. All of this happens completely without sound, indicating the chamber must be well-insulated. Eve cannot hear anything, even when she places her ear against the windowpane.

Then the material starts to vibrate. Eve takes one step to the side, then another, until she no longer blocks the area in front of the chamber. She has an idea of what is about to happen. The vibrations of the pane increase. Eve notices that it moves forward millimeter by millimeter. First it projects one centimeter, then two, then three. How thick is the locking mechanism? At 15 centimeters the pane briefly stops. *That can't be it,* Eve thinks, and indeed, soon afterward fog hisses from a narrow gap that has formed between the lock and the wall of the chamber. Then the front side moves forward again.

Eve sees now that it is held by four strong rods sticking out from the upper and lower corners of the honeycomb. The fog is cold and heavier than air, so it sinks. Soon Eve can see details on the inside again. The couch still seems to be in place. The alien has changed the position of its feet, but she knew that already. Now the couch starts moving, following the windowpane. At first it seems to float, but then Eve recognizes it rests on two metal rails that disappear into the inside of the chamber. The couch and the glass front move forward gradually, as if proudly presenting its owner. Eve feels a shiver running down her spine. Their first encounter is about to happen. She has cold sweat on her palms.

The extraterrestrial lies on its side, though she cannot tell whether the front or the back is facing her, as the eyes are distributed all around. Once she imagines the creature hopping like a kangaroo, she can tell by the position of the legs that she is looking at its back. She hasn't seen it in motion yet, though. At this closer position, the eyes are even more impressive. The dark blue of the huge iris looks inviting, like a tropical ocean in which you can dive down, directly into the soul of this being. Even though the rest of the body might seem repulsive, the eyes are really beautiful.

Eve takes a step backward. She is still waiting for the first sign of life. Would the alien first move its hands or its legs? It would be best to stay out of reach, in case there are involuntary spasms. She realizes that the creature must breathe somehow. How does fresh oxygen get into its body? Through the skin? Considering the body size and the related energy expenditure, that should be difficult. There is nothing indicating breathing, no chest moving up and down. Could this creature be sick?

She walks around the couch that has by now been completely extended. The lamp to the left of the chamber is still blinking. Is the chamber waiting for something? Or should she do something? Under normal circumstances, would there be a team waiting to place an artificial respiration tube on the alien's belly? She does not know. With every passing second she feels more and more convinced she has made a terrible mistake.

She approaches the couch until she can touch the skin of the creature. In front of her lies a huge, ugly frog-like creature, which at the same time is the only intelligent creature within a radius of several light years. She has to force herself to touch the alien. The tips of her fingers graze against the skin. It is not as slick as she imagined, but instead feels more like leather—cold leather. Sure, these beings might be cold-blooded, but this specimen is definitely too cold. It can't be more than ten degrees. The revival process must have failed. A dead individual lies in front of her. This being slept for many years, until a human broke into its house to awaken and kill it.

She has to make amends. Eve overcomes her repulsion and gently touches the leathery skin. She touches the extremities that are just as cold. Then she tries to move its arms, but they feel like they are frozen. There is no trace of life. Before long this creature will start to decay, until it turns into dust again. It might have a glorious past, though she doesn't know that, but she took away its future. Eve places her ear on the body above the skin flap. She is still full of hope, but she hears nothing. Nothing is moving. This creature is dead. She can no longer suppress her tears. They roll across her cheeks and drip onto the alien's skin. Eve would like to sing it a lullaby, but the words stick in her throat. She cannot comfort the alien being, nor herself. Now she has become a murderer as well.

What is that? Eve hears a sound behind her, a soft bubbling noise. She is shocked and turns around. The sound comes from between the legs of the creature. The pointed appendages discharge a slimy liquid. The stuff stinks abysmally. Eve cannot grab her nose quickly enough. She immediately feels nauseous. She throws up right next to the opened honeycomb.

May 4, 19

'FORTUNE FAVORS FOOLS.' THAT'S WHAT I CAN HEAR MY MOTHER saying right now, the same as she always did when she was patching me up with vodka—as an antiseptic—and a band-aid after one of my risky pranks went awry. My front section is completely functional, while my rear has been splintered into many tiny parts. The accident cost me a third of my nano-fabricators, which is particularly annoying. The repair is not as extensive as after the encounter with the pleated wall, but it will take almost as long.

Seeking to use the time wisely, I prioritize a task I had planned to do at the control center of the life support system. Just before the accident, I had sent my legs on their way as ISUs. They are supposed to be exploring the labyrinth of rooms and pipes and, if possible, finding Eve. And sending their findings to me, of course, now that I've survived.

This situation has its positive aspects, I think as I let my mind wander. For one thing, the way to the control center is now free. In addition, the crash also exposed electrical wires and coolant lines. Thus I find enough resources here for a truly extensive repair. The builders of this facility used lots of rare earths. Therefore I can use the optimal raw material for each purpose.

I pull myself back on task—I use the forced downtime to monitor my mobile sensors. The ISUs actually found the control center very quickly. If I interpret their data correctly, data I had hoped to be collecting myself, almost the entire building has been shut down. According to the information they send, some areas are not supplied with fresh air. I can already exclude those from my search. Even if Eve might have reached them, she could not have survived without oxygen.

Most of the rooms run in standby mode, without heating or other services, but they are pressurized. Eve might be anywhere in those sections. Yet there is one room that receives a higher than average quantity of fresh air and uses an unusual amount of electricity. I have no idea where any of these sections are located or what they are like.

The ISUs did not find any maps of the building. They only measured where resources are sent, and how much of which ones. Now their task is to follow those tracks. I ordered two of them into the most promising area, while the remaining four have been ordered to cover everything else. The sensors possess enough intelligence to select the least dangerous path that will lead them, sooner or later, to the preprogrammed destination.

Tock... tock... tock. The sound comes from the destroyed pipe in front of me. I check the locations of my ISUs, but none are nearby. The noise sounds like metal hitting against metal. The rhythm is slow and regular. I imagine an old grandfather walking barefoot while tapping his walking stick against the ground. Tock... tock... tock... tock. Now he is walking faster, but only a few steps. This is definitely not a mechanical process, like a clockwork. This thing adapts its behavior to the environment. Tock... tock... tock... tock... tock. It sounds almost playful, like a cat on the prowl.

Damn. I am probably pretty close to the truth. The destruction I caused here must not have gone unnoticed, and now someone comes looking. Perhaps it really is a pet that is hunting intruders... or is it one of the inhabitants? No, I rather suspect it is a machine—a guard. It has to be able to reach all rooms, including the ones not supplied with air. Furthermore, machines simply last longer... unless they constantly let themselves be destroyed in accidents. It would be wise to retreat from here. If that thing investigates the scene it will quickly find the cause for the incident—something that does not belong here. Me. Unfortunately, my legs are currently far away. I can't get away from here, and the thing that makes the tock-tock-tock sound coming from around the curve is getting closer and closer.

I am watching the hole from which it must emerge. It is cautious. At first it sticks out a kind of proboscis that it is using to peek around the corner. Tock... tock... tock... tock... Now the noise sounds cheerful. The guard seems to be glad to have found the damage. I see an object with six legs, about the size of a German shepherd, with smooth, black skin and no head. Instead it has the afore-mentioned proboscis—in front, of course—that is surely full of sensors and is being used to examine the former rotor. The thing touches the suspensions, of which only a few parts remain. Unfortunately the corpus delicti is one of them, the hub with a part of my prehensile tail stuck to it.

The guard sits down on two hind legs and starts investigating its find with the proboscis and the four other legs. It rips apart the material with two legs. I had not expected it to be so strong. Finally it throws away the hub. Then it walks toward me. Tock... tock... tock... tock... It is taking its time, aiming it proboscis in all directions. It seems to enjoy its job, like a railroad worker cheerfully checking a few kilometers of track. I am clearly the goal. How intelligent might this thing be? If it is all alone here, its designers must have given it more than a weak AI. I would like to make myself as flat as possible, but I lack even that capability.

Tock. 'The inspector,' as I will call this thing from now on, comes to a stop directly in front of me. Its proboscis hovers close to my body. It is probably scanning me. It seems to like what it finds, because a claw now reaches out from the end of its proboscis. The opening claw moves down at me and digs itself into my body with great force. I feel that I am being picked up. The thing drags me away. What does it want to do with me? Why doesn't it simply toss me into a corner, like the useless hub? It must have recognized that I am something special. Do I really want to know its instructions for such cases?

We get going. The inspector carefully lifts me over the damaged section, managing to do so without bumping me into anything—quite some achievement, considering the inspector must be about my height and weight. It keeps moving through the large pipe. I suspected as much. The inspector probably wants to deliver this unusual find to the control room. Thus it can't be alone, because otherwise it would have dismantled and examined me then and there. There is probably a higher-ranking unit responsible for the analysis of problematic cases.

We reach the control room. The shape of the room is a regular octagon with a diameter of approximately 15 meters. The ceiling is about three meters above me. It is dark, but not completely so, as multi-colored symbols glow on various devices in the middle and on the walls. Pipes both large and small emerge from the walls wherever the walls are not covered with switches. In addition, each side of the octagon has an area without technical devices—probably doors. If I were not in such a predicament I would feel in paradise, because there are so many things I could explore. This would probably keep me busy for weeks. I look at giant boards on four sides of the octagon. They are covered in numerous symbols. *Why,* I want to ask, *do some display glowing lights while others are dark?*

In the middle of the room my radar sees several technical consoles about one and a half meters tall, forming a circle. There are two entrances, and the inspector drags me through one of them. Inside are two high-backed chairs that look very comfortable but must have been designed for giants. One of them is empty. The other chair is turned away from me, and the inspector places me on the floor in front of that one. Then he uses a tentacle to turn the chair in my direction. This chair is occupied. Everything inside me urges me to flee immediately. I'm frightened to death, but the irony still strikes me as funny. My legs have not come back yet. A mummy stares at me through empty eyes, the mummified shape of an enormous frog.

At first the weird-looking thing really does frighten me! Then I take a closer look. The frog consists of lots of skin and a few bones, suggesting a once very-corpulent body. The eye sockets near the top are impressive. I can only see three, but symmetry would indicate there is a fourth one. There are four upper and two lower extremities. I would have to crawl closer to examine them in more detail. The leg bones are very strong. Eve's hand could not reach around them. Could this be one of the former inhabitants? This specimen must have been dead for a long time. I experience a sense of cautious optimism. If this is the boss the inspector wanted to present me to, then I don't have to be afraid of it.

I am lifted up again. Does the inspector intend to place me on the lap of the dead frog? I look around and am shocked to see that I have misinterpreted the inspector's intentions. The thing sits on its hind legs, while it uses its front extremities to open an apparently heavy octagonal plate that covers a hole of the same shape in the floor of the room. I am already suspended above the hole. This stupid machine did not want to show me to its lord and master. I am much too insignificant for that. It decided to dispose of me. While I am still processing this, my body already plunges into the dark shaft. A thud indicates that the inspector has closed the hatch above me.

The shaft, through which I am moving without being able to stop my fall, has an oval shape. That is all I can tell. I am not even sure how fast I am falling. According to my acceleration sensors, it should be approximately three meters per second, but if that value is correct, I ought to be outside the building by now. The inhabitants of Proxima b managed to construct an extraordinary building, even restructuring space and time. Or perhaps I am simply confused. Considering I had been about to start a major repair for the second time in two days, that is a possibility.

I hope that at least the ISUs can hear me. I ordered them not to move out of radio range. But who knows how deep I have already fallen? Once they can no longer reach me, the sensor units will launch a special search mode that eventually should lead them to me. That is, unless the area where I am going to land can only be reached via the octagonal hatch—the snake-shaped ISUs could not open that by themselves.

Splash! I have landed in a puddle. Yet I seem to be mistaken, because I continue moving further downward. I did not land at the bottom of the puddle but in a full-sized pond within a huge container. I'm not sure what its purpose might be. Might this merely be a safe storage for everything not wanted above? I look around. The floor of the container rises spherically on all sides. Around me lie parts of strange forms, the origins of which are unclear to me. The only things I can recognize are bones. They look quite similar to those of the mummy up there. Did the inhabitants dispose of their dead here?

To make things worse, now my energy management system sends an alert. For the last four days I have been living off my reserves. I should have tried to find more resources a while ago, but when would I have had the time? I had been chasing Eve because she needed me, and I could not have anticipated that I would be lying immobile at the bottom of a water tank, nor could I have prepared for it. I must concentrate on my energy supply if I want to help Eve. I am going to build micro-probes that can examine this tank for potential energy sources. My remaining energy should be sufficient for that.

May 4, 19

Eve drops the empty water bottle. Her eyes follow the plastic container. It seems to fall in slow motion. The bottle hits the ground, tilts, and then rolls on for half a meter. The noise hits her ear canal with a delay. Then it takes a few seconds until her consciousness notices the shock. The meager rest of her life seems to be moving slowly, as if she had activated the parking brake. She is still sitting next to the alien corpse, unable to get up. No, she simply cannot find the will to do it. She leans her head against the honeycomb behind her and closes her eyes. It makes little difference. The blackness remains, and she even thinks she can see relics of the infrared lines on the inside of her eyelids.

She jerks her head forward and back so it hits the hard cover material of the honeycomb-shaped chamber. A gong sounds in her head, then another one, a third and a fourth one. The pain hits her later. It enters her thoughts like a single wave, pushes the fog aside, and suddenly she feels a clarity that amazes her. It is incredibly stupid that she is sitting next to the dead alien, feeling sorry for herself.

She is not yet dead, so she had better go on. She has to get up. Eve looks at her legs. She orders them to move but nothing happens. Fog is seeping into her consciousness again. Gong, gong, gong—she bangs the back of her head against the wall again, clearing her thoughts. Suddenly her limbs react. She gets up. Then she is standing, a bit wobbly at first, but standing. She slaps her cheeks twice with her palms.

The stench is so horrible that she almost topples again. Everything around her stinks. Does the repulsive odor come from the stuff the alien discharged before its death—or was it afterward? Yet there is also a smell of putrefaction that is getting stronger by the hour. Eve takes two steps sideways. Now she realizes she stinks as well. She is the center of her own cloud of hydrogen sulfide, ammonia, and butyric acid. She desperately needs a shower and she should eat something, even though she is not hungry.

She should also do a status check. She is alone. She has to set her own goals. Over there is a railing. Eve stands next to it and looks at the wall. The honeycombs still show up in infrared. This means they are supplied with energy. A violet light is blinking next to the chamber she opened. She remembers that it was orange yesterday. Does the color indicate something about the status of the chambers?

She walks down to the control panel with the countless symbols. Then she pushes circle-buttons at random to activate about 50 lights scattered across the entire console. She turns around and counts the results. There are eight yellow honeycombs, six orange ones, and nine red ones. Most are blue, and exactly three are violet, just like the light at the chamber of the dead alien. Violet is the end of the optical spectrum. Therefore the three occupants of the chambers marked in violet are probably already dead. That is only a theory, though, until she checks it out herself. Eve uses the in-between keys to turn all three honeycombs transparent. Then she walks back up to see for herself.

She reaches the first chamber in the middle of the second floor. Her heart skips for a moment when she sees what's inside—a creature, lying on a couch that is much too large for its small size. It is strange, but she immediately recognizes that this is not a different sex of this species, but a far-from-mature being. She does not even know what gives her this impression. Is it because this creature put his two precision arms into the belly fold? If that is an organ for food intake, then the position would resemble a human baby sucking on a finger.

The eyes of the alien child are covered by a thin layer of skin, perhaps for protection. The legs resemble more the second, strong pair of arms than the powerful jumping limbs of adults. And the child has hair on its back, or some other kind of skin protrusions that it would likely have shed later in its life. What really makes Eve sad is the overall condition of the body. It is quite obvious this individual will never again wake up. Its skin is thin and almost transparent, and the body lies in a puddle of liquids that flowed from its corpse despite the cooling. The child must have died a while ago.

It takes her a bit longer to reach the second chamber. She places both hands against the window and mentally prepares herself before looking inside. The creature here is lying on its back instead of on its side. It is completely desiccated, practically mummified. The body is only two meters long. It is hard to say whether this is a female or an adolescent. The system failures must have started a long time ago. How long might this facility have been in operation? Could it be 100 years, or 1,000?

By now Eve thinks nothing could shock her anymore, but she is wrong. The third chamber, almost at the very top of the shaft, looks like a battlefield. Hoses and surgical instruments hang from its ceiling. Perhaps the chamber tried to save its occupant, but the numerous seemingly random cuts in the body point toward the opposite. It seems the chamber tried to kill its inhabitant. It is interesting that the body shows no signs of decomposition. The chamber's cooling function still seems to be working. However, the medical technology apparently intended to perform a little massacre. Eve can't help but imagine what it would be like to sleep in such a cryo-chamber, only to be cut apart alive by a robot surgeon gone haywire. Hopefully the alien did not consciously experience its own death.

The results are clear. She no longer has to check any other violet chambers. The color code definitely indicates the status of the frozen extraterrestrials. This means, though, that the entire system must have been in a state of decay for some time. Something went wrong. Perhaps the remaining inhabitants retreated into this building to shelter from the large flare, hoping their brothers and sisters would come for them later. Maybe the system was supposed to wake them 100 years afterward—but nobody heard the alarm. Eve knows these are only speculations. Had the inhabitants of Proxima b written down their history? It would certainly be exciting to study such a document. To do so, she has to get out of this shaft, which seems to be a dead end in this labyrinth.

First she has to solve a different problem. She needs drinking water. Yesterday she considered setting up a condensation tent to obtain water, but that takes a long time. The opened honeycomb might offer a different option. If her assumption is correct, the chamber would provide water to the occupant, at the latest after the awakening. So far she has not found a single faucet outside of the chambers. Eve walks back all the way. The closer she comes, the stronger the smell.

She stands once more in front of the couch with the dead alien. Should she push the creature off the couch? Then it might roll away a short distance, and the stench would not be as strong. She begins, but then she doesn't have the heart for it. The extraterrestrial does not deserve this. When she awakened the creature, the light was not violet. Without her, the alien might have lived to be rescued. Was that the meaning of the call for help received on Earth?

The water. Eve kneels down and examines the design of the chamber. The couch moves on two rails. There is a gap of about 20 centimeters between the rails and the floor. On the rear wall she can see a few air-exhaust ducts, but no other technology. She should look for a source of water in the upper part. To do so, she has to step on the couch. In her mind she asks the extraterrestrial for forgiveness and then pushes his front part slightly to the side. The skin feels different from the way it was right after the awakening, slicker and colder.

Eve flinches, but there is no other option. The plan works. Now she can kneel next to the corpse and crawl to the rear of the chamber. The cavity is lit from the side walls. She steps off the couch. Here she can only crouch. Now she sees that she was right. Back here are the technical systems she has been seeking—short metal pipes sticking out of the wall, ending in rubbery arms. These arms are flexible and hollow. They probably contain artificial muscles that help the creatures move. Does one of them provide drinking water, and if so, which one? And how could she get it to discharge some water?

What if one of the occupants woke up and was thirsty? There must be conventions for marking sources of water—blue color, certain symbols—but they would certainly be too foreign for her to recognize them. But what would be the most comfortable way a just-awakened creature could drink? How would it signal its intention to get fluids into its body?

Eve imagines a baby who knows nothing about the world or its conventions. Yes, the baby would possess a sucking reflex. You need to create suction to move water in a certain direction. That is a mechanism that should work anywhere where drinking water and gravity exist, including on Proxima b. Could it really be this simple? Eve takes the first hose into her hand and puts it to her lips. And then she sucks on the hose, very carefully. After all, it might deliver some nutrient solution that could be poisonous to her. Nothing happens, even when she sucks more vigorously.

Second attempt: the next hose also remains empty.

Number three leads to the same result. Eve wipes the sweat off her forehead.

She suctions harder from the very start on the fourth attempt and is clearly successful. A liquid materializes in her mouth before she can tell what it is. She is panicked and spits it out, but she notices her mucous membranes have not come into contact with anything corrosive. The liquid still flowing from the rubber tube is completely clear and does not smell of anything. While she has no analyzer, this could only be water. Finally, a success after all this time! This really perks her up.

The water flow stops after 20 seconds. There is obviously an automatic shutoff. Eve takes off her suit and her underwear. This is the opportunity she has wished for after she awoke today—a shower! The water is lukewarm, but at least it is refreshing. She has to suck on the hose several times to keep the water flowing, can only take a shower while crouching, and can't avoid splashing her nearby clothes, but it is still a fantastic experience that she enjoys with her eyes closed. This way she manages to block this bizarre situation from her mind—a meter and a half away there is still the alien's corpse whose death she might be responsible for, while she is naked and splashing herself with fresh water in its sleeping chamber.

To finish things off, Eve replenishes her water supply. After she has crawled back out she is so exhausted she feels like collapsing right next to the chamber. However, the stench reminds her of another task. She has to get to the central control room! She picks up her clothes and walks down to the control panel. Then she presses the key with the reversed S that will move the couch with the dead alien back into its chamber. The window closes and becomes opaque. Only the blinking violet-colored lamp and the trail of wet, naked human footprints indicate something extraordinary must have happened here.

She cannot slack off now. It feels good to be active. She can't go further down in the shaft. Yet walking back does not make sense to her either. What about the air vent she noticed? She stands next to the rear wall of the shaft and feels for it. Yes, this is the structure from which she heard noises yesterday. Today, there is nothing to hear.

Eve has to stretch her arms to reach the edge of the vent. The curvature tells her that the diameter of the pipe must be about two meters. That should be more than sufficient for her. It seems almost oversized for ventilation purposes, but perhaps it also fulfills another function. She tries to pull herself up with her arms, but she is not strong enough. She makes a second attempt, gasps, and wiggles her legs, but she has no chance because the wall is too smooth. A stool would be good, a table or a chair. She wonders what she could stand on. She can only think of her backpack. Eve sighs. That would need to be the next farewell.

She places the backpack on the ground right next to the wall and steps on it. Due to the integrated frame it can carry her weight. Then she tries to pull herself up. The added 50 centimeters are sufficient. She manages to push off with her forearms and crawl into the hole. A new victory—and also a loss, because she won't be able to take the backpack with her. If Marchenko only could be here! He could have easily lifted her with his third arm. The pain of this loss rises in her mind. She quickly suppresses the feeling as she climbs back out.

In the dim light of the lamps on the honeycombed wall, she checks what she might still need from her backpack. Surprisingly, many items. She puts on her clothes again, not because she feels cold, but because the pockets in the jacket and the pants offer a lot of storage: the toolset, just in case; the universal device, even though it is almost out of energy; and as much food as possible. She eats what she can't stow, even though she still does not feel hungry.

"Let's go," she calls out into the silence. No one answers.

Shouldn't she try to wake another one of the aliens? If anybody knows how to find the central room it would be the creatures sleeping in those chambers. She might have a better chance if she chose a honeycomb with a light still glowing yellow. But what if the revival system is failing in general, due to lack of energy, for instance? No, she does not want to make the decision about the life or death of another creature.

"Goodbye, backpack," she says. When she hears her words echoing through the shaft they sound odd, as if the backpack were a living creature. Yet for Eve it is a very emotional farewell. She has the impression she is taking one of her last steps. First Adam, then Marchenko, then the alien, and finally the backpack. Afterward there won't be anything or anyone else she can leave behind. Fate cannot demand more of her now except for her life.

She steps on the backpack, grabs the edge of the vent, and pulls herself up. Then she puts her weight on her forearms, pulls the right leg after her, and moves it over the edge. She lets herself fall forward and lifts the other leg inside. She has made it! After pulling herself forward with both hands she cautiously gets up on her knees. It is dark in here. Her hands reach upward. The pipe is in fact at least two meters wide and high, so she can stand up without any problems.

She can still see her way vaguely for the first few meters, but then... darkness. Not even her infrared perception can help her. Eve thinks about this. Blackness by itself is not threatening. She has already spent weeks in complete darkness, and she doesn't think there are any dangerous animals here. Nothing is alive here, outside those chambers. There is also no danger if the pipe were to curve.

The only thing she worries about is the possibility of holes in the floor. Perhaps the builders included a drainage system —or the pipe might suddenly turn 90 degrees downward. Walking upright is risky. She will have to crawl, her hands cautiously extended. That way she should be safe from such surprises. If she is lucky the pipe won't be too long. She can manage to crawl on all fours for a few meters. Eve crouches and then sinks to her knees. At least the floor does not appear to be muddy. She can live with a few smudges on her pants. She starts to crawl.

Eve quickly notices that humans are not designed for crawling. If she only had kneepads! Or at least nice, soft mud. She imagines crawling through the soft sand at the shore of an ocean. Waves touch her hands and the sun shines on her back. She has never experienced this, only seen it in pictures. Yet her imaginings feel real. She manages to distract herself from the harsh reality.

Then she hears a rustling noise.

Eve stops and holds her breath. Or did she just imagine it?

There it is again. It sounds like a leaf that the wind blows in her direction. Yet there is no breeze, and certainly no leaf. She has to listen very closely. It might be far away, amplified by the echoes in the metal pipe. There is definitely something, and it is coming toward her. On Earth, as she learned, all kinds of animals run around in sewers—rats, for example, that live off garbage. Yet there is nothing here such an animal could feed on. She remembers those mini-frogs that had been about to use her as food. A shiver runs down her spine. *Did it just get colder in here?*

"Hello," she calls out, attempting to sound calm. Some animals are easily impressed if you act self-confident, she knows. What might be considered self-confident behavior here on Proxima b? She stands up. While she still does not see anything, this might not hold true for whatever is causing the rustling sound. On two legs she might look less like potential prey than on all fours. After all, the inhabitants of this building moved as bipeds.

There is more rustling. The noise is louder, but still so faint that Eve imagines an object no larger than a cat. Aren't cats supposed to move on silent paws? *Couldn't whatever is coming toward me be a cute little cat, please?*

Eve takes a few steps forward and then stops again. She should not be careless, just because of the noise. There still could be a hole in front of her. She feels the ground with her foot before each step, even though this makes her look insecure.

"Watch out," she yells. "Here I come!" The likelihood of this thing understanding her is rather low. It might not even be able to hear. "You'd better get out of my way!"

The softer a noise is, the harder it is to localize. She might actually step on the animal, which would then have to defend itself, of course. She had better avoid unnecessary conflict.

Suddenly a red dot appears in the dark, only four or five meters ahead. Eve stops abruptly. There is also a red dot on her suit jacket. It must have a laser. Whatever it is that faces her can hardly be an animal. Is this thing aiming at her? She spreads her hands to show she is unarmed. The point of light scans her body, jitters around on her chest, moves down, then up again, up to her neck and chin. She closes her eyes and quickly opens them again because she feels dizzy. *That damned thing.* If it wants to shoot her, she stands no chance anyway. She walks directly toward the red dot. She hopes that this is no trick, that there is no abyss right in front of her!

The strange object retreats slightly, but not backward. It moves to the side, to the curvature of the pipe. It seems to be climbing the wall. Without hesitation it moves to the ceiling and remains stuck there.

"Nice trick," Eve says. Crawling up the smooth tunnel wall doesn't look very easy. Perhaps it is a kind of maintenance robot especially designed for this. It doesn't seem to be hostile, merely curious at most. Maybe that will change once she damages something around here. She stands below the object.

"Come here," she jokes, as if talking to a pet, "come to Mama."

Eve raises her arms. She does not expect what happens next. It follows her invitation and drops down. It lands on her shoulder with ease. She wants to reach for it but isn't fast enough. She only briefly touches its tail. What is it, anyway? It seems to have the shape of a snake.

Now it is on the collar of her jacket. The stupid thing is crawling into it! Eve wants to rip off her jacket. The creature slithers across her back and then is in her sleeve. What did she catch here? Eve trembles and suddenly becomes very calm. The snake has wrapped itself around her hand. The red eye looks at her, or at least it appears that way. This is definitely no animal. It is artificial, and its metal skin is warm. She has never seen anything like it, yet it seems familiar.

"ISU 2," she suddenly hears a soft voice say. The thing can speak! Eve's mouth drops open. A sensor unit, a terrestrial product! It must come from Marchenko. Her mind rejoices when she realizes what this means: *Marchenko is probably still alive!* Did he really survive the collision with the wall? But why is he not contacting her via radio?

"What are you doing here?"

"Partial mission 1: Generate plan of building. Partial mission 2: Find missing person. Partial mission 2 completed."

It is an automaton, a robot with the limited abilities of a weak AI. It looks like it has no online connection with Marchenko. Eve is disappointed.

"Can you lead me to Marchenko?"

"Logging partial mission 3: Locating a missing person. Please assign priority."

"Marchenko is missing?" Did the ISU express this vaguely —or has she just received more bad news?

"Current location of person Marchenko unknown."

"When were you last in contact?"

"Twenty-two hours, eight minutes, and seventeen seconds ago."

"And where?"

"Sector 17, room 2FC of the preliminary map, which has not been synchronized with the other sensor units."

"There are other ISUs?"

"Overall, six ISUs are on their way fulfilling partial order 1."

"Can you lead me to the location where the contact with Marchenko broke off? Priority 1."

"Confirming authorization by Eve. New partial order 1: Joint travel to sector 17. Room 2FC. Reprioritizing partial order 1 to 2."

"Where is the route?"

"Suggesting subject should put ISU 2 down and then follow sensor unit."

A good idea. "Are you able to select your path in such a way that survival of the person is the highest priority?"

"That is part of my basic programming."

"Good, because I cannot see obstacles in the dark."

"Should ISU 2 execute the implied order?"

"You are right, yes, turn on the light if you can."

The sensor unit does not answer. Instead, it activates a lamp at its front. It is not very bright, but sufficient to avoid holes and other obstacles. Then it says, "According to the preliminary map data, we will leave the area of insufficient illumination in seven minutes."

"Good, ISU 2."

"Thanks, Eve," the little robot says. Politeness also seems to be part of its basic programming.

"What happened to Marchenko?"

"Current status of person Marchenko is unknown."

"I mean earlier, before the contact broke off."

"You would like a chronological summary?"

"Exactly."

"I can tell you about the past forty-six hours, seventeen minutes, and thirty-seven seconds."

"Yes, please."

"In second number seventeen I registered a fall from a slight height. I hit the floor in sector 14, room 1AA. Then I moved 2.21 meters in a northeasterly direction."

"Just a moment, I don't need it told so precisely. I am mostly interested in facts concerning Marchenko."

"I understand. Generating a reprioritization of past events." The ISU takes a short break.

A reprioritization of past events, Eve thinks, feeling she would sometimes like to be a weak AI. Life could be so simple. Did the ISU really understand what she wanted from it?

"When I was activated, the person Marchenko was immobile in sector 14, room 0AA. Later he moved through rooms 1AA, 1AB and—"

Eve impatiently says, "You can leave out the room coordinates. But add descriptions of the rooms."

"Understood. Marchenko moved through a technical sector and from there entered a pipe, which first expanded and then ended in a fan assembly. Marchenko caused the fan to be destroyed but was damaged during this."

"But did he survive?"

"Correct. He was busy repairing himself when he sent all ISUs on a search with the already mentioned partial orders. After seventy-two minutes and thirteen seconds the contact broke off."

"So you do not know what might have happened to him?"

"I do not possess that piece of information. But I am very glad to have successfully finished partial order 1."

Does its voice express something like pride? Perhaps that is part of the internal reward and motivation system of the AI that allows it to make decisions in the absence of an explicit input.

"Can you speculate about Marchenko's current status?"

"I am able to develop predictions based on probability. Would that fulfill the definition?"

"That's perfect. Then I ask you for a prediction."

"The contact was interrupted very rapidly. Among possible scenarios, I therefore must rate the one most probable in which Marchenko was destroyed by a violent event."

"Couldn't he have walked into an area with bad reception?"

"That is unlikely, because contact would have been lost only after increasing connection problems. These did not occur."

Sounds logical, Eve admits to herself. She sighs. That was a very short period of hope. She should not have fallen for it to begin with. Now everything feels much worse.

"It is not impossible, though," the ISU adds, almost as if it wanted to comfort her.

"Are there alternative scenarios to explain the sudden loss of contact?"

"Yes, though they must be assigned lower probabilities. For instance, Marchenko might consciously reject any contact. In rare cases, strong AIs can develop such personality disorders. Or he is within a Faraday cage that is shielding him. It can also not be excluded that he might have covered a great distance in some unknown way. His body was damaged twice, so that might reduce the range of his radio signals. Finally, he might have run out of energy. All these would match the actual events."

ISU 2 seems to have no special talent for raising her hopes. Eve decides that the Faraday cage or the lack of energy will give her the best reason for believing in Marchenko's survival. Her private probability calculus is disconnected from reality—that's at least one ability in which she surpasses ISU 2.

• • •

"WE WILL SOON REACH SECTOR 17. WATCH OUT, THERE IS considerable damage ahead. I have to warn you especially of sharp edges."

The pipe curves ahead of them. From there, light shines on the opposite wall. Now she can finally see the shape of ISU 2. The sensor unit looks like a slightly-too-fat serpent. It has no feet and moves like a snake. Marchenko really came up with an interesting design.

"I notice that this room was not lit during my last inspection."

That is an interesting fact, Eve thinks. She leans against the wall and cautiously peers around the corner.

"Is there anybody here?" she asks the ISU in a whisper. The robot wriggles into the room. She loses sight of it for a few seconds, but then it reappears on her side of the tunnel.

"Nobody is present," the sensor unit says. "However, I notice changes."

"What kind of changes?"

"Somebody has started to repair the damage caused by Marchenko."

"When?"

"It must have happened during the past twenty-two hours. I cannot be more precise."

At least something still seems to be working down here. That might be a good sign. "That's good," she says. "Isn't it?"

"The repairs were not done very professionally and stopped in an early stage."

Still. Eve considers this a good sign. The building is not completely dead. "Go ahead," she says.

The ISU follows her command and wriggles across the building site. Eve is impressed. Marchenko really made a good job of it. Something seems to have gone wrong, though.

"What happened? Why was Marchenko damaged?"

"According to the information available to me, this was part of the plan."

"Marchenko blew himself up on purpose?"

"This plan had a success probability of seventy-five percent."

"That is an enormous risk. Wasn't there an alternative?"

"A detour would have cost us two days."

"Two days is an acceptable delay."

"Not if finding the missing person Eve has such a high priority."

Suddenly Eve is glad she has met ISU 2. Its weak AI tells her Marchenko's deepest secrets without displaying any emotion.

"Which goal had the higher priority, your own survival or finding the missing person?" Eve has an idea which answer the sensor unit will give her. And she does not feel bad about snooping on Marchenko's thoughts this way. She will ask him herself once they meet again. "No, wait," she says, "I don't want to hear the answer."

"Room 2FC is directly ahead, around the next curve."

"What does that mean?"

"This is the room where the contact ended."

"And what will be waiting for us there?"

"I do not have any information about this."

"But you mapped the room, didn't you?"

"No, I only assumed there is a room there based on Marchenko's last position upgrade and that it should be labeled 2FC based on the internal coordinate system."

"Good that we clarified that. We should therefore be particularly cautious."

"I can confirm this. The reason for the loss of contact might still be in the room."

"I would suggest that you crawl ahead and keep out of sight, if possible."

The sensor unit waves with its tail and starts crawling. They should have agreed on some kind of signal.

Eve carefully reaches into her pants pocket and pulls out

the universal device. The ISU certainly could stream live video to its display. However, she should have recharged the device beforehand. Why didn't she think of this earlier?

Eve is startled when something touches her foot. It is the ISU. "No signs of life in the room," it says.

"No machine activity either? Any robots?"

"Until a few seconds ago, a sensor unit was active there."

What a jokester. Eve is glad to have some company again. There seems to be no danger in the room, at least for the moment. She leaves the tunnel. The room is huge and well-lit. Its walls form an octahedron. This reminds her of the honeycombs right away. Six corners, seven fingers, eight corners. She shakes her head. That's nonsense.

In the center of the room there are a few scattered cabinets that block her view. She cautiously approaches them, looking to the right and the left, even though the ISU told her there was no danger. She knocks on the rear of one of the cabinets. It is made of metal, painted green, and it sounds hollow. There is an odd, familiar smell in the air. She walks between two of the cabinets in order to reach the center of the room.

Eve screams and then quickly puts a hand to her mouth. An extraterrestrial seems to be staring straight at her. She is still trembling from the shock, even though now she laughs at herself. It is obvious the alien has been sitting here for a very long time. The creature definitely won't be able to hurt her. No biological activity, the ISU has claimed. Oh well. Strictly speaking, the ISU is right. Eve sits down in a second chair that is in the opposite corner from the mummified frog. She definitely has to talk to the ISU.

Sleepiness descends on her like a soft blanket. She tries to resist it. She is amazed at how quickly something has become normal that recently would have frightened her to death—that she sits across from her second corpse today and still does not manage to hold off the inevitable sleep.

May 5, 19

THE BASIN I AM IN MUST BE SOME KIND OF COOLANT CONTAINER. From above, warm water keeps flowing in, which over time releases its energy outward. I am probably in the lowest part of the building, inside the ice layer. The continual heat output might have melted a part of the ice below us.

I am not quite sure what is being cooled. The incoming water is slightly radioactive. This might indicate a fission reactor, a safe and long-lasting energy source, but I had expected more from the inhabitants of this planet in terms of technology. They at least managed to evacuate a large portion of the population in spaceships. Or had that only been a nice plan, and they ran out of time in the end? Perhaps we have been too optimistic in interpreting the pictograms.

My energy problems should be over by tomorrow at the latest. The temperature difference between the warm water on top and the cold layer where I am lying provides the necessary energy supply. So it was lucky after all that I ended up in the coolant container.

The one thing that worries me is that the inspector deliberately threw me down here. This strongly suggests there is no easy way out. The machine seemed to possess at least a weak

AI that might be able to make such decisions. And, from its perspective, I had already caused a lot of damage to the structure.

One thing I wonder about is why the inspector did not destroy me outright. Does it have a programmed-in restraint that keeps it from using this solution—which would indicate the inhabitants of Proxima b possess a high standard of civilization? Too bad we cannot communicate directly with them.

Another one of my microprobes returns. They only have minimal equipment, and I have no connection with them while they are out there. Now that the energy supply has been secured, their new task is to find a way out of this container, just in case. The probe integrates itself into my body so that I can gain access to the data it has collected. The result is sobering. The probe swam along the outer walls of the container. As I suspected, it has the shape of a hemisphere.

In the lower third are several drains that are protected by fine mesh grates. From an engineering perspective, it makes sense to keep trash from entering the coolant circuit. Since I myself am part of this trash—with the exception that I am looking for a way out—this becomes a problem. The microprobe thoroughly examined one of the grates. It consists of a steel plate, nine millimeters thick and with numerous tiny holes. Nothing larger than two millimeters in any dimension has a chance to get through.

However, I fell into the water in one piece. Therefore there must be openings without grates. Obviously, these would not be underwater. I will have to wait for one of the microprobes investigating the water surface.

Will my nanofabricators enable me to flee? I might move to one of the drains and have the fabricators take me apart atom by atom. Microprobes could then transport me to the other side in tiny portions, where the fabricators would then reassemble me. In theory that should work. I simulate the procedure. Unfortunately there are two problems: First of all, the process would take too long. If Eve has not managed to find water, she would be close to dying of thirst. I have to get out of here as quickly as possible! And second, I have no clue how the transfer of my consciousness would work. I cannot simply cut *myself* into micro-portions.

Should I use violence again? I do have ways and means to blow my way out of here. If I electrochemically separate water into hydrogen and oxygen, the mixture only needs a certain concentration and a spark to explode and become water again. Last time this less-than-elegant method only got me halfway to my goal, though. I have to correct myself: I am farther away than ever from my goal of finding Eve, not just concerning the distance.

The distance. Right. That is an issue I must focus on. On my way here I covered several kilometers, first voluntarily, then involuntarily. At least that's what the data from my atomic clock and my acceleration sensor tell me. That does not at all fit the image of this building we gained from gravity measurements. Where is the catch?

To be on the safe side, I run a diagnostic program for my sensors. They are working flawlessly. Acceleration and time have been recorded precisely. Newton could have readily used this to calculate the distance covered. So if my sensors work correctly, but the result is still wrong, shouldn't this be a problem for Newton? His motion equations no longer work when one gets into the area of the theory of general relativity. Yet this is absolutely impossible for the distances and speeds we are talking about. Or is it?

Not if a 'singularity'—something that distorts space and falsifies measurements—is involved. I barely dare to think this, as the idea seems so crazy. Physicists hate singularities, because these take them to the limits of their theories. When I think of a singularity, I imagine a huge, all-devouring black hole, but I know quite well that is only a cliché. A singularity develops when the density of mass exceeds a critical value. In the case of the typical black hole, there is a singularity at its core equal to the mass of several suns—or even thousands of them. This is not necessary here, though, as the decisive factor is the density, not the mass.

Of course it helps to gather a lot of mass in one place if you want to create a singularity. I remember the irregularities of our gravitational measurements taken from orbit. A large concentration of mass would explain the measured deviations, which I had considered measurement errors until now. An even crazier idea tentatively reports in. I let the thought come forward. *What if the extraterrestrials use a singularity as an eternal source of energy?* At the limits of normal reality—the event horizon—pairs of particles constantly emerge from nothingness. Normally they extinguish each other in a very short time, in order to pay the energy debt to the universe. Yet when one of the particles ends up on the wrong side of the event horizon, it has no chance of finding its partner out there. That partner is suddenly available as energy that comes from nothingness.

Right now, my imagination seems to be running wild. The technical control of a singularity would be an enormous feat. After all, it has the constant tendency to grow larger. Whatever enters its radius of influence will be swallowed. Therefore it would have to be perfectly insulated so that the whole planet won't disappear into its gaping mouth. On the other hand, this might explain the odd distance measurements. A singularity bends space so that everything in it, even light, adapts to its structure. What I perceived as a straight line might in reality have been a loop, curving several times, leading me around the singularity into the lowest level of the building. That would be incredibly fascinating! Mankind is still millennia away from controlling forces of nature this way.

Therefore, it is also rather likely that my ideas are pure

speculation. In practical terms it does not matter. It does not change my most urgent goal of finding Eve as quickly as possible.

Another microprobe approaches. It brings data from the surface of the water. The probe discovered 17 openings in the dome of the container. None of them are closed with grates. However, to reach them I would have to be able to jump up seven meters. Or fly.

May 5, 19

EVE'S STOMACH IS GROWLING. SHE FINALLY FEELS HUNGRY AGAIN. Yet she needs to reduce her intake to 800 calories per day in order to survive a few days longer. Her body does not like that. She places her hands on her belly to calm it down. She almost started talking to her body parts. She has to get up and move around.

The dead extraterrestrial is still sitting across from her. She walks around its chair and looks at the creature from all sides. What brought about its death? Somehow the alien looks content, she thinks. She knows nothing about it or its species, but there appears to be some basic empathy. Perhaps this is wishful thinking. Who would not want to die with a happy smile on his face? The next visitor here will find the corpses of a human and a giant frog in one room. Eve smiles at the idea of how confusing this will be for an observer. How long will it take before someone else arrives here? A hundred years? A thousand? How quickly does a corpse turn into dust?

"Can you tell me anything about the alien's cause of death, ISU 2?"

"I am not equipped for that."

Eve nods. Marchenko certainly would have been able to

tell her more. He would have X-rayed the alien, developed a model of its biology, and then arrived at reasoned conjectures about the cause of death.

"It doesn't have any visible injuries," she says. The alien she had moved from its hibernation chamber had looked much worse. The extraterrestrial in front of her appeared as if it would wake up refreshed from a long slumber once you put it in a tub full of water.

"I lack any material for comparison," ISU 2 says.

"What else can I use you for?"

"I am an explorer unit. I can map areas and follow tracks."

"Could you find out where Marchenko is currently located?"

"I could check all possible paths using a process of elimination."

"How long will that take?"

"That is impossible to predict. So far I have mapped one twenty-seventh of the spatial volume of this building. In the worst case, I will find Marchenko within a month. Should I start right away?"

"No, wait, I am thinking about it."

Eve walks around the alien once more. What had been its task here? The room definitely seems to fulfill some central function. There certainly should be a 3D map of the entire building here. If the aliens are really as technically advanced as it seems, it might show in real time which rooms have occupants. She just has to find out how to use the alien technology. Perhaps then she could even send a message. The fact is, everything is collapsing here. If nobody intervenes, and soon, the aliens sleeping in the honeycombs are doomed. Nobody will be able to help her anymore, unless she somehow finds Marchenko, but it would be nice to know that she saved the lives of several thousand beings during her last days.

She stands next to the alien's seat and places her head at

about the height of the upper end of its body, where its eyes are located. Where was the creature looking during its final minutes? What is the most important object in this room? No, this does not work. The four eyes of the creature confuse her. One looks forward to the left, to a small cabinet with a large number of symbols, and another to the front right where she sees an object as tall as a man and resembling a wardrobe. And then there are also two eyes that are aimed backward. There are two quite different objects in those directions. One is a pillar reminiscent of a Greek column. The other is a chest with figures on top of the lid. The figures look like something carved by a mad artist. Eve memorizes which object lies in each direction and then pushes against the seat of the alien. As she suspects, it is a swivel chair. The alien could use his four arms to operate two devices simultaneously and keep two more in view. Very efficient!

The column seems the easiest to identify. It has an octagonal footprint and tapers in the middle. Eve touches the material. It looks like gray stone, but it feels warm and smooth. The column reaches up to her belly button. She stands next to it and looks at the top part. Because it is curved inward, it reminds her of a basin. A baptismal font? No, that idea comes from too much of a human perspective. She also detects switches around the edge that are marked with unknown symbols. Without Marchenko, she once again has no chance to find out their meaning. Eve focuses on the infrared image. It is significant that most symbols are connected below the surface by a mysterious pattern of fine red lines. That must be electrical wiring. Two elements stand out. From these, thicker lines run directly into the basin. At its bottom they form a loop and then join exactly in the center. Now she also sees that the material there is a bit shiny.

Some kind of process must be triggered there. Would the basin fill with water, or with another liquid? The numerous switches around the edge of the base then could determine the exact composition, and when you press the two buttons from which the lines emerge, the liquid is discharged. Eve rubs her hands. She would like to discuss her ideas with someone, but only ISU 2 is here, and the sensor unit probably would say that it does not have enough information. Instead, she turns around and looks into the alien's backward-looking eye.

"What do you think I should do?"

She waits, but the alien offers no reply. Well, the alien is right. She has to decide for herself. Eve reaches across the basin and touches two symbols she has selected. Then she presses down on them. They move a few millimeters. Eve hears a soft humming sound that gradually is increasing in volume. Then a golden ball grows from the deepest spot of the basin. At first it is the size of a marble, then that of a tennis ball, and then a soccer ball. Eve takes two steps back and bumps against the dead alien's chair. The ball is still swelling, until its diameter reaches about a meter and a half.

The ball now fits perfectly into the curvature of the basin. It still has a golden glow but is slowly becoming transparent. At the same time a structure develops in its interior, consisting of a central fireball orbited by a tiny marble. The orb's golden skin disappears so that Eve understands the function of this column: It is a three-dimensional star chart. The star in the center should be Proxima Centauri, and the tiny marble orbiting it the planet she is currently on. It should be possible to zoom in and out of the display, but Eve would first have to decipher the numerous symbols.

The 3D chart is breathtakingly beautiful. It appears to be a hologram, because Eve can reach into it with her hand. This does not tell her much, though, as she already was aware of her location. She would have preferred a spatial representation of the building. Eve presses other buttons at random, but that does not change the display. She probably would have to enter coordinates in some way unknown to her.

What now? Eve feels a growing sense of disappointment. She activated a technical device belonging to an alien civilization. She should be proud of that! Nevertheless, she would have preferred specific and useful hints. Even though she has accepted her impending death pragmatically, she subconsciously still hopes to be saved.

"ISU 2?"

"Yes, Eve?"

"We have to find Marchenko quickly."

"The search has top priority for me."

"That's not what I mean. The systematic search you are planning would take much too long."

"We do not have other options."

"We have to find out by some other means what happened to Marchenko."

"I do not understand."

Eve suspected that this would be beyond the mental capacity of the sensor unit's limited AI. But the mere fact of having someone to talk to quickens her imagination.

"You said that the connection was interrupted in this room."

"That is correct."

"Where did you last see Marchenko?"

"At the site of the accident. From there he sent out all sensor units to search."

"Why didn't he himself start to search?"

"He was unable to move."

"Then how exactly did he get into this room?"

"I do not have any information about it. When he sent us out, he was still busy repairing himself."

"When was the repair supposed to be finished?"

"The following day."

"And when did the connection break off?"

"Three hours after I started my search."

"Do you notice the contradiction, ISU 2?"

"Yes. Marchenko could not have been in this room when the contact ended, yet he was here."

"Are you really sure concerning the place and the times?"

"Both values are 99.9998 percent certain."

"Fine. If he did not get here by walking with his own legs, then someone or something must have carried him."

"That would resolve the contradiction."

"There must have been a reason for that. Marchenko was certainly rather heavy. It would take a lot of energy to transport him here. Why was this energy expended?"

"The—"

Eve interrupts ISU 2. "I am just thinking out loud. He caused quite a mess back there with that explosion. Avoiding further destruction sounds like a good reason. There could have been an attempt to neutralize him. If they wanted to destroy him completely, they could have done that right then and there without carrying him this far."

"That is logical."

"Then he was neutralized by some process in this room, without being physically destroyed. But how?"

"I do not have any—"

"I know, ISU 2," Eve says, cutting him off again. "I don't see any device in this room that could do that. Maybe I am too stupid to recognize it. That's possible. It could be simply hidden in one of these cabinets."

"These cabinets must be perfectly insulated," the ISU says. "Otherwise I would definitely receive something from such a short distance."

"It was just an idea. I am afraid we won't be able to find the hiding place by ourselves."

"Should I delete the search for Marchenko from my program memory?"

"No. If we can't find it ourselves we just have to ask the thing that brought Marchenko here."

"I am not aware of such an object."

"I have no idea what it looks like, either. I don't think it was one of the inhabitants. It would not have left its colleague sitting here like that. I think we should rather look for a machine."

"I cannot detect any movement or energy signatures."

"It probably turned itself off after finishing its task. Then we have to call it again."

"How can we establish contact with an unknown machine?"

"Exactly like Marchenko. By breaking things."

EVE TURNS AROUND ONCE AND WALKS ACROSS THE ROOM. SHE tries to push over one of the cabinet-like objects but it is firmly anchored in the floor. She also cannot see any tool she could use to destroy things. There must be some detection threshold they would have to exceed. Scratching up the floor would not be enough to get the 'police' unit to come.

"Hello, is there anyone here?" she yells as loud as she can. Perhaps noise would be enough. She stops and listens. Nothing. She pulls out her tool bag and sees at first glance that she won't get far with it. Marchenko obviously called attention to himself through an explosion. She lacks the means to do so. In addition, she only wants to talk to the alien machine and avoid being attacked by it. She could run away, unlike Marchenko, but how would she then find out what happened to him?

She walks around the room once more, and then again and again. During her fourth round she almost stumbles over ISU 2.

The little robot seems impatient. "I ask permission to continue the search for Marchenko."

"Why are you in such a hurry?"

"Finding him has top priority for me."

"One moment," she replies.

The sensor unit must have a self-destruct mechanism. If it explodes loudly enough, that might attract the machine she is looking for. She hopes she won't be in danger then, because she wouldn't be the obvious source of the disturbance.

"I have a suggestion that might shorten the search time considerably." She must describe her idea in cautious terms in order to avoid any conflict with the motivation of the AI. The sensor unit would then no longer be able to fulfill its explicit task of locating Marchenko. Of course she directly contributes to this fact. The AI of the sensor unit must accept this as a valid opportunity to fulfill its mission.

"Asking for a description of the improved search strategy," ISU 2 says.

"You will form a technical-biological unit with me. The technical part of this unit triggers the self-destruct mechanism. The biological part then determines what happens to the remains, thus finding the location of Marchenko in a very short time."

The ISU does not answer. Its AI seems to have a hard time making this decision. "This method would end the existence of ISU 2," it finally says.

"I am very sorry," Eve says, and she means it. She likes the electronic snake—it has become almost a pet for her. After all, it is currently the only companion she can talk to.

"Its own existence does not have priority for ISU 2," the sensor unit replies. "However, the uncertainty factor of the suggested strategy is high. If it fails, ISU 2 can no longer search for Marchenko."

"You will just have to trust me," Eve says.

"How would this work?"

"Your self-destruction is not going to fail, is it? Then the only free variable is my behavior afterward. You define this variable as one, or one hundred percent. This mathematical procedure is called 'trust' by humans."

"I understand. Thank you for explaining the concept of trust to me. Should I initiate my self-destruct mechanism now?"

"Just a moment while I gather my thoughts."

The sensor unit does not answer. It is probably waiting for a sign.

What is the best thing to say in such a moment? 'Thank you for your efforts?' The AI will soon die voluntarily. The mechanical pet is sacrificing itself for her. It is an odd feeling, and somehow rubs her the wrong way. The fact that the ISU can speak made Eve feel close to it right away.

"You can start the self-destruct sequence now," Eve finally says dryly.

"Starting sequence. Please step back two meters for safety reasons."

"Make it as loud as you can," Eve says. She sits down again in the empty chair. From here she has a good view of the dying ISU. First, something happens in the infrared range. A thick red line develops under the skin of the snake.

"Are you still there?" Eve asks.

"Yes," ISU 2 simply says.

Now smoke curls above that line. The skin seems to expand, as if a cavity were forming inside the unit.

"Termination in ten nine eight seven six five four three two one." A second later there is simultaneously a loud bang and a flame spurting from the center of the unit, reaching about one meter upward. The machine breaks apart sideways. Once the smoke has cleared, Eve sees the scorched insides of the ISU.

"Are you still there?"

She receives no answer. Grief suddenly overwhelms her. She cries for the machine she had just recently met.

Eve collapses in her chair while the tears are drying on her cheeks. She feels hardly more alive than the extraterrestrial across from her. Her stomach is growling, and she allows herself a piece of dried food. Now she must wait and stay alert, even though her eyes are drooping from fatigue. From which direction might the cleaning unit appear? How large will it be?

"Eve, you have to stay awake now," she says out loud to herself. Then she bites her lip. She hopes she did not just scare away the visitor she is waiting for. The smell of scorched cables still hangs in the air. Would the cleaning unit follow the smell?

Eva wakes up startled. *Damn, I fell asleep!* She looks at her universal device. Half an hour has passed. Luckily the pieces of ISU 2 are still here. *When is that thing finally coming?*

Tock... tock... tock. She hears the metallic clacking sound first, and then she sees the object. The cleaning unit moves on six legs. It is approximately the size of a large dog, and its head and back are covered with smooth, black skin. Instead of a snout, the machine has a kind of proboscis on its head that it moves back and forth.

It is getting closer.

Eve hopes her theory is correct and she will escape unscathed! And what if that thing recognizes she is just as much out of place here as the remnants of the sensor unit? The machine walks straight toward her. Eve puts her hand in front of her mouth. She is sitting directly alongside the shortest path between the site of the explosion and the hatch this thing emerged from. It must approach her if it wants to reach the goal. She should not—must not—move.

Tock... tock... tock. The machine walks past her without paying her any attention. Eve feels an enormous sense of relief. The cleaning unit does not look frightening at all. It also does not seem to be particularly intelligent. It probably only received the knowledge it needed to fulfill its intended purpose. Now its proboscis is checking the spot where the ISU self-destructed. It looks as if the cleaning unit wants to log all data in detail. Then a pincer appears at the end of the proboscis. The strange machine grabs the leftover parts and carries them through the room. Once again, Eve is its destination. *Calm. Stay totally calm,* she tells herself. She hopes her loud heartbeat won't give her away.

The cleaning unit stops close to her chair. It sits down on two hind legs and uses the other four legs to open a hatch in the floor. Was that hatch there before? Eve can't remember. The lid of the hatch seems to be heavy. It is several centimeters thick and obviously made of metal. Now the cleaning unit extends its proboscis so that the fragments of the sensor unit are directly above the hole that the hatch revealed.

Eve feels she has to act now. She sees the hole into which the pieces of the ISU are being dropped. It is large enough for her. Two steps, a jump, and she would probably end up at Marchenko's current location. *A garbage dump? A shredder? A dark dungeon?* Eve can't make up her mind. Who says Marchenko is still alive? Perhaps she will only find his remains. And she is doing relatively well up here! She knows she should jump now, but she is scared of the dark hole. She really wants to jump, but her legs won't obey her.

She admits she lacks the strength needed in an emergency. She cannot save those she loves. She was unable to do anything for Adam, and now she fails when it comes to saving Marchenko. And she even sacrificed the ISU for this, the only one she could talk to! Slowly, the hatch closes in front of her eyes. Eve bites the hand she has placed over her mouth to prevent herself from screaming. The hatch once more sits flush in the floor. Her chance has passed. The cleaning unit clack-clack-clacks away on its six legs.

May 6, 19

THE HOURS IN THE TANK PASS UNEVENTFULLY WHILE I AM gathering energy. I have to be patient, even though I know that I am desperately needed up there. My mind is racing, and I try to solve a problem which cannot be solved. Sometimes I feel flashes of lights or shocks, but when I check the relevant sensors I find no data. Are those the first signs of insanity?

Suddenly I feel the presence of a sensor unit. ISU 4 is sending me location data. How could this be? Is it a faraway echo that somehow got through to me? I reply and confirm, but the ISU is out of range again.

Once again I feel a weak pressure wave thumping me. I am about to skip checking the data. I seem to be overly sensitive. Yet my sense of duty will not allow it.

I read the pressure sensor's displays that are distributed across my entire body. Indeed, it was not just my imagination! The individual parts of my splintered consciousness are reassembling. What happened? Based on the individual data points I can extrapolate the origin of the pressure wave. It propagated in a circle around a spot on the surface of the water and finally reached me at the bottom.

Something must have fallen into the water. There is no other explanation. There is a hole above the spot where it dropped. As I know the water's composition, I can calculate the object's weight, which by now has probably reached the bottom. The thing weighs as much as... one sensor unit!

My excitement is turning into a sense of foreboding. I send two microprobes to the assumed crash site. The object might have tumbled when diving into the water, so I can only mark an approximate position. The probes will have to scan the ground there, record images, and return them to me. Then I can compare the photos with prior images.

The probes are on the way. Why doesn't this work faster? If I could only convince myself to be more patient! I assume it is no coincidence that something seems to have been dropped into the water right now. It might not happen very often that something in this building gets destroyed to such a degree that it has to be disposed of by the inspector. As I am lying here immobile on the bottom of the tank, I assume it has something to do with Eve.

The first probe is back. It starts with the data transfer. A shape that looks like a thick earthworm emerges from the darkness. I recognize it as one of my sensor units. I might never know which one, as it seems to be totally destroyed. What disfigured the unit so much? I am waiting for the data of the second microprobe. Together, both recordings create a three-dimensional image. I am surprised. The ISU must have self-destructed. The unit must have overheated its circuits, with the damage spreading from the inside outward so that it burst like an overripe piece of fruit. So it was no external force —and unfortunately, that leaves a lot of questions unanswered. Most of all, why did this happen?

What caused the sensor unit to self-destruct? Usually that is the very last option, used to avoid falling into enemy hands. The first requirement is that something is identified as hostile. If the ISU ran into one of the inspectors, that machine would have to act in an openly hostile manner, and flight could not have been an alternative. Did the explosion I caused trigger something I am no longer aware of?

Are inspectors now roaming all corridors to remove things that don't belong there? And what does this mean for Eve? I am trying to come up with additional scenarios. The unit might have self-destructed because successful completion of the mission seemed impossible. Such an option is defined very specifically—the situation must be 100 percent certain and a return to me has to be impossible. Not 99.999 percent, but 100.000 percent. One example would be if the ISU found Eve's corpse. I don't even want to consider this scenario. No, I would rather believe the sensor unit was threatened by an enemy.

One thing is certain, I absolutely must get up there. My energy level has only reached 75 percent, but I need to know what happened. I can wait no longer. Yet I would have to learn to fly in order to leave the tank by the channel through which I came. While that is not impossible in principle, it would take a long time to modify my body in this way. I don't have that much time. This only allows for plan B: I will cause a small explosion in order to get through one of the holes covered by grates. There is no other way out of here. We will be listed in the annals of the inhabitants of Proxima b as the alien race that always resorts to violence. Unfortunately, I can't take that into consideration. Eve needs me up there. At least I really hope so.

FIRST I HAVE MY NANOFABRICATORS ASSEMBLE A BALLOON. WHEN fully inflated, it should have a capacity of several cubic meters and very tear-resistant skin.

HALF AN HOUR LATER I START SEPARATING WATER MOLECULES into hydrogen and oxygen. This will require a large part of my stored energy, but there is no other way. I plan to keep at least a quarter of my energy. That should suffice for a day-long search for Eve. I don't have to worry about the ratio of oxygen and hydrogen in my mixture, as the electrochemical decomposition of water automatically creates the perfect oxyhydrogen mixture of 1:2. However, I have to be very careful not to detonate the contents of my balloon prematurely. A tiny spark would suffice.

THE OXYHYDROGEN SYNTHESIS TAKES THREE HOURS. DURING IT, I suddenly hear the soft sounds of an old Russian folk song. My mother used to sing it to me when I was three or four years old. The song touches me in a strange way, but it must be just my imagination.

While the balloon was growing, I had the currently unemployed nanofabricators build me four new legs. They are not perfect, but they will allow me to flee once the path is open again. They work well under water. Dragging the balloon behind me, I slowly move to one of the drainpipes. I hope my legs will be able to carry my weight once they are no longer supported by buoyancy. I attach the balloon to the grate and move away again.

THE BALLOON IS COMPLETELY FILLED. MY INTERNAL ATOMIC clock states it is late in the morning of May 6, year 19, standard time. I hesitate. Everything is actually well-prepared. Yet so far there has always been something that went wrong. Our voyage has been star-crossed so far, and that scares me, even though I am usually an optimist. *Do I have a choice?* The idea of passively waiting for help that may never come pleases me even less. I still believe that Eve is waiting for me somewhere in this building. I don't even dare to think about Adam anymore.

It is strange. More than 18 years ago I awoke aboard a tiny space probe. I grew along with it, raised two children who by now have turned into adults, and—before all that, decades before—I was one of the first humans to set foot on a planet in a far-away solar system, encountering the remnants of an alien civilization. I have had a fulfilled life, but still, saying farewell to it is not at all easy for me. I do not want to die, nor do I want to stay in this dark, wet hole, waiting forever for something that will never come. Therefore, I have to do something.

From my battered body a long, thin wire loop leads to the balloon filled with the perfect oxyhydrogen mixture. If I run electricity through the wire, it will heat up, becoming so hot that it will glow and supply the activation energy for a catastrophic chemical reaction. The entire contents of the balloon will suddenly turn into water, giving off a great deal of energy at the same time. This energy will create a blast wave in the water that will cave in the grate next to the explosion site. That is the plan. It only has one weakness: The blast wave might destroy more than the grate. Yet I don't have a choice. I can only hope things will turn out okay.

I start the flow of electricity. I watch in slow motion as the explosive reaction tears through the balloon. It starts at the wire loop and then moves evenly in all directions. The water molecules are hot, move fast, and try to expand their volume. In doing so, they cool down, until the water vapor eventually condenses into water and forms drops. *Can we imagine the Big Bang to have been like that?*

I return my consciousness to normal speed and am shocked. The explosion loses its mysterious charm. What remains is brute force. The balloon's contents once again consist of water, but the balloon itself no longer exists. Instead, an invisible wave races through the medium. Water does not compress well. It passes on the pressure caused by the explosion, almost like a piece of iron hit by a hammer.

My plan to cave in the grate in order to free my way has succeeded. I slowly move toward the now open channel. At that moment the blast wave reaches me. I am afraid of being swept away, but the wave only presses me against the bottom. I use the radar to track the spread of the blast wave through the entire tank. And then something happens that I feared without admitting it—the intense pressure expands the entire lower part of the tank. The material does not seem sturdy enough to withstand such forces. It is brittle, like porcelain… and it develops cracks, like a teacup in which a firecracker exploded.

The way into the building's interior is free, but I won't be able to reach the channel. The water is already looking for a way outside. There seem to be cavities below the building, likely created by the thermal radiation of the edifice. And now the water rushes into them. I try to hold on, but my legs were not constructed for this kind of stress. They are supposed to carry my weight. They are powerless against the freight train hitting me from behind.

I notice that my legs bend and are about to break. I had better let go. This body is not up to resisting this force. It will pull me outside. My plan has failed. I had thought my situation could get no worse. I was wrong. Now I am leaving this mysterious building, but certainly not the way I had hoped to do it. I am back in the icy world of Proxima b.

Well, Eve, I hope you are doing better than I am. I am saying farewell. Perhaps I will soon meet Adam again. While I do not believe in a better afterlife, the thought gives me some comfort. The water sucks me through a crack one meter wide, down to unknown depths. I am outside.

Marchenko, over.

May 6, 19

A GIANT SPIDER ON WOODEN LEGS LOOMS ABOVE HER. EVE knows it, though she is squeezing her eyes shut. It is the spider Adam found in that pit in the forest. Somehow it must have crept into their camp. Where is Adam? He has to save her. She knows he can talk to the spider. He will convince it to leave them alone. After all, Eve did not hurt the creature. The spider bends its legs and lowers its belly. It will touch Eve in a moment. The intense smells of forest and fungi get stronger. Eve must not open her eyes. Not even when she notices that a stinger extends from the spider's abdomen. Eve knows that the animal uses it to ingest. It will dig the stinger into her belly and drink from her. She can feel the great thirst the spider experiences. She feels sorry for the creature. 'Just help yourself,' she feels like saying, but she is also afraid of pain and death.

Something stings her foot. Eve notices her lips are dry. She is thirsty. She slowly opens her eyes. There is no spider. She is sitting in the control room of the alien building, directly across from a shriveled-up frog. She is alone. Once again something pinches her toes. Eve jerks back and sits bolt upright. On the floor in front of her is an ISU.

"ISU 2? Where are you coming from?"

No, of course it's not Unit 2. That one self-destructed right in front of her. Eve saw how it disappeared in that hole in the floor. She did not dare follow it. ISU 2 died for nothing. Eve feels nauseous. Is that due to her cowardice or because she hasn't eaten?

"ISU 4 reporting in," the unit says.

"That's great," Eve replies. At least she is no longer alone. The unit is indistinguishable from ISU 2, so it looks like an old acquaintance to her.

"What was your mission?"

"Finding person Eve."

"Good, then you have accomplished your task."

"I can confirm this. However, I am not able to complete the second part of my mission. I therefore ask for new objectives."

"What was the second part about?"

"Delivering this information to unit Marchenko."

Eve nods slowly. "Right. Marchenko is at some unknown location. According to ISU 2, the contact broke off in this room."

"I had my last contact with unit Marchenko yesterday. At that time I was not here."

"You were in contact with Marchenko yesterday?" Eve gets up from her chair and sits down next to the ISU. The unit wriggles and turns until its front is facing Eve again.

"That is correct."

"Where was he located at that time?"

"The contact was too short to exchange location data."

"Can you tell me anything about him?"

"He was obviously functional. The signal delay was unusually large, so he must have been far away."

"When exactly did the contact occur?"

The ISU transmits a time to her. Eve compares this with the log of her universal device. A perfect match.

"That was the moment when the hatch here was briefly open," she says.

"I have insufficient information about this."

"That was a piece of information."

Eve gets up again and places a finger against her lower lip. Marchenko is still alive, or at least was alive yesterday. That is good news. The channel here in the floor probably leads to him. Should she repeat yesterday's attempt?

She looks at the sensor unit. She could talk it into self-destructing. But would she manage to jump into the dark hole this time? What is smarter, to repeat a failed attempt, or to start an entirely new experiment? She sits down and holds her head with both hands. Who is reacting in there? Is it cowardice that wants to keep her from a leap into the darkness? Or is it intelligence that wants to prevent her from repeating an unnecessary failure? Could the force controlling her actions please speak up?

"We have to establish contact with Marchenko," she says, more to herself than to the sensor unit.

"I have insufficient information about this," the ISU replies. "Should I search for the unit Marchenko?"

"No, this is not about physical contact. There must be a possibility of establishing a connection between different rooms in this building."

"I have insufficient information about this."

"I know, but this was not meant as a question. Can you help me find a communication device?"

"I don't know. Please define task more specifically."

"I assume there is a wired connection. We can see that radio contact is impossible through the closed hatch. There are surely more of these hatches around here. Therefore a secure connection through the entire building is only possible by cable."

"What kind of cable?"

"I don't know the technology the aliens use. We have to

look for something... anything. Fiber-optic cable, electrical wiring, perhaps something more exotic. Back on Earth they used to communicate via vacuum tubes. We need to be open to any technology. But we can assume that the technology should be present in every room here. Can you look for possible devices?"

"My sensor suite is limited, as I was built for mapping rooms."

"So you cannot see what is hidden behind a wall or in the floor?"

"That is correct."

This means the ISU is almost useless for this search. Yet she has the ability to see differences in heat. "Perhaps there are visible structures indicating communications channels," Eve suggests.

"I am going to check the adjoining rooms for this," ISU 4 says, then wriggles away.

Eve sits down and closes her eyes in order to gather her thoughts. She is in a central room, perhaps even the control room of the building. So everything should lead to this place. It is definitely the wrong place to start a search, because the floor and the walls might contain hundreds of lines leading to all kinds of devices. As this technology is so foreign to her, she can't tell which of them are used for communication. Therefore she has to go to one of the adjoining rooms.

Eve stands up. She nods at the dead alien who by now seems to be an old friend, and then she turns towards a passage on the right. She walks through an oval arch into an area that looks like a living room. When she looks at the furniture she feels like she's that uninvited guest who secretly snoops through your bookshelves. In a corner, two sections, each measuring approximately 2.5 by 1.5 meters, are fenced off by wires. Inside each there is a two-meter-long roll that is almost one meter thick.

Eve moves in closer. The cover material is soft. Could

those be beds? If she imagines the anatomy of the giant frogs, such a bedroll would be well-suited to rest their legs at night. Next to the two beds are two chairs and a table. They seem to have practical shapes. Apart from their size, these items of furniture could have come from Earth.

There are no wardrobes, though. The aliens didn't seem to wear clothing, at least not inside the building. Did they have special suits for going out on the ice sheet?

Eve detects something that looks like a trough in another corner of the room. Slightly above it two thick pipes and a thin one emerge from the wall. The thin pipe has a rotary valve and Eve resolves to turn it. She has to use all of her strength. Suddenly a warm liquid flows from the pipe. She tastes it: water, relatively salty but potable. She does not find a faucet on the two thick pipes. Perhaps they provide food?

Eve turns around. She is still too close to the central room. The living room has only one exit. The next room might have been an office or a movie theater. The wide rear wall is covered by a reflective disc. A screen? Two meters in front of it are four chairs with tilted backs. There are pedals placed in front of the chairs, and the armrests contain lots of switches with symbols on them, which she has already seen. Should she see whether the TV programming is any good here?

No. She first ought to finish her task. She leaves the office. The following room is long and narrow. For the first time she sees decorated walls. The entire surface is covered with colors. The patterns remind her of psychedelic graffiti. She touches the surface. These are not simply drawings. She feels bumps, textured areas, and lines that are sometimes parallel to the colors, but often intersect or complement them.

Sensation seems to play a bigger role in the aliens' perception than they do for humans. Perhaps the thin probe arms with their seven fingers are really well suited for feeling shapes. She imagines the frog creatures standing in this corridor, viewing and touching the works of art on the walls. This would also explain why all switches are covered by symbols.

There are no recognizable technical devices in the corridor where she is currently located. This is ideal for her plan. She tries to concentrate on her infrared sense. This form of perception is still so new to her that she has to consciously engage it.

She slowly looks across the wall. Shortly above the floor she finds three lines, a bright one and two of lesser brightness. Eve makes sure of one thing: They are coming from a room further back. They appear to run at a constant height until they enter the office. She follows the lines. Around the center of the office, two other lines join them. Shortly before reaching the living room, one of the two thin lines moves upward.

The thick line divides itself twice inside the living room. The branches run across the room to the head of the beds and end in a barrel-shaped container. Eve cannot do anything with it, as there are no switches. The thick heat line continues to the control room. There it ends in one of the tall electrical cabinets. Has she found the communication device she was looking for? It cannot be just a power supply, as in that case the other devices would have to be connected to it.

Eve sits down on the floor. If she lowers her face enough, she can see a whole network of lines inside the floor. She crawls through the room. Too bad she isn't a robot. If she could record what she sees, this might generate a kind of wiring diagram for the entire control center. However, almost all of the cables disappear deeper under the floor. There is almost certainly a technical level, she figures, where all the water pipes and electrical cables are located. She doesn't have to worry about that.

Eve sits back down in her chair. She looks at the dead alien, who by now does not appear quite so dead to her. She has quickly become used to seeing him like this. "I am Eve. What is your name?" she inquires.

The alien does not reply. She doesn't mind. He probably doesn't understand her language.

"I am going to call you George." She hopes that this doesn't mean anything offensive in his language. Perhaps these creatures don't have names, but are associated with particular scents or symbols?

"George, I would like to activate that device over there." She points at the cabinet. "Can you tell me anything about it?"

Did he just shake his head? No, that is impossible. And of course she does not receive an audible answer.

"I understand, George, you don't want to help me. I am supposed to help myself. Right you are."

Eve stands up. She wouldn't be surprised if George now winked with one of his eyes. However, he remains sitting ramrod straight. Eve smiles at him. Perhaps there is some kind of connection, because she feels as though there is some leftover soul in this desiccated body, laughing at her futile efforts.

"Yes, George, I see you want to test me," she says. Then she turns around and looks at the cabinet where the thick infrared line ends. Eve sighs. It is probably totally useless to bother with this thing. It was a crazy idea to use infrared to look for a cable. The chances of her coming to the correct conclusion are about as high as the possibility of George's name really being George. But it's been fun.

Why hadn't she ever entered the adjoining room during the last two days? Now she won't die of thirst, and she is sure to figure out how to coax food from the system. She might be able to survive here for weeks or months. So why is she so obsessed with finding a means of communication?

She needs to know for sure what happened to Marchenko, that's why. Otherwise she will go insane. She knows that. Total solitude is worse than death. She could become friends of a sort with George, and share all her secrets with ISU 4. Yet that would not save her from madness. She would rather kill herself by jumping into that dark hole. *Where did that sensor unit go?* she suddenly wonders. It was supposed to look for traces of communication cables as well. It must not have found anything yet.

Eve kneels next to the slab-like cabinet. It is approximately 1.5 meters high, 1 meter wide, and 30 centimeters deep. The front, which she is looking at, is almost completely covered by symbols. She doesn't find anything familiar to her. In the center she discovers a circular indentation with a diameter of about 20 centimeters. At the edge of the circle, near the 4 o'clock position, a ball the size of her pinkie finger rises halfway from the surface. One could take it for a simplified diagram of the Proxima system, but the star in the center is missing.

Eve follows the outline of the circle with her fingers. It is warm. Afterward, her fingertips are gray with dust that has collected there. The symbols, which most probably are also buttons, are distributed around the entire circle. Eve tries to find a pattern. Some symbols are repeated. Above the circle they seem to be upside-down, while right and left they are placed sidewise. That is not very practical for reading.

She imagines one of the aliens placing the thumb of its probe hand with the seven long fingers in the center of the circle, moving its fingers like a pair of compasses and reading the symbols with the sensitive fingertip. She tries to do it but her fingers are too short. It was a nice idea, but it isn't going to work this way. Why are there all these other symbols grouped concentrically around the circle? Even the aliens' fingers are not that long.

Without suspecting what might happen she presses one of the symbols at the outer edge. Suddenly she hears a short, deep sound. Eve flinches and turns around. The sound came from the ceiling. There must be a loudspeaker hidden in here. Is that a warning—an alarm system—indicating that an intruder is using the device? She stands up and looks around nervously, but nothing happens and nobody appears. Yet she is not entirely sure. The cleaning unit took some time to react to the small explosion. Just to be on the safe side, Eve sits back down in her chair. This way the cleaning unit might not notice anything has changed.

EVE WAITS FOR ALMOST AN HOUR AND THEN DECIDES THERE IS NO danger. She kneels down at the same spot. This time she presses the key right next to the one she had previously selected. Now a slightly higher-pitched sound can be heard. She is startled again but doesn't get up.

The next key produces a sound in between the previous two ones. She presses all the keys in reverse order and gets Do – Re – Mi. Eve smiles. Has she discovered a musical instrument? Then the thick red line might transport her input to other rooms. Nonsense. Why would they have installed a music system in the central control room?

The cabinet in front of her probably has a serious purpose. The sounds might just be part of the user interface. This way, everyone can hear whether the navigator pressed the correct keys. Eve tries the next symbol in this sequence. No reaction. She is disappointed and looks up to the ceiling, where the sound should come from. Is the key defective, or perhaps the whole device, because of the small explosion she caused?

Eve memorizes the symbol she just pressed and looks for its double. And she does indeed find one in the second row from the outside. Once again there is no sound. It would be an odd coincidence if two keys so far apart should be defective, while the neighboring ones are working. Perhaps she cannot hear the sound because it is in the ultrasonic or subsonic frequencies, outside her hearing threshold. Once the

ISU is back she is going to ask it. Where is that little snake, anyway?

Eve tries out more keys. Each one creates a specific sound. But nothing else happens. Sometimes she cannot hear anything at all. These aliens seem to have a better sense of hearing than humans. She selects the keys she needs for 'Bajushki Baju,' the lullaby Marchenko used to sing to them. She remembers the tune quite well and cannot help crying when she plays it herself. Eve wipes the tears from her face and turns toward George.

"That surprised you, didn't it?" she asks. She imagines him giving her a thumbs-up with all four hands.

Four hands. "Four hands," she mumbles to herself. Of course. Why should the designers of this device base it on the one-finger search system she employs with it? The intended users have four hands. The keys are too far apart for all 22 fingers to be used. But one finger on each hand, that would be possible. The frog creatures must have knelt in front of the device, just like she has been doing.

Perhaps she can raise it a bit more from the floor to operate it more easily. Eve looks at the four sectors to find similarities. How could she have overlooked this? The four pie shapes on the top left, top right, bottom left, and bottom right are identical—in other words, axially symmetric. Turn one of the quarters by 90 degrees, and it is congruent with the next one. Therefore, pressing one key after the other doesn't appear to be enough, as it seems all four must have to be activated at once. Eve imagines the harmony in several parts this should create. The aliens seemed to have known how to combine work and pleasure. Each meaningful action in this system, whatever it might achieve, also created a tune.

How might this have sounded? Eve's shoulders sag. She will never find out, because she only has two hands. What about her feet? She changes her sitting posture but cannot find a position in which she can operate the keys with fingers and toes simultaneously. Being a frog would be nice! For a moment she wonders whether she should sever the dead alien's arms and then... No way, that is out of the question!

"No signs of a communication infrastructure detected," she hears ISU 4 saying behind her.

Eve is so startled she bumps against another cabinet. "You scared me!" she says.

"I am sorry."

"But it is good to have you here. I have a new task for you." Eve looks at the sensor unit. It is not perfectly suited for the task, but she has no choice.

"What is my task?"

"I need your help operating this panel." Eve points at the device, which so far only serves as a musical instrument.

"I do not have sufficient information about this."

"I will tell you. I want you to press your front end and your back end against two of the symbols I will point out to you."

The sensor unit definitely isn't long enough to reach all the keys. But it should be able to handle the right or left half of the lower quadrants, perhaps up to the sixth symbol row. Eve does not yet know whether this will be a problem. And if it is, she will find a solution. At some point the four other ISUs will arrive here. *Where are they, anyway?* The building must be much larger than she imagined.

"I understand. Task accepted. Waiting for input." The ISU crawls into position.

Eve kneels in front of it. Then she wonders which symbol to use. There are many choices, and none of the icons seems familiar. She shrugs her shoulders. It doesn't matter. One symbol is just as good as any other. "Pick a symbol on the left and another one on the right," she orders the ISU.

"Based on which system?"

"Randomly generated."

She herself presses two spontaneously selected keys and

holds them down. Two pleasant notes sound from the ceiling. Eve waits until the ISU is in position. She notices it when two new notes are sounded. A beautiful four-note chord! Yet an unpleasant humming noise disturbs the music, and she gets goosebumps. What is that? She turns around, but there is nothing to see. The noise comes from in front of her.

Eve stands up without letting go of the two symbols. Something blue has appeared on the other side of the cabinet. It reminds her somewhat of a hologram, seeming to consist entirely of light rays, and it glitters magnificently. Her experiment has been worthwhile. Unfortunately she cannot see the entire object from her current position.

The aliens are significantly taller and would be able to look over the cabinet. She needs an object to stand on. Eve stretches and straightens her body. In doing so, one of her fingers slips. The three-dimensional image fades away.

"Wow," she says, "that was something special."

"Indeed, I do not have an entry for such an object in my database," the ISU confirms. Even the ISU sounds a bit proud. Its AI probably has a bit of pride-of-discovery programmed into it, in order to give it some motivation.

"I need an object approximately 30 centimeters high that can withstand my weight."

"I could call ISU 1, 3, 5 and 6. They could change their configuration so they would carry your weight and provide the required height."

"You are in contact with the other sensor units? Why didn't you tell me before?"

"You did not ask, and I assumed you know our abilities."

"That was an incorrect assumption, but you are correct, I should have asked. No problem, though. So far I haven't needed the others. Where are they now?"

"Number 1 can be here in five minutes. It was already on its way back. ISUs 3, 5, and 6 will cancel their search mission and return. ISU 6 will take the longest, arriving here in two hours."

"Search mission?"

"The ISUs have the mission to search for person Eve."

"But you've already found me."

"It was not my task to inform the other ISUs. Normally I would have reported my success to unit Marchenko and returned to him. The loss of contact led to gaps in our programming."

Not bad, Eve thinks, *the ISUs can even analyze their own mistakes.*

"We might as well rest until ISU 6 arrives."

EVE WONDERS WHETHER SHE SHOULD WALK AROUND THE ROOMS and corridors a bit. Who could guess what else she might discover here? Where and how, for instance, did the inhabitants take care of hygienic needs? Was there a pool for swimming, or a swamp for mud baths? What about facilities for adolescents? She could probably spend months exploring the everyday life of the inhabitants and the inner workings of their technology. Yet during this time the sleeping aliens would be dying in their hibernation chambers.

While she had found out how to open such a chamber, she has no idea what she could do to save the aliens. The entire system is breaking down for reasons unknown to her. Proxima b is dying. Perhaps her confidence is naive, but if anyone can help, it would be Marchenko. Therefore she has to get in contact with him first, and if that is not enough, she has to reach the inhabitants' relatives who left for the stars untold ages ago. Eve decides to remain in her seat, and she waits patiently until the time has come.

As promised by ISU 4, ISU 1 reports back after a few minutes. Almost an hour later, ISU 3 and ISU 5 follow. Then

Eve becomes noticeably nervous. She wiggles her toes and kneads her hands. Should she start right away? Four units might be enough to allow her to look over the cabinet. No, those few more minutes won't matter.

She hears a rumbling sound from far away. Her seat vibrates slightly. Eve jumps up and almost stumbles over one of the sensor units. She cannot distinguish the units from each other.

"Did you feel that, too, ISU 4?"

The answer comes from behind her. "I registered a loud noise in the distance, followed by a slight shock."

"Could you be more precise?"

"No, because the event was too far away."

Eve massages her temples, feeling overwhelmed. She is almost sure this has something to do with Marchenko. What might have happened? Maybe now the structure of the building is starting to fail, after its functions have deteriorated. That would be an odd coincidence. Or had their mere presence finally triggered a self-destruct mechanism? That is unlikely. If so, the building would kill all of its still-living occupants just because of two strangers it is trying to get rid of. In addition, one would expect a shrill alarm to sound in the corridors.

No, this was certainly Marchenko. What can this possibly mean? Are these the sounds of fighting, or an explosion he caused? Did his plan work? *If I could only talk to him!* She walks around in a circle through the control room, faster and faster, until she is breathless.

Girl, that's no good, she thinks to calm herself down. *Sit down now, take a deep breath, and then finish your plan.* Yet her body refuses and won't let her stop. She will walk in a circle until she can present a solution. Hadn't she feared she might go insane? She already is insane.

ISU 6 rescues her from her musings. The sensor unit falls from the ceiling, directly in front of her feet. Eve is startled, stops, and looks up. She sees that a hatch is still closing up there.

"ISU 6 reporting in," says the fat snake as it is quickly wriggling sideways.

"Very good," Eve says. Suddenly she feels quite calm again. The shock stopped her thoughts from spinning, like someone deliberately startling you when you have the hiccups. She has to remember that.

"I need four ISUs in a configuration suitable as a platform for me."

Nobody answers. It looks as if the units are putting their heads together, whispering to each other. Then they all crawl in parallel to the device that, so far, has only produced beautiful sounds and the blue hologram. Four ISUs interlace in such a way that Eve can stand securely on them with both feet. She tests her new position. Her hands still reach the two upper sectors of the keypad, but now she can also look over the cabinet.

"Great," she says, "this will work." One single ISU is still lying next to the platform. "Is that you, ISU 4?"

"That is correct."

"I need you to activate the two lower symbols again. The same ones as earlier."

"Understood."

Eve turns forward. She hopes the blue projection will appear again soon. She looks for the keys she pressed before.

"Now," she says. Two sounds indicate ISU 4 has followed her order. She waits for a few seconds and then presses her two symbol keys. Once again a soothing chord is heard in the room, before the crackling and humming starts. *Static electricity,* she thinks. Her individual hairs are being charged and they stand up. This time she has a good view of the shiny marvel appearing above a seemingly-empty area.

The projection technology must be hidden in the walls, the ceiling, or the floor. It is hard to tell what she is seeing. If only

Marchenko were here, he certainly could decipher this structure. Eve has seen images of the large-scale structure of the universe, and this projection reminds her of it. However, it possesses significantly more elements. She might be seeing something that is otherwise not observable, the dark matter whose structures span space. That is fascinating, but it seems to serve no obvious purpose.

She also does not think this is a form of art. Why would they put in all the effort to place this in the control room? Eve glances down to the keypad. Right now she and the ISU have activated symbols in the outermost of the concentric rings. Would it be possible to zoom in on the image? She lets go of one of the symbols in the right upper quadrant and touches the symbol next to it. The hoped-for effect does not occur, but the image slides a bit to the left. She tries the same method on the upper left sector. The image slides down. Okay, so these two sectors seem to handle the x- and y-axes.

"ISU 4, in your left sector please press the symbol to the right of the current one."

The projection moves to the back. Now she has found the z-axis. And what about the circles? Eve selects the symbol directly below the current one with her right hand. Nothing at all happens. She moves one further key to the right. Now the image moves to the left, but not as much. The rings seem to change the distance by which the image is moved. On her universal device she just slides two of her fingers apart for such changes. However, she is only a human with two hands and ten fingers. If the user had twice as many hands and 22 fingers, this strange-looking interface might be significantly more efficient.

She must zoom into the image as precisely as possible and establish contact, if that is even feasible. The lower right quadrant should be responsible for that. She has the ISU test several symbols and indeed finds the zoom mechanism this way. However, zooming in on a precise location is difficult.

Shouldn't it be easier to move toward a specific place? She thinks of the maps people once used on Earth. You only had to know the coordinates of a place to call it up. Perhaps the inhabitants possess electronic lists they use for navigation, or there is a voice interface that she has not noticed yet—but which would be useless to her anyway.

One moment. The hemisphere visible in the inner circle is marked with a symbol. She tries to reach it with her right hand but the shape is too far below. Now the entire hologram disappears again. It seems to turn itself off when fewer than three keys are pressed for a certain length of time. She activates a random symbol to bring the image back. Can she reach the planet symbol with her knee? *A kingdom for a third arm!*

She stands on one leg and carefully presses the right knee against the hemisphere. The image flickers, briefly disappears, and then rebuilds itself on a completely different scale. She sees a mirror image of the building. Eve is fascinated. She has finally found a diagram of the building! In this depiction the edifice looks like a living being. A strong heart—a pulsating sphere—beats in its center. This must be the building's energy source. Is this image realistic? If so, the building would exhibit very different proportions from what *Messenger's* mass scan indicated.

The farther that one advances into the interior, the larger the rooms and corridors become. Scales seem to shift. Distances appear to increase. Is that technically even possible? Eve zooms in more on the image with the aid of ISU 4. First she finds the honeycomb chambers where the aliens sleep. Here the image flickers in many spots. From there she tries to retrace her own path into the central room. There is the pipe, and here... yes, this is the room. The octagonal shape is unique, and there is also a special symbol, a dot blinking blue and white. This is either the device she is operating now—or the building has noticed her presence.

The idea gives her hope, because if she can be seen on the map, then Marchenko could be found as well. From the central room a thick line leads briefly down and then to the side. Near the energy center it expands and then moves down to the bottom of the building. Eve holds her breath. She should find Marchenko soon. The line ends in a spherical room, which in her display appears to be empty. There is no blinking dot, as in the central room.

She is paralyzed by disappointment. This has also been futile. She stares intensively at the map, as if she could force it by sheer willpower to reveal Marchenko's location. The only thing she notices is a broken wall at the bottom of the spherical room. Eve's hands tremble. She hopes Marchenko did not fall through this hole.

Suddenly the humming sound of the holographic image really stresses her. She lets go of the symbols and returns to her chair. She urgently needs to rest now. She sits down carefully, props up her elbows, and places her heavy head in her hands. It is just too much. She can't do it. This back and forth between hope and despair, this fear of solitude—she just can't stand it any longer. She would like to cry now, let the tears flow, but she can't even manage to do that anymore. It's a complete fiasco.

And who is to blame, who got her into this situation? Marchenko? That would be unfair. The Creator sent her on this voyage without ever asking her. For many years she was thankful for this. What is normal, after all? She did not know anything different. Yet now she feels an anger that must have always been hidden deep inside her. She slaps her hand against the armrest.

No matter. She is not yet finished here. Some day she will be able to tell the Creator what she really thinks of him, even though right now the idea seems absurd. He will have to face her. And therefore she has to survive.

The blue hologram had to be more than just a map. For

one thing, the column already provided a kind of 3D map of the system. *Two different devices fulfilling the same function? That is unlikely.* She stands up and walks back to the cabinet. The ISUs have not moved from their spots.

"Nice ISUs," she says.

"I did not understand this command," ISU 4 replies.

"It was an expression of praise."

"Thanks."

She once again steps on the artificial platform. "The symbols that were previously selected," she says. One sound rings out, the other one might be inaudible to her.

"Can you confirm that the system emits sounds in the ultrasonic range?"

"Confirmed," the sensor unit replies.

Eve nods. She guessed right. She presses a knee against the hemisphere so that the image centers on the building. She navigates through the edifice using the symbols in the upper quadrants but finds no trace of Marchenko. The strange heart is still beating. She asks the ISU to increase the scale using the lower quadrant. The building gradually shrinks and then disappears into the surface of the planet.

By now the imaginary observer, from whose perspective the scene is displayed, is floating in space. Eve briefly looks for *Messenger,* but then remembers they used the spaceship to clear their way. She sighs. The way back to space is barred. Now the planet becomes smaller. There is the asteroid belt. She expects the sun to come into view when she notices a mass glowing in an intensive blue at the edge of the display. Is that Proxima Centauri?

She shifts the field of view until she realizes this object is also orbiting the central star. What has she found here? Eve's heart is beating faster. Why didn't they see this when onboard *Messenger*? There can be only one reason—it was not there earlier. The object must have arrived after them. Probably after they crashed *Messenger,* as otherwise the ship would have warned them. If something can *arrive* somewhere it probably is not a natural object. Just the enormous size would argue against it.

The sphere is smaller than Proxima b, but certainly surpasses the size of Earth's moon. In the holographic display, it shines brighter than any other object, even than the star Proxima Centauri that now comes into view. Does this mean something? If there only were a manual on operating this device!

Eve looks at the entire control panel again, without letting go of the keys. The symbol on the hemisphere shines in white. Is that an invitation? She moves her knee into position. The image jumps. The center no longer shows the building, but the glowing blue sphere. Her knee vibrates. This must be the hemisphere that serves to center the display. Does it have an additional function? She won't find out using her knee. Therefore her left hand reaches for the lowest of all symbols. This way she can bend down and still just reach the hemisphere on the right. She takes away her knee and places her hand there. The ball is pleasantly warm and still vibrates slightly. It seems to be waiting for something.

Eve moves her hand slightly and looks at the hologram. Could the bright sphere have moved as well? *Hello, extraterrestrials,* she thinks, *come to me. I am on this planet.* She moves the hand on the hemisphere in the direction of Proxima b. The hemisphere turns in its mounting and vibrates more vigorously. A bit more—she seems to be on the right track. Could she really steer the alien spaceship in her direction?

The vibration increases, but the intensely glowing sphere doesn't seem to be quite on the right course. Eve overcomes the resistance of the mounting and keeps turning the control. The hemispherical surface is no longer warm, but quite hot. *Don't let me down,* she thinks. She ignores the pain from the heat and moves it a bit more. Now the strange object is definitely moving toward Proxima b. She has made it!

Suddenly the vibration stops. The hemisphere can no longer be turned, no matter how hard she tries. Its surface stays hot. The soft tones of the device have turned into an unpleasant jumble. She lets go of all keys, but this time the hologram remains where it is. The awful tune keeps on playing. What has happened? Why doesn't the hologram disappear? Did she annoy the system by being too aggressive?

She steps off the artificial platform, walks around the cabinet blowing on her hand, and goes to stand in the middle of the hologram. All around her are blue lights, objects blinking blue, and blue bodies. It would be beautiful if the sounds playing were not so distorted. She stands in front of the glowing sphere and touches it with a finger. Of course there is only emptiness.

Eve draws a straight line following the object's direction of travel. After a while her finger meets Proxima b, the world on which she lives. What if this isn't a spaceship, but something else hurtling towards the planet? She shakes her head. How could another object get into an orbit around the local star so quickly? This thing must have arrived here under its own power. Unless they somehow overlooked it earlier… Slowly, she feels terror creeping up her spine. *No, that is totally impossible.* Yet the cacophony of sounds coming from the loudspeakers in the ceiling seems to confirm her rising fears. She feels that something terrible is about to happen, even though she does not yet know what it is.

Eve sits back down in her chair. She realizes quickly that she won't be able to sit still for long. She has to escape these horrible sounds. However, she wants to look at the dead alien's face one more time.

"George," she says, "couldn't you have warned me?"

The alien does not reply, but his head moves imperceptibly, left, right, and back to center.

May 7, 19

Another 96 kilometers. Marchenko 2 deactivates his scanner again. Moving underwater is considerably slower than traveling on the ice sheet. He checks his energy supply. Everything is within the normal range. Then he receives a radio message from his base. His underwater home, which used to be a spaceship, reports detecting an unusual mass shift.

"'Mass shift?'" Marchenko 2 asks.

"The gravitational situation in the Proxima Centauri system has changed dramatically," the system replies. It is good that he had already installed his own background software before the other crew appeared.

"What does this mean? Will there be a collision?"

"No, but if the current trend continues, the orbit of Proxima b will become unstable. The planet will crash into its sun, or at least get much too close to it."

All life on this planet is as good as dead. Marchenko 2 feels no emotion. He can burrow deep into the rocks and survive almost any catastrophe, like a cockroach. He likes cockroaches. They are creatures able to survive in almost any condition, just like he can. Yet the message also offers him a chance. Perhaps he can still take his revenge. He falls silent.

Author's Note

Welcome back to the comfort of your room, or wherever you are while reading this note. Exploring the dark side of Proxima b is no easy task, not for me, nor for Adam, Eve, and the two Marchenkos. Everything seems lost at this time, and maybe it really is. On the other hand, this is a trilogy. The third part is called *Proxima Dreaming*, so there might be some happier hours to come. I wish the team on Proxima b the best of luck, that's for sure, and thank you for staying with them so Eve is not alone.

This will not be for long, I promise. In fact, there is something happening right now that Eve has yet to notice. I have had similar experiences quite often in my life, and they have shaped me into a very optimistic person. Whenever things looked bad for me, there was something going on that I was unable to observe at the moment, but which would soon reveal itself and open up new possibilities. Maybe, I realize, it works the other way around—if you are optimistic, you will see new options. Anyway, I have been, and I am, a pretty lucky person, and I'm very thankful for that. Especially now that I have found a new reader—maybe even a fan—in you.

I love getting messages from my readers. Would you like to ask me anything, such as what it was like growing up behind the Iron Curtain? You can contact me by e-mail at brandon@hard-sf.com or via Facebook. And if you liked this book, would you mind writing a review on Amazon? You can use this link:

hard-sf.com/links/652146

Thank you so much!

Proxima Dreaming is now available. You can get it here:

hard-sf.com/links/705470

Due to the fact that dark matter plays an important role here, I have provided a section entitled *A Guided Tour of Dark Matter* following this note. If you register at hard-sf.com/subscribe/ you will be notified of any new Hard Science Fiction titles. In addition you will receive a color PDF version of *A Guided Tour of Dark Matter.*

facebook.com/BrandonQMorris
amazon.com/author/brandonqmorris
bookbub.com/authors/brandon-q-morris
goodreads.com/brandonqmorris

Also by Brandon Q. Morris

The Death of the Universe

For many billions of years, humans—having conquered the curse of aging—spread throughout the entire Milky Way. They are able to live all their dreams, but to their great disappointment, no other intelligent species has ever been encountered. Now, humanity itself is on the brink of extinction because the universe is dying a protracted yet inevitable death.

They have only one hope: The 'Rescue Project' was designed to feed the black hole in the center of the galaxy until it becomes a quasar, delivering much-needed energy to humankind during its last breaths. But then something happens that no one ever expected—and humanity is forced to look at itself and its existence in an entirely new way.

3.99 $ – hard-sf.com/links/835415

The Death of the Universe: Ghost Kingdom

For many billions of years, humans—having conquered the curse of aging—spread throughout the entire Milky Way. They are able to live all their dreams, but to their great disappointment, no other intelligent species has ever been encountered. Now, humanity itself is on the brink of extinction because the universe is dying a protracted yet inevitable death.

They have only one hope: The 'Rescue Project' was designed to feed the black hole in the center of the galaxy until it becomes a quasar, delivering much-needed energy to humankind during its last breaths. But then something happens that no one ever expected—and humanity is forced to look at itself and its existence in an entirely new way.

3.99 $ – hard-sf.com/links/991276

The Death of the Universe: Rebirth

In the 1980s, physicists at a lab in the Soviet Union find traces of strange data in the cosmic background radiation. Because powerful forces in the military believe these findings can be turned into a weapon for use in the cold war, the information gleaned by the physicists is kept under strictest secrecy.

The scientists are limited to primitive 1980s' technology, but what they find has roots in much, much older times. They finally try an experiment that they hope will win the world over for communism.

But will they be able to maintain control over an enormous power that has its own, dangerous plans?

3.99 $ – hard-sf.com/links/1060781

The Enceladus Mission (Ice Moon 1)

In the year 2031, a robot probe detects traces of biological activity on Enceladus, one of Saturn's moons. This sensational discovery shows that there is indeed evidence of extraterrestrial life. Fifteen years later, a hurriedly built spacecraft sets out on the long journey to the ringed planet and its moon.

The international crew is not just facing a difficult twenty-seven months: if the spacecraft manages to make it to Enceladus without incident it must use a drillship to penetrate the kilometer-thick sheet of ice that entombs the moon. If life does indeed exist on Enceladus, it could only be at the bottom of the salty, ice covered ocean, which formed billions of years ago.

However, shortly after takeoff disaster strikes the mission, and the chances of the crew making it to Enceladus, let alone back home, look grim.

2.99 $ – hard-sf.com/links/526999

The Titan Probe (Ice Moon 2)

In 2005, the robotic probe "Huygens" lands on Saturn's moon Titan. 40 years later, a radio telescope receives signals from the far away moon that can only come from the long forgotten lander.

At the same time, an expedition returns from neighbouring moon Enceladus. The crew lands on Titan and finds a dangerous secret that risks their return to Earth. Meanwhile, on Enceladus a deathly race has started that nobody thought was possible. And its outcome can only be decided by the

astronauts that are stuck on Titan.

3.99 $ – hard-sf.com/links/527000

The Io Encounter (Ice Moon 3)

Jupiter's moon Io has an extremely hostile environment. There are hot lava streams, seas of boiling sulfur, and frequent volcanic eruptions straight from Dante's Inferno, in addition to constant radiation bombardment and a surface temperature hovering at minus 180 degrees Celsius.

Is it really home to a great danger that threatens all of humanity? That's what a surprise message from the life form discovered on Enceladus seems to indicate.

The crew of ILSE, the International Life Search Expedition, finally on their longed-for return to Earth, reluctantly chooses to accept a diversion to Io, only to discover that an enemy from within is about to destroy all their hopes of ever going home.

3.99 $ – hard-sf.com/links/527008

Return to Enceladus (Ice Moon 4)

Russian billionaire Nikolai Shostakovitch makes an offer to the former crew of the spaceship ILSE. He will finance a return voyage to the icy moon Enceladus. The offer is too good to refuse—the expedition would give them the unique opportunity to recover the body of their doctor, Dimitri Marchenko.

Everyone on board knows that their benefactor acts out of purely personal motivations… but the true interests of the tycoon and the dangers that he conjures up are beyond anyone's imagination.

3.99 € – hard-sf.com/links/527011

Ice Moon - The Boxset

All four bestselling books of the Ice Moon series are now offered as a set, available only in e-book format.

The Enceladus Mission: Is there really life on Saturn's moon Enceladus? *ILSE,* the International Life Search Expedition, makes its way to the icy world where an underground ocean is suspected to be home to primitive life forms.

The Titan Probe: An old robotic NASA probe mysteriously awakens

on the methane moon of Titan. The *ILSE* crew tries to solve the riddle—and discovers a dangerous secret.

The Io Encounter: Finally bound for Earth, *ILSE* makes it as far as Jupiter when the crew receives a startling message. The volcanic moon Io may harbor a looming threat that could wipe out Earth as we know it.

Return to Enceladus: The crew gets an offer to go back to Enceladus. Their mission—to recover the body of Dr. Marchenko, left for dead on the original expedition. Not everyone is working toward the same goal. Could it be their unwanted crew member?

9.99 $ – hard-sf.com/links/780838

Proxima Rising

Late in the 21st century, Earth receives what looks like an urgent plea for help from planet Proxima Centauri b in the closest star system to the Sun. Astrophysicists suspect a massive solar flare is about to destroy this heretofore-unknown civilization. Earth's space programs are unequipped to help, but an unscrupulous Russian billionaire launches a secret and highly-specialized spaceship to Proxima b, over four light-years away. The unusual crew faces a Herculean task—should they survive the journey. No one knows what to expect from this alien planet.

3.99 $ – hard-sf.com/links/610690

Proxima Dying

An intelligent robot and two young people explore Proxima Centauri b, the planet orbiting our nearest star, Proxima Centauri. Their ideas

about the mission quickly prove grossly naive as they venture about on this planet of extremes.

Where are the senders of the call for help that lured them here? They find no one and no traces on the daylight side, so they place their hopes upon an expedition into the eternal ice on Proxima b's dark side. They not only face everlasting night, the team encounters grave dangers. A fateful decision will change the planet forever.

3.99 $ – hard-sf.com/links/652197

Proxima Dreaming

Alone and desperate, Eve sits in the control center of an alien structure. She has lost the other members of the team sent to explore exoplanet Proxima Centauri b. By mistake she has triggered a disastrous process that threatens to obliterate the planet. Just as Eve fears her best option may be a quick death, a nearby alien life form awakens from a very long sleep. It has only one task: to find and neutralize the destructive intruder from a faraway place.

3.99 $ – hard-sf.com/links/705470

The Hole

A mysterious object threatens to destroy our solar system. The survival of humankind is at risk, but nobody takes the warning of young astrophysicist Maribel Pedreira seriously. At the same time, an exiled crew of outcasts mines for rare minerals on a lone asteroid.

When other scientists finally acknowledge Pedreira's alarming discovery, it becomes clear that these outcasts are the only ones who

may be able to save our world, knowing that *The Hole* hurtles inexorably toward the sun.

3.99 $ – hard-sf.com / links / 527017

Silent Sun

Is our sun behaving differently from other stars? When an amateur astronomer discovers something strange on telescopic solar pictures, an explanation must be found. Is it merely artefact? Or has he found something totally unexpected?

An expert international crew is hastily assembled, a spaceship is speedily repurposed, and the foursome is sent on the ride of their lives. What challenges will they face on this spur-of-the-moment mission to our central star?

What awaits all of them is critical, not only for understanding the past, but even more so for the future of life on Earth.

3.99 $ – hard-sf.com / links / 527020

The Rift

There is a huge, bold black streak in the sky. Branches appear out of nowhere over North America, Southern Europe, and Central Africa. People who live beneath The Rift can see it. But scientists worldwide are distressed—their equipment cannot pick up any type of signal from it.

The rift appears to consist of nothing. Literally. Nothing. Nada. Niente. Most people are curious but not overly concerned.

The phenomenon seems to pose no danger. It is just there.

Then something jolts the most hardened naysayers, and surpasses the worst nightmares of the world's greatest scientists—and rocks their understanding of the universe.

3.99 $ – hard-sf.com/links/534368

The Triton Disaster

Nick Abrahams still holds the official world record for the number of space launches, but he's bored stiff with his job hosting space tours. Only when his wife leaves him, however, does he try to change his life.

He accepts a tempting offer from a Russian billionaire. In exchange for making a simple repair on Neptune's moon Triton, he will return to Earth a multi-millionaire, enabling him to achieve his 'impossible dream' of buying his own California vineyard.

The fact that Nick must travel alone during the four-year roundtrip doesn't bother him at all, as he doesn't particularly like people anyway. Once en route he learns his new boss left out some critical details in his job description—details that could cost him his life, and humankind its existence...

3.99 $ – hard-sf.com/links/1086200

Mars Nation 1

NASA finally made it. The very first human has just set foot on the surface of our neighbor planet. This is the start of a long research expedition that sent four scientists into space.

But the four astronauts of the NASA crew are not the only ones with this destination. The privately financed 'Mars for Everyone' initiative has also targeted the Red Planet. Twenty men and women have been selected to live there and establish the first extraterrestrial settlement.

Challenges arise even before they reach Mars orbit. The MfE

spaceship Santa Maria is damaged along the way. Only the four NASA astronauts can intervene and try to save their lives.

No one anticipates the impending catastrophe that threatens their very existence—not to speak of the daily hurdles that an extended stay on an alien planet sets before them. On Mars, a struggle begins for limited resources, human cooperation, and just plain survival.

3.99 $ – hard-sf.com/links/762824

Mars Nation 2

A woman presumed dead fights her way through the hostile deserts of Mars. With her help, the NASA astronauts orphaned on the Red Planet hope to be able to solve their very worst problem. But their hopes are shattered when an unexpected menace arises and threatens to destroy everything the remnant of humanity has built on the planet. They need a miracle—or a ghost from the past whose true intentions are unknown.

Mars Nation 2 continues the story of the last representatives of Earth, who have found asylum on our neighboring planet, hoping to build a future in this alien world.

3.99 $ – hard-sf.com/links/790047

Mars Nation 3

Does the secret of Mars lurk beneath the surface of its south pole? A lone astronaut searches for clues about the earlier inhabitants of the Red Planet. Meanwhile, Rick Summers, having assumed the office of Mars City's Administrator by deceit and manipulation, tries to unify the people on Mars with the weapons under his control. Then

BRANDON Q. MORRIS
MARS
NATION
PART 3

A Guided Tour of Dark Matter

Introduction

In this exact moment a particle of dark matter might be passing through your field of view, but you will not see it. It's not because you need glasses. Even the most powerful microscope—one that can display individual atoms—could not see dark matter, not even as a black dot. 'Dark' in this sense means that it does not interact with light, or electromagnetic waves in general. Light penetrates dark matter as if it were not even there. It actually could be called 'invisible matter.' Yet even that term would not do it justice, as it refuses interaction with other forces of nature as well. The only exception is gravitation. A more precise term might therefore be 'matter that interacts exclusively with gravity.'

Why do scientists even assume that something so strange exists? What clues do physicists have, and how do researchers hunt for the particles it consists of?

Indications for the Existence of Dark Matter

AMONG PHYSICISTS, THE EXISTENCE OF DARK MATTER IS generally accepted. Cosmology, the branch of science that examines the origin and structure of the universe, has made the Lambda-CDM, aka ΛCDM, its standard model. CDM stands for cold dark matter. It is 'cold' because it does not—like light particles do, for instance—gain its energy from movement, which is equal to heat, but mostly from its resting mass. The models currently accepted by the majority of scientists who study the Big Bang, and the time soon after it, cannot do without this form of dark matter. This does not mean that there couldn't be hot dark matter as well, only that it is not necessary to these models.

The ΛCDM model is far more than a speculation, it has become a mature theory. All the knowledge we have about the world consists of theories. Some are well-proven, like quantum physics and the theory of general relativity. We know that they contain gaps, but that does not mean they are wrong. In order to turn mere speculation into a theory, it must be verifiable and falsifiable. Both require that it generates measurable predictions about reality. All this applies to dark matter. We know how it works, and its effects can also be measured.

Yet there is a problem that makes some physicists uneasy, and it has given dark matter a generally bad reputation: We only know it exists, but not what it consists of. Basically, this is a completely normal state of things. Phenomena including electricity, X-rays, and radioactivity were discovered and employed before they were thoroughly understood. Some present-day researchers, though, have forgotten about those times and make the unreasonable demand that we should immediately know what something is made of. You should not let yourself be confused by this. While there are alternative theories regarding dark matter, that is also the case for quantum physics. The existence of multiple theories does not mean there are serious doubts about dark matter. In reality, there are always new experiments trying to disprove the standard model that often end up confirming it.

How did we get on the trail of dark matter? Through its effects! In 1932, the Dutch astronomer Jan Hendrik Oort examined the numerical density and velocity distribution of various star populations vertically aligned to the disk of the Milky Way, and at various distances from the disk. From this, he calculated a mass density much greater than what was then known. In 1933 the Swiss physicist and astronomer Fritz Zwicky noticed that the Coma galaxy cluster could not be held together by the gravitational effect of its visible components. It would take 400 times the visible mass to keep the cluster from disintegrating. Zwicky seems to have been the first one to come up with the idea that the missing mass might exist in the form of 'dark matter.' However, he was not exactly applauded for this proposal.

In 1960, though, there were new indications. The American astronomer Vera Rubin measured the orbital speed of stars in relation to the center of the galaxy. Due to the fact that the visible mass is concentrated in the center, the stars on the outside should move considerably slower, due to Kepler's third law and the law of gravity. In reality, their velocities remain constant or even increase. Therefore, there has to be mass in the exterior sectors which is not visible in the form of stars, dust, or gas.

This observation made the idea much more convincing, and by now, dark matter has been proven for almost all large astronomical systems. Further indicators included:

•The gravitation lens effect: The mass of a heavy object can bend the space around it in such a way that it acts as a lens for light. The strength of the effect depends on the mass of the object. For many gravitation lenses, though, not enough mass was found to create the measured effect.

•The cosmic background radiation: This developed 380,000 years after the Big Bang, and is not completely isotropic, meaning that it is not distributed through space in an absolutely even manner. Special anisotropies measured by satellites represent clear indications for the existence of dark matter.

•The creation of structures in space: In a very early stage, space was evenly filled with energy. At some time there must have been random variations that, due to their gravitation, coalesced into stars and galaxies. If there were only normal matter in space, as we can calculate, these random deviations would have been too small to persist.

•The shape of the universe: The universe, as measurements have shown, is almost flat. Its total energy density, therefore, should be close to 1. From the expansion velocity of the cosmos we can calculate the density of dark energy, and through observation of visible matter, we can determine the density of normal matter. Whatever is missing compared to 1 must correspond to dark matter.

•Baryonic acoustic oscillation: The distance between

normal galaxies is 147 megaparsecs 1 percent more often than it is 130 or 160 megaparsecs. This is a small but significant indication for the existence of periodic density fluctuations in normal (baryonic) matter, which occurs in the ΛCDM model.

No Universe without Dark Matter

THE FOLLOWING COMPOSITION OF THE UNIVERSE ACCORDING TO matter proportion can be derived from the ΛCDM model: 68.3 percent dark energy, 26.8 percent dark matter and about 4.9 percent normal matter. The 'normal' matter is roughly divided into luminous matter such as stars, and non-luminous matter such as planets and primarily cold gas. Purely in terms of mass, dark matter amounts for 84.5 percent.

This ratio has not been constant across the history of the cosmos, though. For instance, there was no such dominance of dark energy—which is still growing—in the early periods. Shortly after the Big Bang, dark matter fulfilled its most important function. Let's just take a look back at that time.

Scientists today still don't know with certainty what took place at the beginning of time, approximately 13.8 billion years ago. All the matter in the universe today, 10^{53} kilograms, was located at that moment within a point, a singularity, where none of today's fundamental laws of nature had any effect. You can imagine a kind of infinitely-dense proto-soup consisting of particles no longer known today. A single force, the primordial force, prescribed the movements of these particles. The temperature of the proto-soup, if the term temperature even makes any sense in this context, must have been around 10^{32} degrees. There were neither electrons nor photons, so there was also no light. If there had been outside observers—but remember, all that was lurking around outside this soup was just nothing—they wouldn't have noticed that anything at all was happening.

This ultra-hot something was under tremendous pressure—and the cosmos expanded. The length of this time period is given from known laws of nature: it is known as the Planck time, that is, the time that light needs to cover a distance equal to a Planck length. That equals 10^{-43} seconds. However, at this pinpoint of time, time itself didn't yet exist. And, words are unable—unavailable—to accurately portray the paradoxes.

So, 10^{-43} seconds after the Big Bang is the first chance we have to use physics for studying the universe. The minuscule bits of matter are still under an unbelievable amount of pressure. But it has grown a little bit colder, because of the expansion. The first fundamental force to break free from the primordial force is the gravitational force that acts, as a force of attraction, against the expansion of the universe.

However, it is much weaker than the pressure of the Big Bang—so the universe continues to expand at a rapid pace. Because the average energy density of the proto-soup continues to decrease, it contains fewer and fewer exotic particles from the very beginning. After 10^{-38} seconds has elapsed, the strong nuclear force and the electroweak force split off of the primordial force.

Then comes a phase, the so-called inflation phase, in which the universe expands by a factor between 10^{30} and 10^{50}. At the start of this phase it is still the size of a proton, but at the end, it is about as large as a soccer ball. This inflation, which scientists place between 10^{-38} and 10^{-35} seconds after the Big Bang, needs so-called inflatons to form an explanation that is reasonable (that is, one that fits into the cosmological world view). These particles, which never appear again, are not attracted to each other by gravity, they are instead repelled.

Only in this way could the universe have grown so much in such a short time period. The argument that this explanation is not so far-fetched is that it also provides a good explanation for other phenomena observed in the universe today, for example, the homogeneity and low curvature of the universe.

The density of the universe—at an incredibly short 10^{-35} seconds after the Big Bang— has already expanded to the point where particles that are known today can be formed: electrons and positrons, quarks—which later combine to form protons and neutrons—and antiquarks, neutrinos—the precursors of photons—as well as gluons, which are responsible for transmitting the strong nuclear force.

Particles and antiparticles are present in equal numbers. When particles and antiparticles meet, they annihilate each other. There is a constant coming and going. Newly formed particles behave normally under the influence of gravity—they attract each other, which somewhat slows down the expansion of the universe. At this time, a quark-gluon plasma is dominant, which can be simulated today, at least in a computer.

Scientists have not yet reached a consensus, but if the laws of nature are subject to supersymmetry, this process is now broken. The theory of supersymmetry assumes that for each known particle, there is a super-partner that differs by a half spin. Supersymmetry would elegantly unify particles and force particles, which transmit the known interactions.

Such super-partners would have to be so heavy that they could only exist at the start of the universe. Today, however, we only observe conventional particles—supersymmetry is broken. At the moment supersymmetry was broken, it is conjectured that mass was imparted to the particles via the Higgs boson, which was confirmed in 2012.

Approximately 10^{-10} seconds after the Big Bang, the last two of the forces known today arise, the weak nuclear force, which plays a crucial role in nuclear fusion, and the electromagnetic force. Somewhat later, space has cooled to just two trillion degrees, so that quarks no longer have to be alone, so that protons, neutrons, antiprotons, and antineutrons coalesce. Gluons act as the bonding agent.

Matter and antimatter continue to be in balance. But this situation doesn't last much longer. Particles and antiparticles annihilate each other, forming photons, and the universe noticeably empties. It is already 10 trillion kilometers wide, approximately one light-year, and has further cooled to one trillion degrees. The fact that we exist, nevertheless, we owe to a small excess of matter. For every billion particle-antiparticle pairs, there resulted in an excess of one particle that wasn't annihilated. So far there are only theories for where this asymmetry came from. Obviously, the laws of nature do not act symmetrically in every respect.

One-fifth of a second after the Big Bang, the universe is already 500 trillion kilometers wide, or roughly 50 light-years. It has cooled to 20 billion degrees. Now it's time for neutrons and electrons to feel the heat. Unstable neutrons in a free state are torn apart by the weak nuclear force, releasing an electron, a proton, and a neutrino. Electrons and positrons annihilate each other. Here, the excess of matter wins the day again.

Due to the now large distances of the cosmos, approximately one second after the Big Bang, the weak interaction is no longer strong enough to produce interactions between neutrinos and conventional matter. Since then, the neutrinos released at that time have been rushing around the universe as a measurable, constant neutrino background with almost no interactions.

From now on, the universe's development progresses

considerably more slowly. The remaining neutrons are rescued when, approximately two to three minutes after T-zero, deuterium and finally helium nuclei are formed. Here, the strong nuclear force protects the neutrons from destruction. The universe grows and grows all the while, continuing to further cool down.

After approximately 17 minutes, it has become too cold to support any more nuclear fusion. At this point, all the still-available neutrons are then bound into atomic nuclei. Approximately three-fourths of the nuclei are hydrogen nuclei, the rest helium—heavier nuclei can be found only in traces.

As it grows colder and colder, electrons also bind electromagnetically to positively charged atomic nuclei. They are constantly being thrown out of their orbits, however, by photons from the still boiling proto-soup. The universe, whose composition is dominated by photons, would look like a glowing fog to outside observers at this time.

That doesn't change for a relatively long time. Starting around 70,000 years after the Big Bang, the ratio of atomic mass and radiation is 1:1. According to the Lambda-CDM model, the universe is now dominated by dark matter, whose nature can only be described by theories at the time of this writing. It has the result, however, that inhomogeneous areas left over from the inflation phase contract even more strongly, a prerequisite for the later formation of stars.

The dark matter increases the inhomogeneities in the structure of the cosmos so that areas with a higher concentration of hydrogen appear. Gigantic bubbles—so-called halos—form, even before the creation of galaxies, and implement the structure that inflation and dark matter impress on the universe. While dark matter is invisible, its gravitation acts on the matter known to us. Therefore, interstellar hydrogen agglomerates in the halos of dark matter. The closer the particles get to each other, the more the pressure in the gas increases—until pressure and gravitation are balanced. The cloud cools off because of the radiation emitted after particle collisions. This lowers the pressure and the cloud can contract further. The more matter gathers in a small space, the stronger it attracts atoms in the vicinity.

Once again temperature and density increase inside the cloud and start radiating in the infrared range. Now the proto-star stage has been reached. The heavier the cloud becomes, the faster it contracts—and then temperature and pressure are so high, about 3 million degrees Kelvin, that a nuclear fusion process is triggered: Groups of two protons collide and change into a deuterium nucleus with one proton and one neutron, while giving off energy. Then the deuterium reacts with an additional proton and becomes a helium-3 (3He) nucleus, while once more releasing energy. If the interior of the star is hot enough, above 10 million degrees Kelvin, the 3He nuclei can later merge into 4He nuclei, releasing two protons. This has the following effect: About 100 million years after the Big Bang, the first stars begin to shine, one after the other. This would have never been possible without dark matter!

Yet dark matter is still needed. Compared to today, the early universe was a very lively place. Smaller galaxies merged into larger ones. There were collisions and hostile takeovers. Today we know that this development was not completely random. The formation of stars actually focuses on fine structures created in the universe by dark matter, the so-called filaments. Where filaments intersect, galaxies and galaxy clusters develop. Today, the observable universe contains several million of these galaxy superclusters. One of them, the Virgo supercluster, for instance, combines several thousand galaxies in a diameter of 110 million light years, among them the Milky Way as part of the 'Local Group.'

It is not yet definitively known how the different types of galaxies form. It is assumed that dark matter plays an important role in the common spiral galaxies, like our Milky Way. After all, it only interacts via gravitation, while normal matter is also influenced by the radiation pressure of stars. Therefore dark matter should be concentrated in the exterior regions of the galaxy, where it formed the halo. Accordingly, the interstellar gas, which is strongly attracted by the core of the galaxy, and weakly by its outside, moves in a spiral course toward the core. Imagine someone holding a cat by its tail and swinging it in a circle. The force pulling the cat inward is greater than the outward push of the cat's bodyweight.

This model has one problem: The contraction stops eventually, and cosmologists still don't know why. Furthermore, spiral galaxies are very fragile structures. Long ago, galaxy collisions should have deformed them more strongly than seems to be the case. At this time, scientists consider the elliptical galaxy as the end point of this development. This type of galaxy most commonly develops from a merger of smaller galaxies. This, according to a simulation, might also be the fate of the Milky Way and our neighbor M31, Andromeda: In 3 to 4.5 billion years there will be a collision between these two systems of approximately similar weight. The consequence should be the creation of a giant elliptical galaxy.

Of what does Dark Matter consist?

DARK MATTER IS NOT SOMETHING COMPLETELY UNKNOWN. IT HAS to fulfill one single condition—it may only interact with other matter through the attracting force of gravitation. This applies to black holes, for example. Neutron stars, almost extinguished white dwarfs, or brown dwarfs—objects between a star and a planet—might represent the part of the galaxies' mass that astronomers are missing. These are covered by the term MACHO, or Massive Compact Halo Objects. However, there are several arguments against the idea that MACHOs would be sufficient to explain dark matter. For instance, measurements have shown that five-sixths of normal matter interact in other ways than just through gravitation, which rules it out as dark matter.

Accordingly, dark matter has to consist of hitherto unknown particles. Here the candidates have been divided into cold, warm, and hot matter. As described above, this does not refer to a measurable temperature but to velocity. 'Cold' dark matter could not cover long distances in the early universe, 'warm' dark matter had medium speed, while 'hot' dark matter was fast and energy-rich. The standard model, which after all is named 'CDM,' only includes cold dark matter.

What could be candidates for cold dark matter? First we have the axion, a hypothetical elementary particle. Its existence would solve a problem faced by quantum chromodynamics—the theory that describes the strong interaction of quarks and gluons. It predicts that the electrically-neutral neutron should possess a measurable electric dipole moment, meaning that its charge should not be distributed quite homogeneously. However, no dipole moment has been found, not even a much weaker one than the theory predicts. The axion would solve this and explain the lack. It would have to be a very lightweight particle, up to ten billion times lighter than the electron, which is already quite lightweight. Yet due to sheer numbers, they still could account for the overwhelming part of the mass in the universe. If an axion gets in contact with strong magnetic fields it might turn into a photon. This could be happening inside the sun. Therefore scientists seek to detect axions of the sun based on their characteristic radiation in the X-ray range. So far, they have been unsuccessful.

The second candidate for dark matter is the complete opposite of the axion. The WIMP, or Weakly Interacting Massive Particle, certainly does not act like a wimp, but is especially heavy, heavier than most known elementary particles and about as heavy as two gold atoms. Nevertheless, it might traverse entire planets unhindered, which makes it complicated to prove its existence. On the other hand, they move leisurely, which makes it easier for them to clump together in clusters, as dark matter does.

As the WIMPs are heavy, the theory would not need nearly as many of them as in the case of axions. The theory of supersymmetry includes such particles, but none of them have been found so far, and supersymmetry itself still waits for confirmation.

For a long time, neutrinos were considered promising

candidates for dark matter. One huge advantage is that they are already known. On the other hand, we know too much about them by now to assume that they make up the majority of dark matter, since they are too lightweight. What if a so-called sterile neutrino exists? While normal neutrinos are susceptible to the weak interaction—one of the four fundamental forces—the sterile neutrino would be immune to it. It could be relatively heavy and would, as is required for dark matter, only exchange forces via gravitation. Researchers have been trying to detect sterile neutrinos for some time, but so far without success.

How to Search for Dark Matter

DUE TO THEIR EXTREMELY RARE INTERACTION WITH MATTER, WIMPs could be most easily proven indirectly, by their decay. To do so, we have to observe them in areas where our view is blurred as little as possible by normal matter, for instance in far-away galaxies. The decay of a WIMP should generate energy-rich gamma radiation. If we manage to measure more gamma radiation in the area under study than could be produced by the normal matter found there, WIMPs would have been proven indirectly.

The sun might be another source of information about WIMPs. Due to its enormous mass, it also possibly attracts WIMPs. Some of them might become so slow that they are caught by the sun. Accordingly, a pool of WIMPs should have collected in the sun over the course of millions of years. There they would collide and destroy each other. Researchers hope to be able to record decay products such as neutrinos.

Yet they also attempt to find a direct proof. In very rare cases a WIMP might collide with a nucleus that then becomes unstable and radioactive. The detectors necessary for this are usually deep underground in order to avoid the influence of radioactive background radiation and secondary cosmic radiation.

Alternatives to Dark Matter?

The existence of dark matter is derived from Einstein's theory of general relativity, or GR. That theory has been experimentally proven in many ways. Yet there could be a theory that might explain reality better or more completely. In the case of GR, for example, we know that it fails at very small scales and in the case of very, very high energies, such as shortly after the Big Bang.

Researchers have suggested alternatives in order to explain dark matter. These are not yet generally accepted, because they currently have no proofs for certain predictions.

Physicists developed Modified Newtonian Dynamics, or MOND, in which at very low accelerations, inertial mass, i.e. acceleration, and gravitational mass, i.e. gravitation, are no longer equivalent. In this case, Newton's law as you learned it in school does not exactly apply. Such low accelerations occur at an astronomical scale. They don't play a role in everyday life, and we wouldn't notice any of this. Yet for the rotation of galaxies, the equations of motion have to be modified. This leads to the observed measurements without assuming the existence of dark matter. However, in the standard model of cosmic evolution, this theory so far cannot replace dark matter, which would still be needed there. Furthermore, it describes the movement of galaxy clusters less precisely than the good old Newtonian law does.

The tensor–vector–scalar gravity, TeVeS, is derived from MOND and also includes the special theory of relativity. It modifies the relation of the strength of the gravitational field to the distance of the mass causing the gravitation. In doing so, TeVeS can avoid some of the problems of MOND and explain the strength of the gravitation lens effect. However, it also lacks applicability to the early phase of the universe. Furthermore, a researcher showed that under the influence of TeVeS, stars would become very unstable and collapse after a few weeks.

The scalar–tensor–vector gravity, or STVG, assumes that across large distances gravitation becomes stronger than Einstein calculated, but that over short distances it is counteracted by a fifth, repulsive force. On this basis, many of the phenomena mentioned above can be explained without dark matter. This also applies to the accelerating expansion of the universe, that otherwise would require dark energy. However, there are no differences to usual gravitation across the distance scales we can measure with today's technology. This makes it hard to actually prove or disprove STVG. It also has difficulties in explaining the structure of the cosmic background radiation.

Overall, today it looks like dark matter really exists. The theory of general relativity, GR, supports this, one of the physical theories with the best proofs. Of course, this should not keep physicists from suggesting changes, though so far, Einstein has always been proven correct in the end. The theory of general relativity reaches its limits in very small dimensions, such as the singularities of black holes. It is there where dark matter plays no role, as it is a phenomenon defining the large structure of the cosmos.

• • •

If you register at hard-sf.com/subscribe/ you will be notified of any new Hard Science Fiction titles. In addition you will receive a color PDF version of *A Guided Tour of Dark Matter*.

Glossary of Acronyms

AI – Artificial Intelligence
CDM – Cold Dark Matter
DNA – DeoxyriboNucleic Acid
GR – General Relativity
ISU – Independent Sensor Unit
IV – IntraVenous
ΛCDM – Lambda-Cold Dark Matter
LCVG – Liquid Cooling and Ventilation Garment
MACHO – MAssive Compact Halo Objects
MOND – MOdified Newtonian Dynamics
NASA – National Aeronautics and Space Administration
SAI – Semi-Artificial Intelligence
STVG – Scalar–Tensor–Vector Gravity
TeVeS – Tensor–Vector–Scalar gravity
VR – Virtual Reality
WIMP – Weakly Interacting Massive Particle

Metric to English Conversions

It is assumed that by the time the events of this novel take place, the United States will have joined the rest of the world and will be using the International System of Units, the modern form of the metric system.

Length:
centimeter = 0.39 inches
meter = 1.09 yards, or 3.28 feet
kilometer = 1093.61 yards, or 0.62 miles

Area:
square centimeter = 0.16 square inches
square meter = 1.20 square yards
square kilometer = 0.39 square miles

Weight:
gram = 0.04 ounces
kilogram = 35.27 ounces, or 2.20 pounds

Volume:
liter = 1.06 quarts, or 0.26 gallons

cubic meter = 35.31 cubic feet, or 1.31 cubic yards

Temperature:
To convert Celsius to Fahrenheit, multiply by 1.8 and then add 32
To convert Kelvin to Celsius, subtract 273.15

Brandon Q. Morris
--
www.hard-sf.com
brandon@hard-sf.com
Translator: Frank Dietz, Ph.D. Editor: Pamela Bruce, B.S.
Final editing: Marcia Kwiecinski, A.A.S., and Stephen Kwiecinski, B.S.
-- --
Technical Advisors: Michael Paluszek (President, Princeton Satellite Systems),
Dr. Ludwig Hellmann
Cover design: BJ Coverbookdesigns.com

Printed in Great Britain
by Amazon

56730870R00187